The Story of King Arthur
and Other Celtic Heroes

Padraic Colum

Illustrated by
Wilfred Jones

Dover Publications, Inc.
Mineola, New York

Copyright

Bibliographical Note

This Dover edition, first published in 2005, is an unabridged republication of
*The Island of the Mighty: Being the Hero Stories of Celtic Britain Retold from the
Mabinogion,* originally published in 1924 by Macmillan, New York. The color illus-
trations have been moved to the front and inside covers of this edition.

Library of Congress Cataloging-in-Publication Data

Colum, Padraic, 1881–1972.
    [Island of the mighty]
    The story of King Arthur and other Celtic heroes / Padraic Colum ; illustrated
by Wilfred Jones.
        p. cm.
    Originally published: The island of the mighty : being the hero stories of
Celtic Britain : retold from the Mabinogion / by Padraic Colum ; illustrated by
Wilfred Jones. New York : Macmillan, 1924.
    Summary: Episodes from the mabinogion, a collection of medieval Welsh
tales, recount the feats and exploits of King Arthur and other powerful kings and
princes.
    ISBN 0-486-44061-3 (pbk.)
    1. Arthurian romances. [1. Arthur, King—Legends. 2. Knights and knight-
hood—Folklore. 3. Folklore—England. 4. Folklore—Wales.] I. Jones, Wilfred,
b. 1888, ill. II. Mabinogion. III. Title.

PZ8.1.C723Sp 2005
398.2'0942'02—dc22

                                                                2004055436

Manufactured in the United States of America
Dover Publications, Inc., 31 East 2nd Street, Mineola, N.Y. 11501

To

MY CYMRIC FRIENDS

LLEWELYN AND JOHN

COWPER POWYS

Contents

Illustrations

Introduction

I

Long ago, at the time when the Romans were leaving Britain, a Celtic Prince bearing a Roman title organized a people in the southwest of the Island. This people came to call themselves "Cymry." Another people who came across the sea from the northeast named them "Welsh" or "Foreigners." These newcomers were the Saxons. They cut off the Cymry from their kinsfolk in the south, the people of Cornwall, and afterwards they cut them off from their kinsfolk in the north, the Britons of Strathclyde. And cut off from the south and north, and facing the western sea in a land of mountains and moors, the Cymry maintained themselves against the Saxons, and afterwards against the people who had been victorious over the Saxons, the Norman invaders of England.

The Cymry maintained themselves against Saxon and Anglo-Norman because they had in their hearts a passionate devotion to their own racial tradition:

> Their Lord they will praise,
> Their speech they will keep,
> Their lands they will lose
> Except wild Wales.

And holding to their speech they looked upon themselves as the rightful inheritors of the Island of Britain; all that was left of the legendary history, of the heroic story, and of the mythology of the British Celts was embodied in their tradition.

The Cymry in Britain and their kinsfolk across the sea, the Bretons of France, were destined to bring a notable element into European literature. The stories about King Arthur that for hundreds of years made up almost the whole of European romance were purveyed by them; by one way or another the Cymry in Britain and the Bretons in France brought these stories into the literatures that were growing up in the Romance and the Germanic languages.

They brought in these stories from the Celtic romance and the Celtic mythology that they were the inheritors of. But the Cymry of Britain and the Bretons of France were not the only inheritors of the Celtic tradition. Beyond the sea there was another Celtic people, the Gaels of Ireland, who possessed that tradition even more fully. The Gaels of Ireland were further from Europe than were the Cymry and the Bretons; the stories they had were not easily understood by the continental peoples, for the reason that they were more purely Celtic. The Cymry and the Bretons were able to make stories out of their own material that could be understood and admired by the Latin and Germanic nations; they were able, too, to take over Irish material and work it into their own literature. And, being amongst the greatest story-tellers that the world has ever known, they were able to make stories that are, after nearly a thousand years, still beautiful to us.

Their best stories—I am speaking now of the Cymry, the Welsh, as the most of the world now names them—were shaped, scholars tell us, between 1080 and 1260. This was a time of vigorous national life in Wales, a time that produced remarkable men. A scholar whose studies were on the literature that came out of this period, Mr. Alfred Nutt, has said, "It was an age of transition, of assimilation of new ideas, new standards of political and social life, of acquaintance with new examples, new methods of literary art." This period, from the middle of the eleventh to the end of the twelfth century, was the greatest period in Welsh literature and Welsh national life. "On one side," said Mr. Nutt, "Wales felt the influence of the Irish renaissance of the eleventh century, that resuscitation of national life and national literature to which we owe the preservation of the most considerable body of archaic culture in modern Europe; on the other side she was brought into intense and continual contact with the strongest, most vital, and most modern culture of the time—that of the Norman conquerors of England."

Wales was then a little country broken up into separate states and separate lordships. She had internal warfare and border warfare. Her ancient enemies, the Saxons, had been overthrown by the Normans, and the Welsh were fighting the conquerors and making friends with them. The Normans were to treat them badly, but the Welsh understood and admired the half-Celtic Normans as they had never understood and admired the Saxons. And they were ready to take over from the Normans something of that which was "the strongest, most vital, and most modern culture of the time," and to reshape their literary work in accordance with that culture.

The Welsh had at the time, as they had before and since, an organization of bards and story-tellers. It was the business of the bards to relate and reshape the histories, stories, and poems that were the current literature of the time, and that they were the custodians of. There were apprentices to the guild of bards, and an apprentice was called "Mabinog." A story that an apprentice-bard might be expected to know was called "Mabinogi." Some of these stories were written down in a manuscript that was compiled in the fourteenth century, and when these stories and other stories that had been put with them were translated into English, the translator gave them all the title of "Mabinogion," a title that we might translate as "Stories known to an Apprentice-Bard." Not all the stories published in English with that title were "Mabinogion" in the strict sense of the Welsh word.

II

The men who made up the great storybook that is in the Welsh manuscript of the fourteenth century probably did not notice that the stories they brought together differed in character very much from each other. We can see now that there are groups of stories in "The Mabinogion" that have different origins from other groups and that were shaped under different influences. There are four stories that are mythological: these are (I name them according to their original titles) "Pwyll, Prince of Dyved," "Branwen, Daughter of Llyr," "Manawyddan, Son of Llyr," and "Math, Son of Mathonwy." Of these four stories two only are given in this book. Then comes "The Dream of Rhonabwy." This is not a mythological story; it deals with old material, but it deals with it in a style that was new in Wales in the twelfth century. Then there is "Kilhwch and Olwen." This story, like "The Dream of Rhonabwy," is written in a style that was introduced into Wales in the middle of the twelfth century. It is a folk-tale to begin with, but as we have it now it is a folk-tale treated by a well-equipped literary man, a genuine precursor of the Welsh novelist of our day who wrote "The Shaving of Shagpat." Then there are stories that could only have been shaped after the Welsh nobles had taken on the manners and ways of the Norman conquerors of England, and after the Welsh story-tellers had come to know the sort of stories that the Normans admired. These stories, the most modern, so to speak, in the collection, are, "The Lady of the Fountain," "Peredur, Son of Evrawc," and "Geraint, Son of Erbin." They have in them the reflection of later manners, but they are made up out of Welsh material, or rather out of material that had been brought back to Wales by Breton story-tellers. We have to note these Breton story-tellers. They had already told stories that were originally Welsh, or Irish stories taken through the Welsh in France and Italy. Now they had come into England with the Normans; they told stories to the Welsh about heroes whose names had been changed from their Celtic forms, and about a King Arthur who was no longer a Celtic chieftain but a king who had taken on the attributes of the French Charlemagne. This group of stories differs very much from the mythological group, and from the two stories, "The Dream of Rhonabwy" and "Kilhwch and Olwen," that had been made under Irish influences. Then there are two stories that are quite different from both of these groups: these are "The Dream of Maxen Wledig" and "The Contention of Lludd and Llevelys"; these are stories made up out of British legendary history—historical romances we should call them now.

III

In the middle of the nineteenth century, out of a manuscript of the fourteenth century, these stories shaped between the eleventh and the thirteenth century were translated. The manu-script that contained them is known as "The Red Book of Hergest," and it is in Jesus College, Oxford; the translator of the stories was Lady Charlotte Guest, and it was she who gave to the stories in her English translation the title of "The Mabinogion."

The book was published in 1849, and it was printed for the second time in 1877. Since that time only about eight reprints and versions of "The Mabinogion" have appeared in English. This is odd; one might expect for these heroic and beautiful sto-ries something of the wide currency of the "Morte d'Arthur" and "The Thousand and One Nights." Something stands in the way of their having this wide appeal. It may be the names—the names of places and people, that look so unintelligible in their unfamiliar combinations of letters and that often appear, not singly, but in battalions:

> Kai, and Bedwyr, and Greidawl, Galldonyd, and Gwythyr the son of Greidawl, and Greid the son of Eri, and Kynddelig Kyvarwydd, and Tathal Twyll Goleu, and Maelwys the son of Baeddan, and Crychwr the son of Nes, and Cubert the son of Daere, and Percos the son of Poch, and Lluber Beuthach, and Corvil Bervach, and Gwynn the son of Nudd, and Edeyrn the son of Nudd, and Gadwy the son of Geraint, and Prince Fflewddur Fflam, and Ruawn Pebyr the son of Dorath, and Bradwen the son of Moren Mynawc, and Moren Mynawc himself.

Then there is the title that Lady Charlotte Guest gave to the stories in her translation. We look at it and no suggestion comes to us from it. Even those who love the stories and who have read them many times would be puzzled if they were asked what the word "Babinogion" really stands for. The title and the difficult names of the places and the people, names that might be of the lost continent of Atlantis or the sea-sunken Island of Ys, have made "The Mabinogion," one must think, difficult of approach.

I have tried to make the approach to the stories somewhat easier. I have gone over them, and I have broken up the massed battalions of names, and have got rid of such names as were not essential in the telling of the stories. I have put the names that had to be kept in forms less forbidding than the older forms—

making Gwenhwyvar, for instance, over into Gwenhuivar, and Kilhwch over into Kilhuch, and Pwyll over into Puil. This I have done under the direction of a distinguished Celtic scholar. And I have put another title over the stories. In some of the stories a lofty name is used to designate the Britain that great Bran ruled over; it is Ynys y Kedyrn, The Island of the Mighty. I have thought that this lofty name would make an appropriate title for the heroic stories of Celtic Britain.

And in order to make certain incidents clear and to get rid of passages that are obscure or repetitious in the stories as they have come down to us, I have worked over them, making certain condensations and certain rearrangements. But I have not attempted to make any far-reaching changes in the language that now seems so native to these Welsh stories, Lady Charlotte Guest's rhythmical English.

Arthur's is a great and a well-remembered name, and I have thought that it would be well to have it as the first personal name in the opening story. And I have thought, too, that the opening story should be one that would lead easily into other stories. Both reasons have led me into beginning with the story that in other books has for its title "Kilhwch and Olwen, or the Twrch Trwyth." As translated by Lady Guest the story does not begin with any familiar name—"Kilydd the son of Prince Kelyddon desired a wife as a helpmate, and the wife he chose was Goleuddydd, the daughter of Prince Anlawdd." But all this is introductory to the appearance of Kilydd's and Goleuddydd's son at the Court of King Arthur, and it was easy to arrange the story so as to have Arthur's name in its beginning.

This story is, in its intention, a story that furnishes a framework for other stories like certain tales in "The Arabian Nights." I have availed myself of this special structure to put within it four stories that have really an independent existence—"Puil, Prince of Dyved," "The Story of Branwen," "The Dream of Maxen the Emperor," and "The Story of Lud and Levellis."

As we have already noted, a long historical period separates stories like "Kilhuch and Olwen," "Puil, Prince of Dyved," and "Branwen" from stories like "The Knight Owen and the Lady of the Fountain," "Peredur and the Castle of Wonders," and

"Geraint and Enid." These last three stories go together, and I have made them the second part of the book. After them I have put "The Dream of Ronabbway," although I am aware that scholars hold that this last story was composed earlier and under different influences from the stories that it is made to follow. But it has in it the vision of the battle in which Arthur was wounded and in which his companions fell, and when one reads it one knows that the Champion of Britain has passed away from the Island of the Mighty. It is better, I have thought, to have this vision at the end rather than in the middle of the book, and for that reason I have made "The Island of the Mighty" end with "The Dream of Ronabbway."

IV

The knights in the stories about Owen, and Peredur, and Geraint, the knights who wear armour and ride from castle to castle, who act under the instructions of chivalry, and who take part in tournaments, belong to quite another age than the kings and magicians who are in the stories about Puil and Branwen, and the heroes who strive to win the marvellous things that Yspaddaden, Chief of the Giants, demands from his daughter's suitor. And the Arthur of "Kilhuch and Olwen" differs greatly from the Arthur of "The Knight Owen and the Lady of the Fountain" and the two stories that go with it. In the first story he is a Celtic King like Concobar in the Irish stories, ruling over no wide territory and being merely first amongst equals. In the other stories he has been made over into the likeness of the French Charlemagne, and he is thought of as Emperor of Britain. The Bretons have now given back to the Welsh a British King who has been Europeanized.

Two hundred years after these last Welsh stories about Arthur had been shaped, Sir Thomas Malory translated from the French the stories about him that had been developed on the Continent, and made an English masterpiece. The stories about Owen, and Peredur, and Geraint can be compared with the stories of the knights in the "Morte d'Arthur." The feudal life that the Normans developed is reflected in both sets of stories. But for all that we can easily see that an imagination other than the imagination of feudalized Europe and Normanized England has gone into the making of such stories as "The Knight Owen and the Lady of the Fountain," and "Peredur and the Castle of Wonders," and "Geraint and the Maiden Enid." The knights in these stories act, even although they have had an instruction in chivalry, from personal humour, as when Peredur avenges upon Kai the blow given to the dwarf and dwarfess, or when Geraint treats the lovely and faithful Enid with such strange sullenness. The women whom these knights meet have a personality that is as distinct as their own—the unmastered personality of the Celtic women.

No, the feudalized Welsh stories about Arthur have no inner likeness to the romance that Sir Thomas Malory made out of French stories in the fifteenth century. In the "Morte d'Arthur" the knights are held rigidly to the pattern of chivalry; they are all men who have been indoctrinated with a great social ideal, a great social tradition; they are men of convention, and the whim and fantasy that are in Owen and Peredur and Geraint are not in them. Sir Launcelot is much further away from the originals of Sir Gawaine and Sir Perceval than the soldier or administrator of our day is from Sir Launcelot. The purposeful knights who rode from Camelot belong completely to this world, and we can watch them going about the business of mastering the world.

> In the meanwhile came in Sir Ector, with an eager countenance, and found Ulfius and Brastias on foot, in great peril of death, which were foul defiled under the horse's feet. The King Arthur as a lion ran into King Cradlemont, of North Wales, and smote him through the left side, that the horse and king fell down, and then he took the horse by the reins, and led him unto Ulfius, and said, "have this horse, mine old friend, for great need hast thou of a horse." "Gramercy!" said Ulfius.

Here is a fight, half sport, half massacre, that men of our day might engage in.

V

If "Mabinog" and "Mabinogion" were words that were familiar to us, it is probable that we should get from them a sense of

youthfulness that is in the "apprentice-bard." And if that sense
of youthfulness came to us from it the title, "Mabinogion,"
would be singularly appropriate; for no other book in all the
world gives us better than this book youth and youth seen with
youth's eyes. We must think that it is the imagination of youth
concerning itself glowingly with youth going forth that is in the
description of Kilhuch riding to the Court of King Arthur, with
the spears of silver in his hands "of an edge to wound the wind,"
and with the grey-hounds bounding alongside him "like two sea-
swallows," and with his courser casting up "four sods with its
four hoofs like four swallows in the air." And no maiden was ever
more radiantly of the dream of youth than is Olwen when she
comes first upon us, with her head "more yellow than the flower
of the broom," and her skin "whiter than the foam of the wave,"
and her hands and her fingers "whiter than the blossoms of the
wood anemone amidst the spray of the meadow fountain." The
stories may differ in the manners they reflect, but they are at
one in this that they tell of nothing but of youth's appearance
and youth's adventure. The Knight Kynon comes upon two
youths "with yellow curling hair, each with a frontlet of gold
upon his head, and clad in a garment of yellow satin, and they
had gold clasps upon their insteps. In the hand of each of them
was an ivory bow, strung with the sinews of the stag, and their
arrows had shafts of the bone of the whale, and were winged
with peacock's feathers; their shafts also had golden heads. And
they had daggers with blades of gold, and with hilts of the bone
of the whale." We remember Peredur on his bony piebald horse
saying to Kai, "Tell me, tall man, is that Arthur yonder?" And
our first glimpse of Geraint is of "a knight upon a hunter foal of
mighty size; the rider was a fair-haired youth, bare-legged, and
of princely mien, and a golden-hilted sword was at his side, and
a robe and a surcoat of satin were upon him, and two low shoes
of leather upon his feet; and around him was a scarf of purple,
at each corner of which was a golden apple." In these stories we
seem to see immortal youth moving through a world that knows
no change or decay.

If we turn from such glimpses as are in these stories to the
most vernal scene in the "Morte d'Arthur," to the scene where

Queen Guenever goes a-maying, we seem to find ourselves in a world the youth of which has passed:

> And thus it passed on from Candlemas until after Easter, that the month of May was come, when every lusty heart beginnith to blossom, and to bring forth fruit. For, like as herbs and trees bring forth fruit, and flourish in May, in likewise every lusty heart, that is in any manner a lover, springeth and flourisheth in lusty deeds; for it giveth until all lovers courage that lusty month of May in some thing, for it constrain him in some manner of thing, more in that month than in any other month, for divers causes; for then all herbs and trees renew a man and a woman. And, in likewise, lovers call again to their mind old gentleness and old service, and many kind deeds that were forgotten by neg-ligence. . . . Now it befell in the month of lusty May that Queen Guenever called unto her knights of the Round Table, and she gave them warning, that early in the morning she should ride a-maying in the woods and fields beside Westminster; "And I warn you that there be none of you but that be well horsed, and that ye all be clothed in green; and that I shall bring with me ten ladies, and every knight shall have a lady behind him, and every knight shall have a squire and two yeomen, and I will that ye all be well horsed." . . . And those ten knights made them ready in the most freshest manner to ride with the Queen. And on the morrow they took their horses and rode a-maying with the Queen in great joy and delight.

Compared with the freely-moving figures in "The Mabinogion" the knights and dames of Malory move through a world that is, indeed, too much with them.

VI

In one of Mr. Havelock Ellis's essays the suggestion is thrown out that "The Mabinogion" does not belong to the English people. The suggestion comes in an essay on Cornwall and follows a remark upon the courtesy of the people there, courtesy that marks them as having an older civilization than that which belongs to the bulk of the people of England. No, Mr. Havelock Ellis says, "The Mabinogion," with its graciousness and its cour-tesy, belongs to a people of whom the Cornish people are a survival, and does not at all belong to the Saxon-descended English people. "Our hearts and souls are expressed in 'Beowulf,' and 'Havelock,' and more remotely in 'The Chanson de Roland.'" A great scholar makes the suggestion, but somehow one cannot assent to it. The poem "Beowulf" never became part of the English inheritance; and neither Beowulf nor any other Teutonic hero was able to take root in England. As for the Roland of the Normans, he is no more than a name to the English. Celtic Britain, after all, was the Britain to which the English looked back before the break in their tradition; and when Shakespeare made his plays about British history he made them about the Celtic Lear and the Celtic Cymbeline. If the tradition that Shakespeare was in had not been broken, the "Mabinogion" would have become part of the consciousness of the English people long and long ago.

Through language and through law the English go back to the Saxon, but there was no Saxon consciousness in England until a bishop at the court of Elizabeth began a movement for a Saxon revival. This was in the interest of the religious change that had its origin in Germany. The movement ultimately brought about a complete Saxon consciousness; all that was Saxon was made seem near and all that was Celtic was made seem alien and remote. The Saxonism of the English people is now one of the most firmly established facts in the world. But before Saxonism became dominant, and in times since, the English and the English-speaking peoples have heard the birds of Rhiannon— the birds of Celtic enchantment. "And there came three birds, and began singing unto them a certain song, and all the songs they had ever heard were unpleasant compared thereto; and the birds seemed to them to be at a great distance from them over the sea, and yet they appeared as distinct as if they were close by."

PADRAIC COLUM.

BEING THE HERO STORIES
OF CELTIC BRITAIN
RETOLD FROM THE MABINOGION

I

HOW THE YOUTH KILHUCH
CAME TO KING ARTHUR'S COURT

Thus the youth rode to the Court of King Arthur: the horse that was under him was of four winters old, firm of limb, with head of dappled grey, with shell-formed hoofs, having a bridle of linked gold on its head, and on its back a saddle of gold. In the youth's hands were two spears of silver, sharp and well-tempered, of an edge to wound the wind, and swifter than the fall of a dew-drop from the blade of reed-grass upon the earth when the dew of June is at its heaviest. A gold-hilted sword was upon his thigh, the blade of which was of gold, bearing a cross of inlaid gold of the hue of the lightning of heaven, and his warhorn was of ivory. Before him were two brindled, white-breasted grey-hounds, having strong collars of rubies about their necks. And the hound that was on his left side bounded across to the right side, and the one on his right to his left, and like two sea-swallows they sported around him. His horse, as it coursed along, cast up four sods with its four hoofs, like four swallows in the air, about his head, now above, now below. About him was a four-cornered cloth of purple, and an apple of gold was at each corner, and every one of the apples was of the value of an hundred kine. And there was precious gold of the value of three hundred kine upon his shoes, and upon his stirrups, from his knee to the tip of his toe. And the blade of grass bent not beneath him, so light was his courser's tread as he journeyed towards the gate of King Arthur's palace.

When he came before the palace, the youth called out, "Open the gate." "I will not open it," said the porter. "Wherefore not?" asked the youth. "The knife is in the meat, and the drink is in

1

the horn, and there is revelry in Arthur's hall, and none may enter therein except the son of a King of a privileged country, or a craftsman bringing here his craft. Stay thou outside. There will be refreshment for thy hounds and for thy horse, and for thee there will be collops of meat cooked and peppered, and luscious wine, and mirthful songs. A lady shall smooth thy couch for thee and lull thee with her singing; and early in the morning, when the gate is opened for the multitude that came hither to-day, for thee it shall be opened first, and thou mayest sit in the place that thou shalt choose in Arthur's hall." Said the youth, "That I will not do. If thou openest the gate for me, it is well. But if thou dost not open it, I will set up three shouts at this very gate, and these shouts will be deadly to all." "What clamour soever thou mayest make," said the porter, "against the law of King Arthur's palace thou shalt not enter until I go first and speak with the King."

So the porter went into the hall. The King said to him when he came near, "Hast thou news from the gate?" The porter said, "Half my life is past, and half of thine. I have seen with thee supreme sovereigns, but never did I behold one of equal dignity with him who is now at thy gate." Then said King Arthur to him, "If walking thou didst enter, return thou running. It is unbecoming to keep such a one as thou sayest he is outside in wind and rain." Then said the knight Kai who was in Arthur's hall at the time, "By the hand of my friend, if thou wouldst follow my counsel, thou wouldst not break through the laws of thy court because of him." "Not so, blessed Kai," said Arthur. "The greater our courtesy, the greater will be our renown, and our fame, and our glory." And by this time the porter was back at the gate.

He opened the gate before the youth who had been waiting before it. Now, although all comers dismounted upon the horse-block that was at the gate, yet did he not dismount, but he rode right in on his horse. "Greeting be unto thee, sovereign ruler of the Island," he said, "and be this greeting no less unto the lowest than unto the highest, and be it equally unto thy guests, and thy warriors, and thy chieftains—let all partake of it equally with thyself. And complete be thy favour, and thy fame, and thy glory

"Greeting be unto thee, sovereign ruler of the Island."

throughout all this Island." "Greeting be unto thee also," said
King Arthur. "Sit thou between two of my warriors, and thou
shalt have minstrels before thee, and thou shalt enjoy the privi-
leges of a King born to a throne, as long as thou remainest here."
Said the youth, "I came not to consume meat and drink; but if I
obtain the boon that I have come seeking, I will requite it thee."
Then said Arthur: "Since thou wilt not remain here, Chieftain,
thou shalt receive the boon whatsoever thy tongue may name, as
far as the wind dries, and the rain moistens, and the sun
revolves, and the sea encircles, and the earth extends; any boon
thy tongue may name save only my ship and my mantle, my
sword and my lance, my shield and my dagger, and Gwenhuivar,
my wife. By the truth of Heaven, thou shalt have it cheerfully,
name what thou wilt. For my heart warms unto thee, and I know
thou art of my blood." "Of thy blood I am indeed," said the
youth, "for my mother was thy mother's sister, Prince Anlod's
daughter." Thereupon he told the King of his birth and his up-
bringing.

Kilhuch he was called, and he was given that name because
he was born in a swine's pen. Before he was born, his mother
became wild, and she wandered about, without habitation. Then
she came to a mountain where ther was a swineherd, keeping a
herd of swine; there she stayed, and in the swine's pen her son
was born. The swineherd took the boy, and brought him to the
palace of his father, and there he was christened. Afterwards he
was sent to be reared in another place.

His mother died soon afterwards. When she knew she was
going to die, she sent for the Prince, her husband, and she said
to him, "I charge thee not to take a wife until thou seest a briar
with two blossoms growing out of my grave." And she asked him
to have the grave tended, day by day, and year by year, so that
nothing might grow on it. This he promised her, and, soon after,
she died.

For seven years the Prince sent an attendant every morning
to dress her grave and to see if anything were growing upon it.
But at the end of the seventh year he neglected to do that which
he had promised to his wife. Then one day he went hunting. He

passed by the place of burial and he saw a briar growing out of his wife's grave. He knew then that the time had come for him to seek another wife. He sought for one, and he married again, and brought another lady into his palace.

A day came when the lady he married went walking abroad. She came to the house of an old crone, and going within she said to the woman, "Old woman, tell me that which I shall ask thee. Where are the children of the man who has married me?" "Children he has none," said the crone. "Woe is me," said the lady, "that I have come to one who is childless." "Children he has none," said the crone, "but a child he has. Thou needst not lament."

Then the lady returned to the palace, and she said to her husband, "Wherefore hast thou concealed thy child from me?" The Prince said, "I will do so no longer." He sent messengers for Kilhuch, and the youth was brought into the palace.

Now when his step-mother saw him she was fearful that he would take the whole of his father's possessions away from her own child, for it was predicted to her by the crone that she would have a son. So she said to him when she looked on him, "It were well for thee to have a wife." The youth answered, "I am not yet of an age to wed," but although he said this he was well grown at the time. His step-mother said to him, "I declare to thee that it is thy destiny not to be suited until thou obtain Olwen, the daughter of Yspaddaden, the Chief of the Giants, for thy wife."

Hearing that name the youth blushed, and the love of the maiden named was diffused through all his frame, although he had never seen her. He went to his father and he told him that it had been declared to him that he would never be suited until he had obtained the daughter of Yspaddaden for his wife. "That will not be hard for thee to do," said his father, "for King Arthur is thy cousin, and he will aid thee. Go to Arthur, therefore. And ask him to cut thy hair, as great lords cut the hair of youths who are dear to them. And as he cuts thy hair ask it of him as a boon that he obtain for thee Olwen, the daughter of Yspaddaden." Then Kilhuch mounted his steed and rode off to the Court of King Arthur.

"I crave it as a boon," said Kilhuch, "that thou, King Arthur, cut my hair." "That shall be granted thee," said the King. "To-morrow I will do it for thee." Then, on the morrow, King Arthur took a golden comb, and scissors whereof the loops were of silver, and he made ready to cut Kilhuch's hair.

All King Arthur's warriors and chieftains were in the hall, and Gwenhuivar, Arthur's wife, was there also, when the King did honour to Kilhuch by cutting his hair for him. And the chief story-teller of the Island of Britain was there, and to the King, and to the King's warriors and chieftains, and to Kilhuch he told a story.

THE STORY OF PUIL, PRINCE OF DYVED

How Puil Went Into Annuvin, the Realm of Faerie

One day in the summer it came into the mind of Puil, Prince of Dyved, to go hunting, and the place in all the seven Cantrevs of Dyved that he chose to go hunting in was the Vale of the Cuch. Early in the morning he went there; he unloosed his hounds in the wood, he sounded his horn, and he began the chase.

As Puil followed his hounds he lost the companions who had come with him. Still he went on. He came in sight of a glade that was deep in the wood, and then he saw that he was alone. He heard the cry of hounds coming from a direction opposite to that in which his own hounds were going. And as his hounds came to the edge of that glade he saw a stag there; it was at bay before hounds that were not his. Then, as he came on with his hounds, those other hounds flung themselves on the stag and brought it down.

It was a great stag. Nevertheless, Puil did not examine it for a while, so taken was he with the sight of the hounds that had pulled the stag down. For these hounds had bodies that were shining white, and they had red ears, and as the whiteness of their bodies shone so did the redness of their ears glisten. Never in all the world had Puil seen hounds that were like these hounds. For a while he looked on them, and then he drove them off, and he set his own hounds to kill the stag.

Then, just as he had done this, he saw a horseman come out of the wood, riding towards him. He was on a large, light-grey steed, and he had a hunting horn around his neck; he wore a hunting dress that was of grey woollen. And when the horseman came near he spoke to Puil, saying: "Chieftain, I know who thou

7

art—Puil, Prince of Dyved—but I shall not give thee any salutation."

Then said Puil: "Art thou then of such great state that thou thinkest it beneath thee to give me salutations?" "I am of great state," said the stranger, "but it is not the greatness of my state that prevents my giving thee salutations." "What is it then?" asked Puil. "Thine own discourtesy and rude behaviour," answered the stranger.

Said Puil: "What rudeness and discourtesy have I shown, O Chieftain?" "Great rudeness and great discourtesy," answered the stranger. "Greater rudeness and greater discourtesy I never saw than yours in driving away hounds that were killing a stag and then setting your own hounds upon it. That was indeed a great rudeness." "A great rudeness indeed," said Puil, acknowledging the wrong he had committed.

Then said Puil: "All that can be done I will do to redeem thy friendship, for I perceive that thou art of noble kind." "A crowned King am I in the land that I come from," said the stranger. "Lord," said Puil, "show me how I may redeem thy friendship."

Said the stranger: "I am Arawn, a King of Annuvin.[1] Thou canst win my friendship by championing my cause. Know that Annuvin has another King, a King who makes war upon me. And if thou shouldst go into my realm and fight that King thou wouldst overthrow him, and the whole of the realm would be mine." "Lord," said Puil, "instruct me; tell me what thou wouldst have me do and I will do it to redeem thy friendship."

The King of Annuvin then said to Puil: "I will put my own appearance upon thee and I will take thine appearance upon myself, for it is in my power to do these things. And in my semblance thou shalt go into my kingdom. There thou shalt stay for the space of a year from to-morrow, and thereafter we shall meet in this glade." "Yes, Lord," said Puil, "but how shall I discover him whom I am to do battle with?" "One year from this night," said the King of Annuvin, "is the time fixed for combat between him and me. Be thou at the ford in my likeness. With

---

[1]Annuvin, the Realm of Faerie.

one stroke that thou givest him he will lose life. And if he should ask thee to give another stroke, do not give it, no, not if he entreat thee even. If thou shouldst give another stroke he will be able to fight thee the next day as well as ever." "If I go down to thy kingdom," said Puil, "and stay there in thy semblance for a year and a day, what shall I do concerning my own dominions?" "As to that," said the King of Annuvin, "I will cause, for I have such power, that no one in thy dominions, neither man nor woman, shall know but that I am thee. I will go there and rule in thy semblance and in thy stead." "Then gladly," said Puil, "will I go down into Annuvin, thy kingdom, and win thy friendship by doing what thou askest me to do." "Clear shall be thy path, and nothing shall detain thee until thou comest into my kingdom, for I myself will be thy guide." And saying this, the King of Annuvin, who had come into the wood with his hounds for no other purpose than to bring Puil into his realm on that day, conducted him into Annuvin.

And having brought him before the palace and the dwellings, he said: "Behold the court and the kingdom. All is in thy power from this day until a year from to-morrow. Enter the court; there is no one there who will not take thee for me. And when thou seest what is being done thou wilt know the customs of the place." When he had said this the man who had been with Puil went from his sight.

Then Puil, Prince of Dyved, went into that strange court, and there he saw sleeping-rooms, and halls, and chambers, that were the most beautiful he had ever looked on. And there came pages to him who took off his hunting dress, and clothed him in a vesture of silk and gold. All who entered saluted him. Then they brought him into the feasting-hall, and he sat by the side of a lady who had on a yellow robe of shining satin, and who was the fairest woman that he had ever yet beheld. He spoke with her, and her speech was the wisest and the most cheerful that he had ever listened to. There were songs with the feasting. And of all the courts of Kings on the earth this court of Annuvin was, to the mind of Puil, the best supplied with food and drink, with vessels of gold and with royal jewels.

A year went by. Every day for Puil there was hunting and

minstrelsy, there was feasting and discourse with wise and fair companions. And then there came the day on which the combat of the Kings was to take place, and even in the furthest parts of the realm the people were mindful of that day.

Puil went to the ford where the combat was to be, and the nobles of Arawn's court went with him. And when they came to the ford they saw that Havgan, the King against whom the battle was to be, was coming from the other side. Then a knight arose and spake, saying: "Lords, this is a combat between two Kings, and between them only. Each claimeth of the other his land and territory. This combat will decide it. And do all of you stand aside and leave the fight to be between the Kings."

Thereupon Puil in the semblance of Arawn approached Havgan. They were in the middle of the ford when they encountered. Puil struck Havgan on the centre of the boss of his shield, so that his shield was broken in two, and his armour was broken, and Havgan himself was flung on the ground over the crupper of his horse, and he received a deadly blow. "O Chieftain," he cried, "what right didst thou have to cause my death? I was not injuring thee in any thing; I know not wherefore thou wouldst slay me. But since thou hast begun to slay me, complete thy work." "Ah, Chieftain," said Puil, "I may yet repent of what I have done to thee. But I will not strike thee another blow." "My lords," said Havgan then, "bear me hence, for my death has come, and I shall no more be able to uphold you." "My nobles," said Puil, speaking as Arawn, "take counsel, and let all who would be my subjects now come to my side. It is right that he who would come humbly should be received graciously, but he that doth not come with obedience shall be compelled by force of swords." "Lord," said the nobles, "there is no King over the whole of Annuvin but thee." And thereupon they gave him homage. And Puil, in the likeness of Arawn, went through all the realm of Annuvin, and he received submission from those who had been Havgan's subjects, so that the two halves of the kingdom were in his power.

Thereupon he went to keep his tryst with Arawn. When he came into the glade in the wood the King of Annuvin was there to meet him and each rejoiced to see the other. "Verily," said

"But since thou hast begun to slay me, complete thy work."

Arawn, "may Heaven reward thee for what thou hast done for me. When thou comest thyself to thy own dominions," said he, "thou wilt see what I have done for thee."

Then Arawn, King of Annuvin, gave Puil back his own proper semblance, and he himself took on his own. Arawn went back to the realm of Annuvin, and Puil, Prince of Dyved, went back to his own country and his own dominions, and was lord once more of the seven Cantrevs of Dyved.

After he had been a while in his own country and dominions, Puil inquired of his nobles how his rule had been in the year that was past, compared with what it had been before. "Lord," said his nobles all, "thy wisdom was never so great before, and thou wast never so kind or so free in bestowing gifts, and thy justice was never more worthily shown than in this year." "By Heaven," said Puil, "for all the good you have enjoyed, you should thank him who hath been with you, for this is the way matters have been." And thereupon Puil related to his nobles all that had happened. "Verily, Lord," said they, "render thanks unto Heaven that thou hast made so good a friendship."

After that the friendship between Puil and Arawn was made even stronger. Each sent unto the other horses, and greyhounds, and hawks, and all such jewels as they thought would be pleasing to each other. And by reason of his having dwelt a year in Annuvin he lost the name of Puil, Prince of Dyved, and he was called Puil, Chief of Annuvin, from that time forward.

Now when the story-teller had told of Puil's life so far, Kai said, "By the hand of my friend, this hunting was a fair adventure for Puil." Arthur had combed out Kilhuch's hair with the golden comb, and now he took the scissors whereof the loops were of silver, and he began to cut the hair. Then the story-teller who was in the hall, told:

THE STORY OF PUIL, PRINCE OF DYVED

How Puil Won Rhiannon for His Wife, and How Rhiannon's Babe Was Lost to Her

It is told of Puil that once, while a feast was being prepared for him in his chief palace, he arose and went to walk and came to a mound that was above the palace, and went to the top of it. "Lord," said one of those who were with him, "it is peculiar to this mound that whosoever sits upon it cannot go thence without receiving a blow or seeing a wonder." "I fear not to receive a blow," said Puil, "with so many valiant men around me, and as to a wonder, I should gladly see one. I will therefore go and sit upon the mound."

And upon the mound he sat. And while he sat there he and those who were with him saw a lady on a horse of pure white, with a garment of shining gold upon her, coming along the highway; the horse seemed to move at a slow and an even pace, and to be coming towards the mound. "My men," said Puil, "is there any amongst you who knows yonder lady?" "There is not, Lord," said they. "Go, one of you, and meet her," said Puil.

Then one of the men arose, and he came upon the road to meet her, and she passed by, and he followed as fast as a man on foot might follow. But the greater his speed, the further did the lady distance him. And when he saw that it profited him nothing to follow her, he returned to Puil, and he said to him, "Lord, it is idle for anyone in the world to follow her on foot." "Then," said Puil, "go to the palace and take the fleetest horse that thou seest, and go after her."

The man went and took the horse and went forward on the highway. And he came to an open level plain, and he put spurs to his horse. But the more he urged his horse, the further was

13

the lady from him. And yet she seemed to keep the same pace as before. Then his horse began to fail. The man returned to the place where Puil was, and he said: "Lord, it will avail nothing for anyone to follow yonder lady. I know of no horse in these realms swifter than this one, but all its swiftness did not help me to gain on her." "Of a truth," said Puil, "there must be some enchantment in this. Now let us go back to the palace."

So they went back to the palace, and they partook of the feast that was prepared. The next day, after the first meal, they arose, and Puil said: "We will go as yesterday to the top of the mound. And do thou," said he to one of his young men, "take the swiftest horse in the field and bring it along." The young man did so, and they went towards the mound, taking the horse with them.

And no sooner had they sat down on the top of the mound than they saw the lady on the same horse, and in the same apparel, coming along the same road. "Behold," said Puil, "the lady of yesterday. Make ready, youth, to learn who she is." "My Lord," said the youth, "that will I gladly do."

The lady was opposite them then. The youth mounted his horse; and before he had settled himself in the saddle, she passed by, and there was a clear space between them. But her speed seemed no greater than it had been on the day before. Then the youth put his horse into an amble, thinking that for all the gentle pace that his horse went at, he should soon overtake her.

But soon he saw that this pace would not avail him, and so he gave his horse the reins. But still he came no nearer to her than when he went at a foot's pace. The more he urged his horse the further the lady was from him, and yet she rode no faster than before.

When the youth saw that it availed him not to follow her, he returned to the place where Puil was. "Lord," he said, "the horse can do no more than thou hast seen." "I see indeed," said Puil, "that it avails not that anyone should follow her. And by Heaven," said he, "she must have an errand to someone, if her haste would allow her to declare it."

They went back to the palace, and they spent the rest of the day in feasting. The next day, when it came towards evening,

Puil said: "Let us go to the mound and sit there. And do thou," said he to his page, "saddle my horse, and go with him to the road, and bring also my spurs with thee." The youth did as he was bidden.

They went and they sat upon the mound, and ere they had been there but a short while, they beheld the lady coming by the same road, and in the same manner, and at the same pace. Then Puil said: "Bring me my horse." And no sooner was he upon the horse than the lady passed him. He turned after her and followed her. His horse went bounding, and he thought that with the second step or the third he should come up with her. But he came no nearer to her than at first.

Then Puil urged the horse to his utmost speed, but that speed availed nothing; he could not come up with the lady. Then he cried out: "O maiden, for the sake of him whom thou best lovest, stay for me." And when he said that, she turned around. "I will stay gladly," she said, "and it were better for thy horse hadst thou asked me long since."

She stopped, and she threw back that part of her headdress that covered her face. And she fixed her eyes upon him, and began to talk with him. "Lady," he asked, "whence comest thou, and whereto dost thou journey?" "I journey on my own errand," said she, "and right glad am I to see thee." "My greetings unto thee," said he. And saying that he looked on her, and he thought that all the beauty of all the maidens and ladies he had ever seen was as nothing compared to her beauty. "Lady," said he, "wilt thou tell me aught concerning thy purpose?" "I will tell thee," said she, "that my chief quest was to find thee." "Behold," said Puil, "this is to me the most pleasing quest on which thou couldst have come. And wilt thou tell me who thou art?" "I will tell thee, Lord," said she. "I am Rhiannon, the daughter of Heveid."

And then she said: "They sought to give me in marriage against my will, but no husband would I have, and that because of my love for thee, neither will I yet have one unless thou dost reject me. And hither have I come to hear thy answer." "By Heaven," said Puil, "this is my answer: If I might choose amongst all the ladies and damsels in the world, thee would I choose." "Verily," said she, "if thou art thus minded, make a pledge to meet me ere I am given to another." "The sooner I may do so, the more pleasing will it be unto me," said Puil. "I will have it that thou meet me this day twelvemonth at the palace of Heveid, my father," said she, "and I will cause a feast to be prepared so that it will be ready against thy coming." "Gladly," said Puil, "will I keep this tryst." "Lord," said Rhiannon, "keep in health, and be mindful of thy promise; and now I will go hence."

And so they parted. Puil went back to those who were in his palace. But whatever questions they asked him respecting the damsel, he always turned the discourse upon other matters. And so a year went by.

Then it came to the day that was a twelvemonth from the time that Rhiannon had spoken with him. Puil caused a hundred of his knights to equip themselves and go with him to the palace of Heveid. And when they came to that palace Puil was greeted with joy and gladness, and he saw that a feast had been made ready against his coming.

Heveid received Puil as the man to whom his daughter would be given as a bride. And when they went into the feast, Heveid sat on one side of Puil, and Rhiannon sat on the other side, and there were songs with the feasting, and Puil, talking with Rhiannon, found that she was as wise and mirthful as she was lovely.

Now when the feast was at its height, Puil saw a young man enter the feasting-hall; he was clothed in a garment of satin, and he had the bearing of one who had power and wealth. He came to where Puil sat with Rhiannon, and he gave salutation to Puil. "The greeting of Heaven be unto thee, my soul," said Puil. "Come thou and sit down." "Nay," said the young man, "I have a boon to ask thee." Then said Puil, without thinking because of the great joy that was around him, "Whatsoever boon thou mayest ask of me, as far as I am able, thou shalt have it of me." "Alas," said Rhiannon, "wherefore didst thou give that answer?"

But the young man said exultantly: "Has he not given me my answer in the presence of these nobles?" "My soul," said Puil, disturbed now, "what is the boon thou askest?" "The lady whom best I love is to be thy bride this night; I come to ask her of thee—that is the boon I crave. And also I would have the feast and the banquet that is in this place." Then Puil was silent because of the answer he had given. "Be silent now as long as thou wilt," said Rhiannon, "for never did a man make worse use of his wits than thou hast done. This is the man to whom they would have given me in marriage against my will. Now thou hast given me to him. He is Gwaul, the son of Clud, a man of great power and wealth. And because of the word thou hast spoken, bestow me upon him, lest thou be shamed before these nobles for not keeping thy word."

Then Puil was silent, not knowing what to say. "Lady," said he, "never can I do as thou sayest." Then said Rhiannon, speaking in a low voice, "Bestow me upon him, and I will cause that I shall never be his. Do this, I pray thee, and so keep thy word. But tell him that as for the feast and the banquet they cannot be given him, for they have already been bestowed. And I on my part will promise to become his bride this night twelvemonth." "Lord," said Gwaul, "it is meet that I have an answer to my request." "As much of that thou hast asked me as in my power to give, thou shalt have," said Puil. And then Rhiannon said, "As for the feast and the banquet that are here, I have bestowed them on the men of Dyved and the warriors that are with us. These I cannot suffer to be given to another person. But in a year from to-night a banquet shall be prepared for thee in this palace, that I may become thy bride."

Gwaul was content with this. He went away. Then Rhiannon put into Puil's hand a little bag. "See that thou keep it well," she said. "And at the end of a year be thou here, and bring this bag with thee, and let thy hundred knights be in the orchard up yonder. And when he is in the midst of joy and feasting, come thou in by thyself, clad in ragged garments, and holding thy bag in thy hand. Go to him and ask of him for a boon your bagful of food. I will cause that if all the meat and liquor that are in these seven Cantrevs were put into it, it would be no fuller than before. And after a great deal has been put in, he will ask thee whether thy bag will ever be full. Say thou then that it never will, until a man of noble birth and of great wealth arise and press the food in the bag with both his feet, saying, 'Enough has been put therein; and I will cause him to go and tread down the food in the bag, and when he does so, turn thou the bag, so that he shall be up over his head in it, and then slip a knot upon the thongs of the bag. Let there be also a bugle horn about thy neck, and as soon as thou hast bound him in the bag, wind thy horn, and let it be a signal between thee and thy knights in the orchard. And when they hear the sound of the horn, let them come down upon the palace."

After that Puil went back to Dyved, as Gwaul went forth to his possessions. And they both spent that year until it was time for the feast at the palace of Heveid. Then Gwaul set out to the feast that was prepared for him, and he came up to the palace, and was received there with rejoicing. Puil, also, came. He went to the orchard with his hundred knights, as Rhiannon had commanded him, having the bag with him. And Puil was clad in coarse and ragged garments, and wore large, clumsy old shoes on his feet. And when they were at the height of the feast, he went towards the hall, and when he entered the feasting-hall, he went up and saluted Gwaul, the son of Clud, and his company, both men and women. "Heaven prosper thee," said Gwaul, "and the greeting of Heaven be unto thee." "Lord," said Puil, "may Heaven reward thee. I have an errand unto thee." "Welcome be thine errand, and if thou ask of me that which is just, thou shalt have it gladly." "It is fitting," answered Puil. "I crave but from want, and the boon that I ask is to have this small bag filled with food." "A request within reason is this," said Gwaul, "and gladly shalt thou have it. Bring him food," he said then to the attendants. A great number arose and began to fill the bag, but for all that they put into it, the bag was no fuller than at first. "My soul," said Gwaul, "will thy bag be ever full?" "It will not, I declare to Heaven," said Puil, "for all that may be put into it, unless one possessed of lands, and domains, and treasure, shall arise and tread down with both his feet the food that is within the bag." Then Rhiannon said unto Gwaul: "Arise up quickly and go and press down the food." "I will do so willingly," said he. So he rose up, and he put his two feet into the bag.

Then did Puil turn up the sides of the bag, so that Gwaul was over his head in it. Then did Puil shut up the bag and slip a knot on it. Then did he take the bugle horn that was around his neck, and blow a blast on it. The hundred knights who were in the orchard heard the bugle horn; they came quickly into the palace and the feasting-hall; they seized upon all who had come with Gwaul, and they put them in the dungeons of the palace.

Then Puil threw off his rags, and his old shoes, and his tattered array. And his knights, as each one came in, struck a blow upon the bag. "What is here?" one would say to the other. "A badger," the other would say. And so they went on striking on the bag in which Gwaul was held. And every one as he came in would ask: "What game are you playing in this way?" "The Game of Badger in the Bag," he would be told. And this was how Badger in the Bag was first played.

"Lord," said the man in the bag, "if thou wouldst hear me, I deserve not to be killed in a bag in this way." "Lord," said Heveid to Puil, "he speaks truth. It were fitting that thou listen to him, for he deserves not to die in this way." "Verily," said Puil, "I will do thy counsel concerning him." Then Rhiannon said: "Take a pledge from him that he will never seek to revenge himself for what has been done to him. And further: thou wilt have to satisfy minstrels and suitors with gifts. Let him give unto them in your stead out of his treasures. And that will be punishment enough for Gwaul." "Gladly will I do all that," said the man in the bag.

And upon that Puil, taking the counsel of Heveid and Rhiannon, let Gwaul out of the bag, and liberated his henchmen also. "Verily, Lord," said Gwaul, "I am greatly hurt, and have many bruises; I have need to be anointed; with thy leave I will go forth." "Willingly," said Puil, "mayest thou do so." And so Gwaul and his henchmen left the palace, and Gwaul went towards his own possessions.

And then the hall was set in order for Puil and his knights, and Heveid and his people, and they went to the tables, and they sat down, and the feasting began all over again. And now Puil sat with Rhiannon, and they feasted, and had song, and spent the night in mirth and tranquillity. And when the time

Then did he take the bugle horn and blow a blast on it.

came that they should sleep, Puil and Rhiannon went into their own chamber.

The next morning, at the break of day, Rhiannon said to her husband: "My Lord, arise, and begin to give gifts to the minstrels who attended the feast, and to the suitors who have come seeking something for themselves. Refuse no one to-day that may claim thy bounty." "That I will gladly do," said Puil. And he arose and went into the hall, and he caused silence to be proclaimed, and he desired the minstrels and all the suitors to show and to point out what gifts were to their wish and desire. And this being done, the feast went on, and Puil denied no one anything while the feast lasted. And when the feast had ended Puil said to Heveid, "My Lord, with thy permission I will set out for Dyved, for with Rhiannon I would go hence." "Certainly," said Heveid. "And may Heaven prosper you."

So Puil and Rhiannon set out for Dyved the next day. They came to the palace of Narberth and there they abode. And there came to them the chief men and the most noble ladies of the land of Dyved, and of these there were none to whom Rhiannon did not give some rich gift, either a bracelet, or a ring, or a precious stone. And Puil and Rhiannon ruled the land prosperously both that year and the next.

It is told that there came a time when the nobles of the land came to Puil with words that troubled him greatly. Rhiannon, they said, had no children; they asked that Puil take another wife so that a son born to him might rule over them and over Dyved. "Thou canst not always continue with us," they said to him.

Then said Puil, greatly troubled: "Come to me in a year from this, and I will talk this matter over with you." The nobles agreed to this, and they went away. And then, greatly to the joy of Puil, before the end of the year, a child was born to Rhiannon.

Great was Rhiannon's joy when the boy was born, but it was not long until her joy was changed into sorrow. Six women were sent into her chamber to tend the child and to mind Rhiannon. At midnight the mother slept. And the women who were there to watch over her and over the child slept also. The women wakened up before it was day; they looked towards where they had laid the child, and behold! the child was not there. "Oh," said one of the women, "the boy born to our Lord Puil is lost. It will be little punishment for our neglect in watching over him if we are all burned for this." Said one of the women then: "Is there any plan by which we could save ourselves?" "There is," said another woman. "Listen to me, and I will tell you a way by which we can save ourselves."

Then this woman said: "There is a stag-hound with a litter of whelps outside. Let us kill one of the whelps, and rub the blood of the whelp near Rhiannon, and then declare to all that she killed her son in a madness that came on her—killed him and then threw his body to wolves that were outside."

The women agreed to this dreadful counsel. They killed one of the stag-hound's litter, and they spread its blood near Rhiannon. Towards morning she awoke, and the first words that she said were: "Women, where is my son?" "Lady," said they all, "ask us not concerning thy son; we have naught but the blows and bruises got by struggling with thee, and of a truth we never saw any woman so violent as thou, for it was of no avail to contend with thee. Hast thou not thyself slain and flung away thy child? Claim him not therefore of us." "For pity's sake," said Rhiannon, "charge me not falsely. Heaven knows all, and if you say this thing from fear, I declare, before Heaven, that I will defend you." "Truly," said they, "we would not bring evil on ourselves for anyone in the world." "For pity's sake," said Rhiannon, "you will receive no evil by telling the truth." "The truth is that we strove to save the child from being slain by thee, and that we could not save him." And for all her words, whether fair or harsh, Rhiannon received but the same answer from the women.

And when Puil arose, the story that the women told came to his ears, and he was made very sorrowful. The story went through all the land. Then his nobles came once more to Puil, and they besought him to put away his wife, because of the great crime she had done. Puil answered, telling them that he would not put Rhiannon away. "If she has done wrong," he said, "let her do penance for it."

Her husband's words seemed wise to Rhiannon. She preferred to do penance rather than contend any more with the six women. And the penance that she took upon herself was this: that she should sit every day for seven years near the horse-block that was without the gate of the palace, and that she should relate her story to all who came that way and who did not know it, and that she should offer the guests and strangers, if they would permit her, to carry them upon her back into the palace. And so it was with Puil's wife, Rhiannon.

In another part of Dyved there lived a lord whose name was Teirnon, and this lord was one of the best and the kindest of men. And unto his house there belonged a mare than which neither mare nor horse in all the land was more beautiful. On the first day of May every year this mare had a foal, but no one after knew what became of the foal; it was gone before anyone saw it.

One night, when it was coming near May Day, Teirnon was talking with his wife, and he said, "How simple we are, wife! Our mare foals every year, and we have none of her colts. Why should we not watch and mind her when she comes near to foal-ing? The vengeance of Heaven be upon me, if I learn not what it is that takes away her foals." So Teirnon said, and he caused the mare to be brought into the house. And on May Day he armed himself, and he watched the mare through that night.

The mare had a large and beautiful foal. Teirnon saw it stand-ing up beside the mare. And while he was wondering at its size he heard a great tumult, and after the tumult, behold! a great claw came through the window and into the house, and it seized the foal by the mane. Then Teirnon drew his sword, and he struck off the arm that had the claw at the elbow, so that portion of the arm together with the foal, was left in the house with him. And then he heard a tumult and a wailing outside.

Teirnon opened the door of his house and he rushed out towards where he heard the noise, but he could not see the cause of the tumult because of the darkness of the night. Still he rushed in the direction of it. Then he remembered that he had left the door of his house open, and he went back to it. And when he came to his door, behold! there was a child laid, an infant boy in swaddling clothes, wrapped in a mantle of satin.

Then Teirnon drew his sword.

He took the boy, and he saw that he was very strong for the age he seemed to be.

Then Teirnon closed the door of his house and he went into the chamber where his wife was. "Lady," said he, "art thou sleeping?" "I was asleep," his lady said, "but as soon as thou camest in I awakened." "Here is a child," he said, "a boy for thee, if thou wilt, since thou hast never had one." "My Lord," said Teirnon's wife, "what adventure is this?" Then Teirnon told her all that had befallen. "Verily, Lord," said she, "what sort of garments are on the boy?" "A mantle of satin," he told her. "He is then a boy of noble lineage," she replied. And then she said: "My Lord, I will rear this boy as my own."

They had the child baptized, and they gave him a name, and they reared him in their court until he was a year old. Before that year was over he could walk stoutly, and he was larger than a boy of three years old, even one of good growth and size. He was nursed a second year, and then he was as large as a child of six years old. At the end of the fourth year he would get the grooms to allow him to take the horses to water. Marvellously indeed did the boy grow.

One day his wife said to Teirnon: "Where is the colt that thou didst save on the night that thou didst find the boy?" "I commanded the grooms to take charge of it," said Teirnon. "Would it not be well, Lord," said she, "to have the colt broken in and given to the boy, seeing that on the same night thou didst find the boy the colt was foaled?" "I will allow thee," said Teirnon, "to give the boy the colt." "Lord," said she, "may Heaven reward thee; I will give it to him." So the horse was given to the boy, and the grooms broke the horse in so that he was able to ride it.

About this time tidings of Rhiannon and her punishment came to Teirnon and his wife. And Teirnon, because of his friendship for Puil and because of the pity he felt for Rhiannon, inquired closely concerning for all who came to his court. Often he lamented the sad history he had heard, and often he pondered within himself, and often he would look steadfastly upon the boy.

Everything in Puil's appearance was known to Teirnon, for of yore he had been one of his followers. And as he looked upon the boy he had reared, it seemed to him that he had never seen so great a likeness between father and son as there was between this boy and Puil, Chief of Annuvin. Then a time came when he told his wife all that was in his mind, and he told her that they, perhaps, did wrong in keeping the boy with them while so noble a lady as Rhiannon was undergoing a penance that had to do, perhaps, with the loss of him.

Then his wife agreed with him that the boy should be taken to Puil's palace to find out if it might be that he was Puil's son. So Teirnon equipped himself, and no later than the next day he set out for Puil's palace at Narberth, and the boy went with him, mounted on the horse that Teirnon's lady had given him.

As they drew near to the palace they beheld Rhiannon sitting beside the horse-block. And when they came opposite to her, she said: "Chieftain, do not go any further thus; I will bear thee and those who are with thee on my back into the palace, and this is my penance for having slain my own son." "Oh, fair lady," said Teirnon, "think not that I will be one to be carried on thy back." "Neither will I," said the boy. "Truly, my soul," said Teirnon to her, "we will not have it so."

They went forward to the palace, and there was joy at their coming, for Teirnon was liked well by Puil. And when they had washed, Teirnon and the boy sat down to a feast that had been prepared for them, and Teirnon sat between Puil and Rhiannon, and the boy sat at the other side of Puil. And after they had eaten, discourse began.

Teirnon's discourse was all about the adventure of the mare and the boy, and how he and his wife had reared the boy as their own. And all who were in the hall looked on the boy. Then Teirnon said: "I believe there is none of this host who will not perceive that the boy is the son of Puil." "There is none," all of them said, "there is none who is not certain thereof." "I declare to Heaven," said Rhiannon, "if this be true, there is indeed an end to all my troubles." "Teirnon," said Puil, "Heaven reward thee that thou hast reared the boy up to this time, and being of gentle lineage, it were fitting that he repay thee for it." "My Lord," said Teirnon, "it was my wife who nursed him, and there is no one in the world so afflicted as she at parting with him. It were well that he should bear in mind what I and my wife have done for him." "I call Heaven to witness," said Puil, "that while I live I will support thee and thy possessions, as long as I am able to preserve my own. And when he has power, he will more fitly maintain them than I."

After Teirnon had put the boy into Puil's charge, they had counsel together and they agreed to give him over to one of the great men of the land, to Pendaran Dyved, to be brought up by him. "And you both shall be my companions," said Puil to Teirnon, "and both shall be foster-fathers unto him." "This is good counsel," said all who were present.

After that Teirnon set out for his own country and his own possessions. And he went not without being offered the fairest jewels, and the finest horses, and the choicest dogs; but he would take none of them.

The boy was named Prideri by his mother. He was brought up carefully as was fit, so that he became the fairest youth, and the most comely, and the best skilled in all good games, of any in the kingdom. And thus passed years and years away, until the end of Puil's, the Chief of Annuvin's, life came and he died. Then Prideri ruled over the seven Cantrevs of Dyved prosperously, and added three other Cantrevs to his possessions, and he was beloved by his people, and by all around him.

II

HOW THEY SOUGHT THE MAID OLWEN

And now Kilhuch's hair was cut by the hand of Arthur. Then all the champions and warriors in the hall gathered around them to hear what boon the youth would ask of the King. "Whatsoever boon thou mayest ask, thou shalt receive it, be it what it may that thy tongue shall name," said King Arthur. "Pledge the truth of Heaven and the faith of thy kingdom thereof," said Kilhuch. "I pledge it thee, gladly." "I crave of thee then, that thou obtain for me Olwen, the daughter of Yspaddaden, and this boon I seek likewise at the hands of thy warriors. I seek it from Kai and Bedour, and the hundred others who are here."

Then said Arthur, "I have never heard of the maiden of whom thou speakest, nor of her kindred, but I will gladly send messengers in search of her. Give me time to seek her for thee." The youth then said, "I willingly grant from this night to that at the end of the year."

King Arthur thereupon sent messengers to every land to seek for the maiden who was named Olwen. At the end of the year the messengers returned without having gained any more knowledge or intelligence concerning her than on the day they went forth.

And when the year had come to its end Kilhuch said: "Everyone has received his boon, and yet I lack mine. I will depart from this place, and the blame for my going will be upon King Arthur." Then said Kai: "Rash youth! Dost thou lay blame on Arthur? Go with us, and we will not part from each other until thou dost confess that the maiden exists not in the world, or until we obtain her for thee." Kai rose up, and thereupon King Arthur called upon Bedour, who never shrank from any enterprise upon which Kai was bound. None was equal to him in swiftness throughout the Island. And although he was one-handed, three warriors could not shed blood faster than he on the field of battle. Another quality he had: his lance could produce a wound equal to those of nine opposing lances. And Arthur called upon Gwalchmai, because he never returned home without achieving the adventure of which he went in quest. He was the best of footmen and the best of knights. He was nephew to Arthur, the son of his sister and his cousin. And Arthur called upon his guide to go with them; as good a guide was he in a land which he had never seen as he was in his own. And he called upon one who knew all tongues to go with them also, and he called upon another, who, if they were in a savage country, could cast a charm and an illusion over them, so that none might see them whilst they could see everyone. And so, with Kai, and Bedour, and Gwalchmai, with the guide, and the one who knew all tongues, and the one who could cast a charm and an illusion, the youth Kilhuch went forth from Arthur's Court in quest of Olwen, the daughter of Yspaddaden.

They went on until they came to a vast open plain. They saw a castle in the middle of it, and it seemed to them to be the fairest castle in the world. They went towards it; that day they journeyed until evening, and when they thought they were nigh the castle, they were no nearer to it than they had been in the morning. And the second and third day they journeyed, and even then scarcely could they reach so far. But at last they came nigh it. And when they were before the castle they beheld a vast flock of sheep, a flock boundless and without end. And upon the top of a mound there was a herdsman keeping the sheep.

They went nearer, and they saw that a mantle of skins was upon the man, and that by his side there was a shaggy mastiff, larger than a steed of nine winters old. And all the trees that were dead and burnt on the plain that mastiff had burnt with his breath down to the very ground.

Then said Kai to the one who knew all tongues: "Go thou and salute yonder man." "Kai," said he in reply, "I engaged not to go further than thou thyself." "Let us go together then," said Kai. Said the man of spells who was with them: "Fear not to go thither, for I will cast a spell upon the hound, so that he shall injure no one." And this he did.

They went up to the mound where the herdsman was, and they said to him: "How dost thou fare, O herdsman! Whose are the sheep that thou dost keep, and to whom does yonder castle belong?" "Stupid are ye, truly," said the herdsman. "Through the whole world it is known that this is the castle of Yspaddaden." "And who art thou?" they asked. "I am Custennin, and my brother is Yspaddaden," said the herdsman, "but he oppressed me because of my possessions. And ye, also, who are ye?" "We are men on an embassy from King Arthur, and we have come to seek Olwen, the daughter of Yspaddaden." "O men, the mercy of Heaven be upon you, do not do that for all the world. None who ever came hither upon that quest has returned alive."

Then Kilhuch went to the herdsman and told him who he was, and told him who his father and mother were. Also he gave unto him a ring of gold. The herdsman sought to put it on his finger, but it was too small for him, so he put it in his glove. When he went into his house he gave the glove to his wife to keep; she took the ring from the glove that was given her, and she said: "Whence came this ring? Thou art not wont to have good fortune." And he said: "Kilhuch, the son of the daughter of Prince Anlod, gave it to me; thou shalt see him here in the evening. He has come to seek Olwen as his wife." When he said that the herdsman's wife was divided between joy and sorrow, joy because Kilhuch was her sister's son and was coming to her, and sorrow because she had never known anyone depart alive who had come on that quest.

They came to the gate of Custennin's dwelling, and when she heard their footsteps approaching, the woman ran with joy to meet them. They entered the house, and they were all served, and soon after they went forth to amuse themselves. Then the woman opened a stone chest that was before the chimney-corner, and out of it arose a youth with yellow curling hair. Said one: "It is a pity to hide this youth. I know that it is not his own crime that is thus visited upon him." "This is but a remnant," said the woman, Custennin's wife. "Three and twenty of my sons has Yspaddaden slain, and I have no more hope of this one than of the others." Then said Kai: "Let him come and be a companion with me, and he shall not be slain unless I also am slain with him." It was agreed that the youth would go with Kai; then they ate.

Said the woman: "Upon what errand come you here?" "We come to seek Olwen for this youth," said Kai. Then said the woman: "In the name of Heaven, since no one from the castle hath yet seen you, return again whence you came." "Heaven is our witness, that we will not return until we have seen the maiden," said they.

Said Kai: "Does Olwen ever come hither, so that she may be seen?" "She comes here every Saturday to wash her head," said the woman, "and in the vessel where she washes, she leaves all her rings, and she never either comes herself or sends any messengers to fetch them." "Will she come here if she is sent for?" "Unless you pledge me your faith that you will not harm her, I will not send for her," said the woman. "We pledge our faith," said all of them. So a message was sent, and Olwen came.

The maiden was clothed in a robe of flame-coloured silk, and about her neck was a collar of ruddy gold, on which were precious emeralds and rubies. More yellow was her head than the flower of the broom, and her skin was whiter than the foam of the wave, and fairer were her hands and her fingers than the blossoms of the wood anemone amidst the spray of the meadow fountain. The eye of the trained hawk, the glance of the three-mewed falcon, was not brighter than hers. Her bosom was more snowy than the breast of the white swan, her cheek was redder than the reddest roses. Whoso beheld her was filled with love. Four white trefoils sprang up wherever she trod. And therefore was she called Olwen, the Maiden of the White Footprints.

She entered the house, and sat beside Kilhuch upon the foremost bench; and as soon as he saw her he knew her. And Kilhuch said unto her: "Ah! maiden, thou art she whom I have loved; come away with me. Many a day have I loved thee." "I cannot go with thee, for I have pledged my faith to my father not to go without his counsel, for his life will only last until the time of my espousal. But I will give thee advice if thou wilt take

Olwen entered the house.

it. Go, ask me of my father, and that which he shall require of thee, grant it, and thou wilt obtain me; but if thou deny him anything, thou wilt not obtain me, and it will be well for thee if thou escape with thy life." "I promise all this," said Kilhuch.

Olwen returned to her chamber; then Kilhuch and all his friends set out for Yspaddaden's castle.

They came to the castle; they slew the nine guards that were at the nine gates, and they died in silence; they slew the nine watch-dogs without one of them barking. They went through the gates and they went into the hall of Yspaddaden's castle.

"The greeting of Heaven and of man be unto thee, Yspaddaden," said they, when they went in. "And you," said the enchanter, rising up, "wherefore have you come?" "We have come to ask thy daughter Olwen, for Kilhuch." "Where are my pages and my servants? Raise up the forks beneath my two eyebrows which have fallen over my eyes, that I may see the fashion of him who would be my son-in-law." And his pages and servants did so, and Yspaddaden looked at them. "Come hither to-morrow, and you shall have an answer," he said.

They rose to go forth. Then Yspaddaden seized one of the three poisoned darts that lay beside him, and threw it after them. Bedour caught it, and flung it, and pierced the enchanter grievously with it through the knee. "A cursed ungentle son-in-law, truly," said he. "I shall ever walk the worse for this rudeness, and shall ever be without a cure. This poisoned iron pains me like the bite of a gadfly. Cursed be the smith who forged it, and the anvil whereon it was wrought! So sharp it is!"

That night Kilhuch and his friends stayed in the house of Custennin the Herdsman. The next day with the dawn they arrayed themselves and proceeded to the castle. They entered the hall, and they said: "Yspaddaden, give us thy daughter in consideration of the dower which we will pay to thee. And unless thou wilt do so, thou shalt meet with thy death on her account." Then said he: "Her four great-grandmothers and her four great-grandfathers are yet alive, and it is needful that I take counsel of them." "Be it so," answered they. They rose up to leave the hall. And as they rose up, he took the second dart that was beside him, and cast it after them. And the man who could

Yspaddaden seized the second of the poisoned darts and cast it after them.

work all spells caught it, and flung it back at him, and wounded him in the centre of the breast, so that it came out at the small of his back. "A cursed ungentle son-in-law, truly," said he, "the hard iron pains me like the bite of a horse-leech. Cursed be the hearth whereon it was heated, and the smith who formed it! So sharp it is! Henceforth, whenever I go up a hill, I shall have a scant in my breath, and a pain in my chest." By this time, Kilhuch and his friends had gone from the hall.

The third day they returned to the palace. And Yspaddaden said to them: "Shoot not at me again unless you desire death. Where are my attendants? Lift up the forks of my eyebrows which have fallen over my eyeballs, that I may see the fashion of the man who would be my son-in-law." Then they arose, and, as they did so, Yspaddaden took the third poisoned dart and cast it at them. And Kilhuch caught it and threw it vigorously, and wounded him through the eyeball. "A cursed ungentle son-in-law, truly," said the enchanter. "As long as I remain alive, my eyesight will be worse. Whenever I go against the wind, my eyes will water; and peradventure my head will burn, and I shall have a giddiness every new moon. Cursed be the fire in which it was forged. Like the bite of a mad dog is the stroke of this poisoned iron." By this time Kilhuch and his friends had gone from the hall.

The next day they came again to the palace, and they said: "Shoot not at us any more, unless thou desirest such hurt, and harm, and torture as thou now hast, and even more." And after that Kilhuch went to him and said: "Give me thy daughter, and if thou wilt not give her, thou shalt receive thy death because of her." Yspaddaden said to him: "Come hither where I may see thee." They placed a chair for Kilhuch, and he sat face to face with the enchanter.

Said Yspaddaden: "Is it thou that seekest my daughter?" "It is I," said Kilhuch. "I must have thy pledge that thou wilt not do towards me otherwise than is just," said Yspaddaden, "and when I have gotten that which I shall name, my daughter thou shalt have." "I promise thee that willingly," said Kilhuch, "name what thou wilt." "I will name now," said the enchanter, "what I will have to get from thee for her dowry."

Then said Yspaddaden, the father of Olwen, "It is needful for me to wash my head, and shave my beard on the day of my daughter's wedding, and I require the tusk of the boar Yskithyrwyn to shave myself withal, neither shall I profit by its use if it be not plucked out of the boar's head alive."

Said Kilhuch, remembering that Olwen had told him that he must agree to do everything that her father asked him to do, "It will be easy for me to compass this, although thou mayest think it will not be easy."

"Though thou get this," said Yspaddaden, the Chief of the Giants, "there is yet that which thou wilt not get. There is no one in the world who can pluck the tusk out of the boar's head except Odgar, the son of Aedd, King of Ireland."

"It will be easy for me to bring Odgar, the son of Aedd, to the hunt of the boar and get him to pluck the tusk out of the boar's head."

"Though thou do that, there is yet that which thou wilt not do. I will not trust anyone to guard the tusk except Gado of North Britain. Of his own free will he will not come out of his kingdom, and thou wilt not be able to compel him."

"It will be easy for me to bring Gado to the hunt, although thou mayest think it will not be easy."

"Though thou get him to come, there is yet that which thou wilt not get. I must spread out my hair in order to have it shaved, and it will never be spread out unless I have the blood of the Jet Black Sorceress, the daughter of the Pure White Sorceress from the Source of the Stream of Sorrow on the bounds of Hell."

"It will be easy for me to compass this, although thou mayest think it will not be easy."

"Though thou get this, there is yet that which thou wilt not get. Throughout the whole of the world there is not a comb nor a razor nor a scissors with which I can arrange my hair, on account of its growth and its rankness, except the comb and razor and scissors that are between the two ears of the great boar that is called Truith."

"It will be easy for me to get the comb and razor and scissors from the boar Truith, although thou mayest think it will not be easy."

"It will not be possible to hunt the boar Truith without Drudwin, the Little Dog of Greit."

"It will be easy for me to bring to the hunting Drudwin, the Little Dog of Greit."

"Though thou get the Little Dog of Greit, there is yet that which thou wilt not get. Throughout the world there is no huntsman who can hunt with this dog, except Mabon, the son of Modron. He was taken from his mother when three nights old, and it is not known where he is now, nor whether he is living or dead."

"It will be easy for me to bring Mabon to the hunting, although thou mayest think it will not be easy."

"Though thou get Mabon, there is yet that which thou wilt not get. Gwynn, the horse that is as swift as the wave, to carry Mabon, the son of Modron, to the hunt of the boar Truith. His owner will not give the horse of his own free will, and thou wilt not be able to compel him."

"It will be easy for me to compass this, although thou mayest think it will not be easy."

"Though thou get the horse that is as swift as the wave, there is yet that which thou wilt not get. Thou wilt not get Mabon, for it is known to none where he is, unless it is known to Eidoel, his kinsman."

"It will be easy for me to find him, although thou mayest think it will not be easy."

"Though thou get him, there is that which thou wilt not get. Thou wilt have to have a leash made from the beard of Dillus the Bearded, for that is the only leash that will hold the hound. And the leash will be of no avail unless it be plucked from the beard of Dillus while he is alive. While he lives he will not suffer this to be done, and the leash will be of no use should he be dead, because it will be brittle."

"It will be easy for me to compass this, although thou mayest think it will not be easy."

"Though thou get this, there is yet that which thou wilt not get. The boar Truith can never be hunted without the son of Alun Dyved; he is well skilled in letting loose the dogs."

"It will be easy for me to compass this, although thou mayest think it will not be easy."

"And the boar Truith can never be hunted unless thou get the hounds Aned and Aethlem. They are as swift as the gale of wind, and they were never let loose upon a beast that they did not kill it."

"It will be easy for me to bring these hounds to the hunting, although thou mayest think it will not be easy."

"Though thou get them, there is yet that which thou wilt not get,—the sword of Gurnach the Giant; he himself will never be slain except with his own sword. Of his own free will he will not give the sword to thee, either for a price or as a gift, and thou wilt never be able to compel him."

"It will be easy for me to compass this, although thou mayest think it will not be easy."

"Difficulties thou shalt meet with, and nights without sleep, in seeking these things, and if thou obtain them not, neither shalt thou obtain my daughter."

"Horses shall I have, and chivalry; and my lord and kinsman Arthur will aid me in obtaining these things. And I shall gain thy daughter, and thou shalt lose thy life."

"Go forward. And when thou hast compassed all these marvels, thou shalt have my daughter Olwen for thy wife."

III

HOW THEY PERFORMED THE TASKS
SET BY THE CHIEF OF THE GIANTS

They returned to the palace, and they told King Arthur of the tasks that Yspaddaden, Chief of the Giants, had set the youth Kilhuch. Then Arthur sent messengers to find out where the boar was, and the messengers found him in Ireland, in the forests around the Seskin Mountain. And the messengers found that the boar Truith had with him seven pigs that were nearly as fierce as he.

When these tidings were brought back, Arthur summoned all the warriors that were in the Island of Britain, and all the warriors that were in France, and in Armorica, and in Normandy, and he summoned all his chosen footmen and all his valiant horsemen. With all these he went into Ireland. And in Ireland there was great fear and terror on account of his coming with that great host. When he landed there came to him the saints of Ireland, and they besought his protection. And Arthur granted protection to them, and they gave him their blessing.

Then Arthur sent a messenger to find out if the precious things that Yspaddaden spoke of were still between the ears of the boar, since it would be useless to encounter him if they were not there. Arthur's messenger went to seek the boar; he took the form of a bird, and in that form he descended on the top of the boar's lair. He saw that the precious things were between his ears, and he strove to snatch them away. But the boar rose up angrily and shook himself so that some of his venom fell upon Arthur's messenger, and the messenger was never well from that time forth.

Then Arthur, with his hounds and his huntsmen, went to the Seskin Mountain. The dogs were let loose on Truith and his seven pigs from all sides. The men of Ireland went out and fought against the boar. But in spite of dogs and men he was able to lay waste the fifth part of Ireland. The next day the household of Arthur strove with him; but Arthur's household were worsted by the boar, and they got no advantage over him. On the third day Arthur encountered Truith; he fought for nine days and nine nights, and he did not even kill one of the seven pigs that were with the boar.

After that Arthur sent his messenger again, the messenger who took the form of a bird. The messenger alighted on the top of the lair where Truith was with his seven pigs. He said to the boar: "By him who turned you into this form, speak, if one of you can speak." Then one of the seven pigs—the one whose bristles were like silver so that, whether he went through the wood or across the plain, he could be traced by the glittering of his bristles—made answer. "By him who turned us into these forms," said he, "we will not speak with Arthur. That we have been transformed is enough for us to suffer, without a host coming here to fight with us." "I will tell you," said the messenger, "that Arthur has come but for the comb, and the razor and the scissors that are between the ears of Truith." Said the other: "Except he first take his life, Arthur will never get these precious things from Truith. And we will arise up now, and go into Arthur's country, and there we will do all the mischief we can."

On account of this threat, Arthur and his host, and his horses and his dogs, had to go out of Ireland without delay. But he might not leave until he had told the saints of Ireland all that had befallen Branwen, the woman of Britain who came into Ireland when Matholluch was King. Arthur sat in his tent and the saints of Ireland stood before him on the day that he told the first half of the story.

*"Except he first take his life, Arthur will never get these precious things
from Truith."*

THE STORY OF BRANWEN

Her Captivity in Ireland

B ranwen was one of the chief ladies of Britain, and while she
lived there was no maiden in all the world lovelier than she.
Her brother was Bran, the son of Lyr, and he was the crowned
King of Britain, the Island of the Mighty. She had half-brothers
also; because of one of these half-brothers much trouble came
to Branwen.

One day great Bran sat upon the Rock of Harlech, looking
over the sea, and the nobles of his court were with him. As they
were there they saw ships coming from Ireland and making
towards them. The wind was behind them, and the ships neared
very rapidly. And when Bran and his court saw the ships near,
certain were they that they had never seen any that were better
furnished. On they came, with their flags of satin in the wind:
one of the ships outstripped the others, and Bran and his court
saw a shield lifted above the side of this ship, and the point of
the shield was upwards, and this they knew was a token of
peace. And the men on the ship put out boats and came towards
the land.

Now when they came upon the shore great Bran spoke down
to them from the place where he was, from the top of the rock.
"Heaven prosper you," he said, when the men had saluted him.
"Be ye welcome," said he, and then he asked to whom the ships
belonged, and who was chief amongst them. "Lord," said the
men, "Matholluch, the King of Ireland, is here; he is chief
amongst us, and to him the ships belong." "And will the King of
Ireland come to land?" great Bran asked. "Lord," said the men,
"he comes as a suitor unto you, and he will not land unless you
grant him his boon." "What boon does he crave?" asked Bran.

"He comes to ask you for Branwen, the daughter of Lyr, for his wife, so that, if it seems well to you, the Island of the Mighty may be leagued with Ireland, and both become more powerful." Said Bran: "Verily, let your King come to land, and we will take counsel about this marriage." That answer was brought to him, and the King of Ireland said: "I will go willingly." So he landed, and Bran and his court received him joyfully, and, when the counsel was held, it was resolved to bestow Branwen upon Matholluch, the King of Ireland.

And so the marriage was made, and Branwen, the loveliest of the world's maidens, became the bride of the King of Ireland. At the feast the King of the Island of the Mighty and Manawyddan, the son of Lyr, were on one side, and Matholluch on the other side, and Branwen, the daughter of Lyr, beside him. The feast was not in a house; it was under tents, for no house that was built up to that time could hold great Bran. At that feast there were also Branwen's two half-brothers, Nissen and Evnissen: one of these youths was a good youth and of gentle nature, and would make peace between his kindred, and cause his family to be friends when their wrath was at the highest, and this one was Nissen; the other would cause strife between brothers when they were most at peace, this one was Evnissen.

The next day they all arose, and the officers of the court began to equip and range the horses and the attendants. They were doing this when Evnissen, the quarrelsome man, came along. He asked whose might be the horses that they were ranging. "They are the horses of the King of Ireland, who is married to Branwen, your sister," he was told. "And is it thus they have done with a maiden such as she, bestowing her without my consent? They could have offered no greater insult to me than this," said he. And then Evnissen did a terrible thing: he rushed under the horses, and he cut off their lips at their teeth, and their ears close to their heads, and their tails close to their backs, so that he disfigured the horses and made them useless.

One went with tidings of this injury to Matholluch. "Verily, lord," this one said, "it was as an insult to you that this was meant." "An insult indeed," said Matholluch. "But I marvel that they should have given me a maiden of such high rank and so

beloved of her kindred if they desired to insult me." "Lord," said
the one who had come to him, "it is plain that their desire is to
insult you, and there is nothing for you to do but go to your
ships." Thereupon Matholluch, without saying a word to anyone
in Bran's court, set out for his ships that were at some distance
down the coast.

When Bran heard that Matholluch had quitted the court
without asking leave, he sent after him messengers to inquire
why he had done this. The messengers overtook him and asked
him wherefore he went forth. And Matholluch said to the messengers: "I marvel that the insult was not done me before they
had bestowed upon me a maiden so exalted as Branwen." "Truly,
Lord," said they, "it was not the will of any that are of the court
that thou shouldst have received this insult, and indeed, the dis-
honour is greater unto Bran than unto thee." "Verily," said he, "I
think it is. Nevertheless, Bran cannot recall the insult that has
been given me." When they heard him say this the messengers
went back.

They told Bran what reply Matholluch had made to them.
Then the King of the Island of the Mighty sent after the King of
Ireland another embassy, telling him that he should have a
sound horse for every horse that had been injured, and besides,
as an atonement for the insult, he should have a staff of silver, as
large and as tall as himself, and a plate of gold of the breadth of
his face. And Matholluch was to be told who it was who had
wrought the injury and the insult, and that he could not be put
to death by the King because he was the King's half-brother.
"Let Matholluch come and meet me," said great Bran, "and we
will make peace in any way he may desire."

The embassy came to where Matholluch was and gave him
the message of the King, and told him of all the King offered.
He listened to what they had to say; then he had counsel with
his followers, and after counsel he agreed to accept the atonement and to go back. So they turned towards Bran's court. And
when they were sitting together, the King of the Island of the
Mighty and the King of Ireland, the King of the Island of the
Mighty said: "I will make the atonement even greater than I
said, for I will give unto thee a cauldron, the property of which

is, that if one of thy men be slain to-day and be cast therein, to-morrow he will be as well as ever he was at his best, except that he will not regain his speech." And hearing him say this, Matholluch gave Bran great thanks. "I had the cauldron of a man who had been in thy land," Bran said, "and I would not give it except to one from Ireland." "Lord," said Matholluch, "Heaven reward thee."

When the feasting was over, Matholluch journeyed towards Ireland, and Branwen went with him, and they sailed with thirteen ships, and they came to Ireland. At first they were received with great joy, and Branwen for a while enjoyed honour and friendship. But when the injury done to Matholluch's horses became known, the people blamed the King for having submitted to the insult and taken atonement from Bran. Then a tumult arose, and the King's foster-brothers and those who were nearest to him demanded vengeance on the people of Britain for what had been done to Matholluch in their country. Branwen drew their enmity, and in the end they drove her from the King's chamber, and made her be a cook for the court. After they had done this they said to Matholluch: "Forbid now the ships and the ferry boats and the coracles, that they go not into Britain, and such men as come over from Britain, imprison them that they go not back and relate to Bran what we have done unto Branwen." The King gave orders as they had told him, and for three years no ship, nor ferry boat, nor coracle went from Ireland into Britain, and any man that came into Ireland from Britain was imprisoned so that he could not go back again. And so it was for as long as three years.

All that time Branwen was baking bread and preparing food for the court. She reared a starling on the cover of her kneading-trough, and she taught the bird to speak, and she made it know what manner of a man her brother was, great Bran. And after she had reared it and trained it she wrote a letter telling of her woes in Ireland, and she bound the letter under the starling's wing, and she sent it towards Britain. And into the Island of Britain the starling came: it found Bran in Arvon, and it alighted on his shoulder and ruffled its feathers so that the letter was seen. Bran took the letter and read it, and when he had read the letter he grieved exceedingly because of his sister's, Branwen's, woes.

Immediately Bran sent out messengers summoning the men of Britain together. Then all the power of the Island of the Mighty came before him, and he complained to them of the woes that his sister, Branwen, endured. They took counsel, and they resolved to go into Ireland to liberate Branwen from the thraldom that she endured in the King's court. And they resolved, too, that they should leave Britain under the charge of seven knights while they were gone, with Caradog, the son of Bran, as chief of the seven.

The ships of the Britons sailed for Ireland. But Bran did not go in any of the ships. He strode through the sea with what provisions he had on his own back. And so, with the ships sailing before the wind, and with great Bran striding through the sea, the Britons came to where two rivers of Ireland flow into the sea.

Now there were upon the shore two swineherds of the King of Ireland; they saw a strange appearance upon the sea, and they ran back and they came before the King. "Lord," they said, "we have marvellous tidings: a wood have we seen upon the sea, in a place where we never yet saw a single tree. And there was a mountain beside the wood, which moved, and there was a ridge on the top of the mountain, and a lake on each side of the ridge. And the wood, and the mountain, and all these things moved." "Verily," said the King, "there is none who can tell us aught concerning this appearance, unless it be Branwen."

So messengers went to Branwen and told her of what the swineherds had seen, and asked her what she thought the strange appearance might be. "The men of the Island of the Mighty," she said, "who have come hither on hearing of my ill-treatment and my woes." "What is the wood that was seen upon the sea?" they asked. "The yards and the masts of the ships of the Britons," she answered. "And what was the mountain that was seen by the side of the ships?" "Bran, my brother," she answered. "So he comes to shoal-water, for there is no ship that can hold him." "What is the ridge with the lake on each side of it?" "I will tell you," she answered. "On looking towards Ireland,

"So he comes to shoal-water, for there is no ship that can hold him."

Bran, my brother, is angered, and his two eyes that are on each side of the ridge that is his nose, are like two lakes that are darkened."

On hearing this, the lords and the chief men of Ireland were brought together in haste; they took counsel, and after counsel they advised Matholluch to go with all of the men of Ireland to one side of the river Shannon and then to have the bridge over the river broken, so that the river might be between the men of Ireland and the men of Britain. "For there is lodestone at the bottom of this river, so that neither ship nor vessel can pass over it," they told Matholluch. Then the King had the bridge broken down, and he and the men of Ireland kept one side of the river.

"Lord," said his nobles to Bran, when they came to this river, "knowest thou the nature of the river here? Nothing can go across it when there is no bridge over it." Then Bran said words that afterwards became a proverb: "He who will be chief, let him be a bridge." Thereupon he lay across the breadth of the river, and hurdles were placed upon him, and the whole host of the men of Britain passed over him as over a bridge.

Then Bran rose up, and as he did, behold! messengers from Matholluch came before him. They saluted him, and gave him greeting, and said to him: "Matholluch has given the Kingdom of Ireland to Guern, thy nephew, the son of Matholluch and Branwen, and he has done this as an atonement for the wrong that he did to Branwen, thy sister." To this message Bran would return no answer. The messengers he had sent came back to Matholluch and said: "Lord, prepare a better message for great Bran. He would not listen at all to the message we bore him."

Matholluch asked his councillors what he might do to win the favour of great Bran. "Lord," they said to him, "there is no other counsel to be given you except this: it has never been known for Bran to be within a house. Make a house that will hold him— hold him and the men of the Island of the Mighty on one side, and the men of Ireland on the other side, and give over thy kingdom to his will. And by reason of the honour thou dost him in making a house to hold him, he will make peace with thee." Matholluch agreed to this, and messengers went again from him to great Bran. And when the offer was brought to Bran he accepted it, and peace was made between him and Matholluch.

On the second day Arthur sat on the deck of his ship, and the saints of Ireland were in their coracles around the ship, and Arthur told them of the destruction that was wrought in those days in Ireland, and he told of the return of Branwen to the Island of Britain.

THE STORY OF BRANWEN

Her Rescue by Bran

The men of Ireland went to work, and they built a house that was vast and strong. But in building it they had a crafty device in mind. This was the device: on each side of the hundred pillars that were in the house they should put a bracket, and on each bracket they should place a leathern bag, and in every leathern bag they should have an armed man. And this was done so that the armed men might destroy the host of Britain when Bran and his people came within the great house.

Now there had come with Bran, Branwen's two half-brothers, Nissen and Evnissen. Evnissen was the first to come into the vast house that the men of Ireland had built; he came into it before the host of the Island of the Mighty. He searched all through it with fierce and savage looks, and he descried the leathern bags which were around the pillars. "What is in this bag?" he asked of a man of Ireland. "Meal, good soul," said the man. Then Evnissen put his hand upon the bag, and he felt about it until he came to the man's head that was within the bag. He squeezed the head until the man was dead. He went from that bag, and he put his hand upon another, and he asked what was in it. "Meal, good soul," said the man who was by the pillar. He felt about this bag until he felt the head of the man who was in it, and he squeezed that man's head so that he died without making a groan. And from pillar to pillar and from bag to bag Evnissen went, squeezing and killing every armed man who was being hidden there.

It was then that the hosts came into the vast house. The men of Ireland entered on one side, and the men of the Island of the Mighty entered on the other, and they sat down, and there was

peace between them. Then the sovereignty of the land was conferred upon Guern, Matholluch's and Branwen's son and great
Bran's nephew. And when the sovereignty was conferred on
him, Bran called the boy unto him, and he took the boy upon his
vast knee, and from Bran the boy went to Manawyddan, and he
was beloved by all who beheld him. To Nissen he went then, and
he went to him lovingly, and by him he was caressed, and with
him he stayed.

Then said the savage Evnissen: "Wherefore comes not my
nephew, the son of my sister, to me? Though he were not King
of Ireland, yet willingly would I fondle the boy." "Cheerfully let
him go to thee," said Bran, and the boy went to Evnissen.

And when he took him in his arms Evnissen said in his savage
heart that the slaughter that was about to befall was unthought
of by the hosts that were in the house. He arose; he took the boy
by his feet and he flung him headlong into the fire. Then all hurried to the fire, and all hurried about the vast house; never was
there so great a tumult in any house before as was made by them
then, as each man armed himself. And while they all sought
their arms, Bran supported Branwen between his shield and his
shoulder.

Then, in that vast house, there began a battle between the
men of Britain and the men of Ireland. The men of Ireland had
an advantage in that battle: the cauldron that Bran, before this,
had given to Matholluch was in their possession. They kindled a
fire under it, and they cast the dead bodies into it until it was
full, and the next day they came out of the Cauldron of
Renovation, fighting men as good as before, except that they
were not able to speak.

Evnissen cast himself amongst the dead bodies of the men of
Ireland. After he had cast himself down, two unshod men came
to where he was, and, taking him to be a man of Ireland, flung
him into the cauldron. Then Evnissen stretched himself in the
cauldron, so that he burst it into four pieces: he burst his own
heart also in that effort; so died that savage-hearted man.

After that the men of Ireland who were slain did not come
forth as fighting men the next day, and so the host of the Island
of the Mighty gained success. But although they gained success,

they were not victorious: out of their great host seven men only escaped; Bran himself was wounded, wounded in the foot by a poisoned dart.

It was then that Bran spoke to the seven followers who were left to him, commanding them to cut off his head. "And take my head," said he, "and bear it unto the White Mount in London, and bury it there, with the face towards France. A long time you will be upon the road. In Harlech you will be feasting seven years, the Birds of Rhiannon singing unto you the while. And all that time this head of mine will be with you as pleasant company as ever it was when on my body. And in Penvro you will be fourscore years, and you may remain there, and the head with you uncorrupted, until you open the door that looks towards Cornwall. And after you have opened that door, there you may no longer tarry; set forth then to London to bury the head, and go straight forward."

So they cut off the head of great Bran, who was also called Bran the Blessed, and the seven went forward therewith. Branwen was the eighth with them. They came to an island and they sat down to rest. And Branwen looked towards Ireland and towards the Island of the Mighty, to see if she could descry them. "Alas," said she then, "woe is me that I was ever born; two islands have been destroyed because of me!" Then she uttered a groan that all of the seven heard, and her heart broke, and she died! They made a four-sided grave for Branwen, and they buried her on the banks of the Alau.

Then the seven journeyed forward towards Harlech, bearing the head with them. And when they came to Harlech they met a multitude of men and women coming towards them and crying. "Have you any tidings?" Manawyddan asked of them. "We have none," said the people, "except that Caswallon, the son of Beli, has conquered the Island of the Mighty, and is crowned King in London." "And what has become," the seven asked, "of Caradog, the son of Bran, and the seven knights who were left with him to guard the island?" "Caswallon came upon them, and slew six of the men, and Caradog's heart broke for grief thereof; for he could see the sword that slew the men, but the hand that wielded the sword he could not see. Caswallon had flung upon him the Veil of Illusion, so that no one could see him slay the men, but the sword only could they see."

Then the seven men with the head of Bran the Blessed went on to Harlech, and there they stopped to rest, and meat and liquor were provided, and they sat down to eat and drink. And there came three birds, the Birds of Rhiannon, and began singing unto them a certain song, and all the songs they had ever heard were unpleasant compared to this song; and the birds seemed to them to be at a great distance from them over the sea, yet they appeared as distinct as if they were close by. And at the feast they stayed for seven years, and for seven years they heard the music of the Birds of Rhiannon.

And the end of seven years they went forth and they came into Penvro. And there they found a fair and regal spot overlooking the ocean; and a spacious hall was therein. They went into that hall, and two of its doors were open, but the third door was closed, that which looked towards Cornwall. "See, yonder," said Manawyddan, "is the door that we may not open." That night they feasted and were joyful, and of all they had seen of food laid before them, and of all they had heard of, they remembered nothing; neither of that nor of any sorrow whatsoever. And there they remained fourscore years, unconscious of having ever spent a time more joyous and mirthful. And never were they more weary than when at first they came into that hall, neither did they, any of them, know the time they had been there. And having the head with them, it was as if Bran had been with them himself. And because of the fourscore years spent there with the head of Bran, it was called "The Entertaining of the Noble Head."

But a day came when one said to another: "Evil betide me if I do not open the door to know if that is true which is said concerning it." So one opened the door and looked towards Cornwall. And then, when they had looked, they were conscious of all the ills and all the evils they had ever sustained, and of all the friends and companions they had lost from the time when the host of the Island of the Mighty went into Ireland, and of all the miseries that had befallen them. They were conscious of all these things as if all of them had befallen them on that spot, and especially were they conscious of the great ill that had come to them in the death of great Bran, their lord. And because of their perturbation they could not rest, but journeyed forth with the head towards London. They buried the head of great Bran in the White Mount, and when it was buried there they knew that no invasion could come across the sea to the Island while the head was in that concealment.

So ends the story concerning the wrong done unto Branwen, and concerning the entertainment of Bran, when the host of the sevenscore countries and ten countries went over to Ireland to avenge the wrong done unto Branwen; and concerning the seven years' banquet in Harlech, and the singing of the Birds of Rhiannon, and the sojourning of the head of Bran for the space of fourscore years.

IV

HOW THE TUSK
AND THE SWORD WERE WON

Thereafter Arthur and his household were in the Island of Britain. And one day Kai and Bedour went and sat upon a beacon cairn on the top of the mountain Plinlimmon, in the highest wind that ever was in the world.

Then looking around them they saw to the south, afar off, a great smoke that did not bend with the wind. Kai, looking at it, said, "By the hand of my friend, yonder is the fire of a robber." They hastened towards the smoke; they came so near to it that they could see a huge wild man scorching a boar. "Behold, yonder is the greatest robber that ever fled from Arthur," said Bedour. "Dost thou know him?" said Kai. "I know him," said Bedour, "he is Dillus the Bearded." "And there is no leash in the world," said Kai, "that will hold Drudwin, the Little Dog of Greit, save a leash made from the beard of this Dillus." "Even that will be useless," said Bedour, "unless his beard be plucked alive from his face with wooden tweezers; if his beard be plucked out when he is dead, it will be brittle and it will not hold the Little Dog of Greit. What should we do to pluck his beard out?" "Let us suffer him," said Kai, "to eat as much as he will of the meat, and then fall asleep, and after that we may be able to pluck the beard from his face."

They hid, and they watched the huge robber cook and then eat the whole of the boar. While he was cooking it and eating it they made wooden tweezers. And when they knew that Dillus was asleep, when his loud snores came to them, they made a pit under his feet. They thrust the huge robber into the pit, and they filled the pit up with clay so that he could not move in it. And while Dillus the Robber was held in this way, they plucked out his beard with the wooden tweezers, and out of his beard they made the leash that would hold Drudwin, the Little Dog of Greit.

It was Arthur who obtained the Little Dog of Greit. A little while before this a maiden whose name was Creidulad was betrothed to a youth named Gwythur. But before she became his bride Creidulad was carried away by force by Gwyn. Then Gwythur gathered up his forces and he attacked Gwyn. But Gwyn overcame him and captured many of Gwythur's nobles. And amongst the nobles captured was Greit who owned the dog Drudwin.

When Arthur heard of this war he went into the North, and he summoned Gwyn before him. And the nobles whom Gwyn had captured, Arthur caused to be liberated. He made a peace between Gwythur and Gwyn, and the peace was on the condition that the maiden should remain in her father's house without advantage to either of the chieftains who had fought for her, and that they should fight for her every first of May, from thenceforth until the day of doom, and that whichever of them should then be conqueror should have the maiden for his bride.

For having reconciled the chieftains Arthur was given Greit's dog, Drudwin. The leash that could hold the Little Dog of Greit was already in Arthur's keeping, and all was ready for the hunting of the boar Yskithyrwyn.

The boar was in the North and Arthur was in the North. Gado, King of North Britain, was there too. They went to the chase of the boar, the chief huntsman leading the Little Dog of Greit, held by the leash that was made out of the beard of Dillus the Robber. Arthur came leading his own hound, Cavall. And Gado, mounted on Arthur's mare Lamrei, was first to attack the boar. He wielded a mighty axe, and, greatly daring, he came valiantly up to the boar, and clove his head in twain. But the boar was not killed by that stroke. A hound held him while Odgar, the son of the King of Ireland, plucked the tusk out of his jaw. Now the boar was not slain by the dogs Yspaddaden had spoken of, but by Cavall, Arthur's own dog.

Kai and Bedour went through the land together. They came to a vast castle, the largest surely in the world. And, behold! a black man, huger than three of the biggest men they had ever seen, came forth out of the castle. They spoke to him, and said, "Whence comest thou, O man?" "From the castle which you see yonder." "Whose castle is that?" they asked. "Stupid are ye truly, O men. There is no one in the world that does not know to whom that castle belongs. It is the castle of Gurnach the Giant."

Then they said to the huge man, "What treatment is there for guests and strangers who alight at the castle?" "O Chieftains, Heaven protect you," said the black man. "No guest ever returned thence alive, and no one may ever enter therein unless he is a craftsman bringing a craft with him."

On hearing the huge man say this, Kai went towards the castle. "Open the gate," he said. "I will not open it," said the porter. "Wherefore wilt thou not?" "The knife is in the meat, and the drink is in the horn, and there is revelry within the hall of Gurnach the Giant. Except for a craftsman who brings his craft, the gate will not be opened this night." "Verily, porter," said Kai, "I bring a craft with me." "What is thy craft?" said the Giant's porter. "I am the best burnisher of swords in the world." "I will go and tell this to Gurnach the Giant, and I will bring thee an answer," said the porter.

The porter went into the hall, and Gurnach the Giant said to him, "Hast thou any news from the gate?" "There is a man at the portal who desires to come in," said the porter. "Didst thou inquire of him if he possessed a craft?" "I did inquire." "And what answer did he make you?" "He told me that he was a man well skilled in the burnishing of swords." "Then I have need of him. For a long time I have sought for some one who might polish my famous sword, and I found no one. Let this man enter, since he brings with him his craft."

The porter thereupon returned and opened the gate. Kai went in by himself. And when he entered the hall he saluted Gurnach the Giant, and a chair was placed for him opposite the Giant's. Gurnach said to him: "O man, is it true what is reported of thee, that thou knowest how to burnish swords?" "I know full well how to do so," answered Kai. Then Gurnach called on his attendants, and the famous sword was brought to Kai.

Kai took a blue whetstone from under his arm; he asked the

Giant whether he would have his sword burnished white or blue. "Do with it as it seems good to thee," answered the Giant. Then Kai polished one half of the blade and put the sword in the Giant's hand. "Will this please thee?" he asked. "I would that the whole of the blade was like the part you have polished," said the Giant. And then he said to himself, "When the whole of the blade is polished, I will slay him."

After a while he said to Kai: "It is a marvel to me that such a man as thou should be without a companion." "O noble sir," said Kai, "I have a companion, and he is the best teller of tales in the world." "Who may he be?" asked the Giant. "Let the porter go forth, and I will tell him whereby he may know my companion. The head of his lance will leave its shaft, and draw blood from the wind, and will descend upon its shaft again." The porter went to the gate and opened it. Bedour entered the hall and saluted Gurnach. The Giant said to him: "Tell me a tale while your companion is burnishing my sword." Thereupon Bedour began to tell the story that is called, "The Story of Lud and Levellis."

The giant said, "Tell me a tale while your companion is burnishing my sword."

The Story of Lud and Levellis

Said Bedour: Three plagues fell upon the Island of the Mighty, the like of which had never been known by anyone in the Island. The first was a race that had come in, a race of magicians called the Coranians. So great was their power that there might be no discourse on the face of the Island, however low it might be spoken, but what if the wind met it, it was known to this race. And by reason of this, the Coranians were very powerful and the men of Britain could do nothing against them.

The second plague was a shriek, a shriek which came on every May Eve, over every hearth in the Island of Britain. And this shriek went through the people's hearts, and so scared them that the men lost their hue and their strength, and the women their children, and the young men and maidens lost their senses, and all the animals and trees and the earth and the waters were left barren.

And the third plague was this: no matter how much of provisions and goods might be prepared in the King's court, were there even so much as meat and drink for a whole year, none of it could ever be found, except what was consumed on the first night. And of two of these plagues no one ever knew their cause, therefore was there better hope of the people being freed from the first than from the second and third.

That was after the time of Beli the Great who had for sons, Lud, Caswallon, and Levellis. After the death of Beli, the kingdom of the Island of Britain fell into the hands of Lud his eldest son; and Lud ruled prosperously, and rebuilt the walls of London, and encompassed it about with numberless towers. He was a mighty warrior, and generous and liberal in giving meat and drink to all that sought them. And though he had many castles and cities, the city he had rebuilt he loved more than any.

He lived therein most part of the year; therefore was it called Caer Lud, and then Caer London, and at last, London.

Lud loved his brother Levellis because he was a wise and a discreet man. Levellis took the daughter of the King of France for his wife. The crown of the kingdom came with the maiden, and thenceforth Levellis ruled the land of France wisely and happily.

Now when the three plagues spoken of afflicted the Island of Britain, King Lud felt sorrow and care because he knew not how he might free his people from them. And at last he resolved to go to the King of France, his brother, to seek his counsel as to what might be done.

First he caused the men of Britain to make ready a fleet. They had to make it ready in secret and in silence lest the Coranians, that race of magicians, should know of their errand. And when all was made ready they went into their ships, Lud and those whom he chose to bring with him. And then, with no sound from the sailors, the ships began to cleave the seas towards France.

And Levellis, seeing the ships coming, sailed in a fleet to meet his brother. And then, in a single ship, each came towards the other. Levellis came aboard Lud's ship. And when they were come together, each put his arms about the other's neck, and they welcomed each other with brotherly love.

Then Levellis said that he knew the cause of his brother's coming to his land. And in order that the wind might not catch their words, nor the Coranians know what they might say, Levellis caused a long horn to be made, and through this horn they discoursed. But whatever words they spoke through this horn, one to the other, neither of them could hear anything but harsh and hostile words. And when Levellis understood this, he knew that there was a demon thwarting them, and changing what words were said through the horn, and he caused wine to be put therein to wash it. And through the virtue of the wine, the demon was driven out and the brothers talked to each other through the horn without their words being changed.

Levellis assured Lud that he had power to destroy the race of the Coranians. He would give him, he said, certain insects; these insects were to be bruised in water, and the water was to be cast over the Coranians. That would destroy the whole tribe. But the same water cast over the men of Britain would not destroy them.

The second plague, he said, was because, in the Island of Britain, there were two dragons fighting one against the other. The dragon that was being overcome made the fearful outcry. And Levellis told Lud how he might come to see the two dragons fighting, and how he might put them into a place where no outcry could be heard from either of them.

The cause of the third plague, he said, was a mighty man of magic, who took the King's meat, and the King's drink, and the King's store. Through illusions and charms he was able to cause everyone to sleep. Levellis counselled Lud to keep watch himself upon his food and provisions. "And lest he should overcome thee with sleep," he said, "let there be a cauldron of cold water by thy side, and when thou art oppressed with sleep, plunge into the cauldron."

Then Lud returned to his own land. Soon afterwards he brought together in one place the men of Britain and the tribe of the magicians. He had ready the water in which the insects were bruised; he flung it over all who were there. The men of Britain were unharmed by the water, but it no sooner fell upon the Coranians than they ran from the place. Never afterwards were they seen on the Island of Britain.

After this Lud caused the Island to be measured in its length and its breadth. He found the place that was the centre of the Island, and in that place he caused the earth to be dug, and in the pit a cauldron to be set, a cauldron that was filled with the best mead that could be made, and he put over it a covering of fine satin. King Lud himself watched by the pit and the cauldron. And in the middle of the night two dragons came and began to fight with each other. When they had wearied each other out with fighting, they fell down, and they came upon the covering of satin, and they drew it with them to the bottom of the cauldron. They drank up all the mead and they lay in the cauldron, asleep. Then Lud folded the covering around the cauldron, and he had it, with the dragons within it, borne away and carried within a secure place that he had, a place within the mountain of Snowdon. And there he had the dragons closed up, and whether they lived or whether they died there, no man knew, and the fearful outcry that one of the dragons used to make was heard no more in King Lud's dominions.

And after the dragons had been closed in that secure place, King Lud caused a great banquet to be prepared in his palace. And when the banquet was ready, he had a vessel of ice-cold water placed by his side, and he himself, with his arms beside him, watched over the banquet that was spread out in the hall.

About the third watch of the night he began to hear songs that were enchantments. They lulled him, and he became drowsy, and drowsiness urged him to sleep. But then he went into the vessel of ice-cold water, and he became wakeful again. And many times during that night did his drowsiness urge him to sleep, but each time he went within the ice-cold water and became wakeful again.

And at last, behold! a man of vast size, clad in strong, heavy armour, came into the hall. He carried with him a basket of an enormous size, and he set the basket down in the middle of the hall, and he began to put into it all the meat, and bread, and drink that were upon the great tables. And as King Lud watched it seemed wonderful to him that any basket on the earth could hold so much.

The Giant had lifted up the basket to take it out of the hall when King Lud went to him. "Stop," said the King. "You have done many insults to me before this, and you have taken much that was mine away from me, but you will not take away what you have gathered, unless your skill in arms and your valour be more than mine."

Then the Giant laid the great basket down on the floor, and he prepared for battle with King Lud. The encounter was fierce between them, and glittering fire flew out from their arms. But when it was near daylight the Giant weakened; he fell across the great basket and King Lud grappled with him. And then, this third plague that had afflicted him and his people, King Lud threw down on the earth. The Giant besought his mercy. "How can I grant thee mercy," said the King, "after the many injuries thou hast done to me and to my people?" "All the losses I ever caused thee," said the Giant, "I will make atonement for." And after that he brought back to the King basket after basket of provisions, until he had brought back as much as he had taken away. And the provisions that the Giant brought back were spread out in King Lud's banqueting hall, and the people of the country came, and they all feasted well.

And thus King Lud freed the Island of Britain from the three plagues that afflicted it. From thenceforth until the end of his life, in prosperity and peace did Lud, the son of Beli, rule the Island of the Mighty. And thus the story ends.

By this time the sword was burnished; Kai gave it unto the hand of Gurnach the Giant, to see if he were pleased with it. And seeing the burnished blade, the Giant said to himself: "The work is done, and now I will slay the workman." To Kai he said: "I am content therewith." Said Kai: "It is thy scabbard that hath rusted thy sword; give it to me that I may take out the wooden sides of it and put in new ones." He took the scabbard from him with one hand, and he took the sword with the other. Then he came and stood over against the Giant, as if he would have put the sword into the scabbard. But with it he struck at the head of the Giant, and he cut off his head at one blow. Then Kai and Bedour released the captives that the Giant held in his vast castle. Also they took away the great store of goods and jewels that the castle held. Then they went back to Arthur's palace with the famous sword of Gurnach that Kilhuch had need of for his hunting of the boar Truith.

V

HOW THE GREAT SALMON
TOOK THEM TO MABON

Now after they had put into his hands the sword of Gurnach the Giant, Arthur said to them: "Which of the marvels will it be best for us to seek now?" "It will be best," said they, "to seek for Mabon, the son of Modron. But, Lord, stay thou here, thou canst not proceed with thy host in quest of such small adventures as these." The King said: "Kai and Bedour, I have hope of whatever adventure ye are in quest of, that ye will achieve it. Achieve ye this adventure for me."

So they went on until they came to where the Blackbird of Kilgurry nested. Then Arthur's messenger who went with them and who knew all the languages, even the language of birds and beasts and fishes, said to the Blackbird: "Tell me if thou knowest aught of Mabon, the son of Modron, who was taken when three nights old from between his mother and the wall." And the Blackbird answered: "When I first came here, there was a smith's anvil in this place, and I was then a young bird; and from that time no work has been done upon it, save the pecking of my beak every evening, and now there is not so much as the size of a nut remaining thereof; yet the vengeance of Heaven be upon me, if during all that time I have heard of the man for whom you inquire. Nevertheless, I will do that which is right, and that which is fitting that I should do for an embassy from King Arthur. There is a race of animals who were formed before me, and I will be your guide to them."

The Blackbird flew before them, and he brought them to a place where there was a great stag standing. "Stag of Redinvre," said they, "behold we are come to thee, an embassy from Arthur, for we have not heard of any animal older than thou. Say, knowest thou aught of Mabon, the son of Modron, who was taken from his mother when three nights old?" The Stag said: "When first I came hither, there was a plain all around me, without any trees save one oak sapling, which grew up to be an oak with a hundred branches. And that oak has since perished, so that now nothing remains of it but the withered stump; but from that day to this I have been here, yet have I never heard of the man for whom you inquire. Nevertheless, being an embassy from King Arthur, I will be your guide to the place where there is an animal which was formed before I was."

The Stag went before them and led them to the place where was the Owl of Coom Cawlud. "Owl of Coom Cawlud, here is an embassy from King Arthur; knowest thou aught of Mabon, the son of Modron, who was taken after three nights from his mother?" "If I knew I would tell you," the Owl answered. "When first I came hither, the wide valley you see was a wooded glen. And a race of men came and rooted it up. And there grew there a second wood; and this wood is the third. My wings, are they not withered stumps? Yet all this time, even until to-day, I have never heard of the man for whom you inquire. Nevertheless, I will be the guide of Arthur's embassy until you come to the place where is the oldest animal in this world, and the one that has travelled most, the Eagle of Gwern Aby."

So to the Eagle of Gwern Aby the Owl led them. Then Arthur's messenger said: "Eagle of Gwern Aby, we have come to thee on an embassy from Arthur, to ask thee if thou knowest aught of Mabon, the son of Modron, who was taken from his mother when he was three nights old." The Eagle said: "I have been here for a great space of time, and when I first came hither there was a rock here, from the top of which I pecked at the stars every evening; and now it is not so much as a span high. From that day to this I have been here, and I have never heard of the man for whom you inquire, except once when I went in search of food as far as Lyn Liu. And when I came there, I struck my talons into a salmon, thinking he would serve me as food for a long time. But he drew me into the deep, and I was scarcely able to escape from him. After that I went with my whole kindred to attack him, and to destroy him, but he sent messengers, and made peace with me; and came and besought me to take fifty fish spears out of his back. Unless he know something of him whom you seek, I cannot tell who may. However, I will guide you to the place where he is."

So the Eagle guided them to the river where the Salmon was. And the Eagle said: "Salmon of Lyn Liu, I have come to thee with an embassy from Arthur, to ask thee if thou knowest aught concerning Mabon, the son of Modron, who was taken away at three nights old from his mother." "As much as I know I will tell thee," said the Salmon. "With every tide I go along the river upwards, until I come near to the walls of Gloucester, and there have I found such wrong as I never found elsewhere; and to the end that ye may give credence thereto, let one of you go thither upon each of my two shoulders." So Kai and Bedour went upon the two shoulders of the Salmon, and they proceeded until they came unto the wall of the prison, and they heard a great wailing and lamenting from the dungeon. Said Arthur's messenger: "Who is it that laments in this house of stone?" "Alas, there is reason enough for whoever is here to lament. It is Mabon, the son of Modron, who is here imprisoned; and no imprisonment was ever so grievous as mine." "Hast thou hopes of being released for gold or silver, or for any gifts of wealth, or through battle and fighting?" "By fighting will whatever I may gain be obtained."

Then Kai and Bedour went thence, and returned to Arthur, and told him where Mabon, the son of Modron, was imprisoned. And Arthur summoned the warriors of the Island of the Mighty, and they journeyed as far as Gloucester, to the place where Mabon was in prison. Kai and Bedour went upon the shoulders of the fish, whilst the warriors of Arthur attacked the castle. And Kai broke through the wall into the dungeon, and brought away the prisoner upon his back, whilst the fight was going on between the warriors. Then Arthur brought Mabon, the son of Modron, to his castle.

Then at the feast that was given in his honor Mabon told unto Arthur and his court this story of the ancient times in Britain.

Kai brought away the prisoner upon his back.

THE DREAM OF MAXEN THE EMPEROR

Maxen was Emperor of Rome, and he was a comelier man, and a better and wiser man, than any Emperor who had been before him. One day he went hunting with his retinue, and he came to a valley, and to where there was a river that flowed towards Rome. He hunted through that valley until mid-day. Then sleep came upon Maxen the Emperor. His attendants set up their shields around him upon the shafts of their spears to protect him from the sun, and they placed a gold enamelled shield under his head. And so Maxen the Emperor slept.

He dreamt, and in his dream he thought he was journeying along the valley of a river towards its source. Then he thought that he came to a mountain that was the highest in the world, a mountain that was as high as the sky. He crossed over the mountain, as high as it was, and he went through the fairest and most level regions that man ever yet beheld. Then he saw mighty rivers descending from the mountain to the sea, and towards the mouths of these rivers he proceeded. He came to the mouth of the largest river ever seen. He saw a fleet at the mouth of the river, and amongst the fleet he saw a ship that was larger and fairer than all the others. He saw a bridge of the bone of a whale from the ship to the land, and in his dream he went along the bridge, and came into the ship.

Then a sail was hoisted, and the ship was borne along the sea and into the far ocean. Then it seemed to him that he came to the fairest island in the whole world, and he traversed the island from sea to sea, even to its furthest shore.

Then he saw a mountain, and a river that flowed from it and fell into the sea. At the mouth of the river he beheld a castle, the fairest that man ever saw, and he went into the castle. And in it he saw a hall, the roof of which seemed to be all of gold, and the walls of which seemed to be entirely of glittering precious gems, and the doors of which seemed to be all of gold. Golden seats were in that hall, and silver tables.

And beside a pillar in the hall he saw a hoary-headed man, in a chair of ivory, with figures of two eagles of ruddy gold thereon. Bracelets of gold were upon the man's arms, a golden torque was about his neck, and his hair was bound with a golden diadem. Before him was a chests-board of gold, and he was carving out chess-men.

In his dream the Emperor saw another who was there. This was a maiden who was seated in a chair of ruddy gold. A vest of white silk was upon her, with clasps of red gold at the breast; a surcoat of gold tissue was upon her, and on her head there was a frontlet of red gold, and rubies and gems were in that frontlet, alternating with pearls and imperial stones. She was the fairest sight that man ever beheld.

The maiden rose from her chair, and, in his dream, the Emperor put his arms around her. Then they two sat down together in the chair of gold. And it seemed to Maxen that he had his arms about the maiden's neck, and his cheek by her cheek, when, lo! through the sounds in the camp around, through the chafing of the dogs at their leashing, and the clashing of the shields as they struck against one another, and the beating together of the shafts of the spears, and the neighing of the horses and their prancing, the Emperor awoke.

And when he awoke it seemed to him that the world was all empty, and that there was nothing in the world for him since he could look no more on the maiden he had seen in his sleep. Then his household spoke unto him, and said: "Lord, is it not past the time for thee to take thy food?" Thereupon the Emperor mounted his horse, the saddest man that mortal ever saw, and went forth towards Rome.

And still it seemed to Maxen that the world was empty for him. When his household went to drink wine and mead out of golden vessels, he went not with any of them. When they went to listen to songs and tales, he went not with them there; he slept, and as often as he slept he beheld in his dream the maiden he loved best. Except when he slept he saw nothing of her, for he knew not where in the world she was.

One day the page of his chamber spoke to him, and said: "Lord, all the people blame thee." "Wherefore do they blame me?" asked the Emperor. "Because they can get neither message nor answer from thee as men should have from their Lord. And because of this they blame thee and speak evil of thee." "Youth," said the Emperor, "do thou bring unto me the wise men of Rome, and I will tell them wherefore I am sorrowful."

So the wise men of Rome were brought before the Emperor, and he spake to them, telling them of the dream he was wont to have, and of the maiden whom he saw in his dream. Then the sages of Rome counselled him, telling him that he should send messengers for one year to the three parts of the world, to seek for the place that he saw in his dream and the maiden whom he saw in his dream.

Then messengers set out from Rome. They journeyed for the space of a year, wandering about the world, and seeking tidings concerning the place that the Emperor had seen in his dream. They came back at the end of a year, and they knew no more of the place that the Emperor had seen in his dream than they did the day they set forth. Then was Maxen even more sorrowful, for now he thought that he should never have tidings of her whom he loved best in the world.

Then the page of the chamber spoke to him, and said: "Lord, go forth to hunt by the way thou didst seem to go in thy dream, whether it were to the east, or to the west." So the Emperor went forth to hunt, and he came to the bank of the river. "Behold," said he, "this is where I was when I had the dream, and I went towards the source of the river westward."

Then, from that place the Emperor sent forth thirteen messengers, and they journeyed on until there came before them a high mountain, which seemed to them to touch the sky. And when they were over the mountain, they beheld vast plains, and large rivers flowing through. "Behold," said they, "the land which our master saw."

They went along the mouths of the rivers, until they came to the mighty river which they saw flowing to the sea. They saw the largest fleet in the world, in the harbour of the river, and one ship that was larger than any of the others. "Behold again," said they, "the fleet that our master saw." They went aboard the great ship, and they crossed the sea, and they came to the Island of Britain, the Island of the Mighty. They crossed the Island from sea to sea, and they saw the castle at the mouth of the river. The portal of the castle was open, and into the castle they went, and they looked on the hall in the castle. Then said they: "Behold, the hall which he saw in his sleep." They went into the hall, and they beheld the hoary-headed man beside the pillar, in the ivory chair, carving chess-men. And they beheld the maiden sitting on a chair of ruddy gold.

The thirteen messengers bent down upon their knees. "Empress of Rome, all hail," they said. The maiden said: "What mockery is this ye do to me?" "We mock thee not, Lady; but the Emperor of Rome hath seen thee in his sleep, and he has neither life nor spirit left because of thee. Thou shalt have of us therefore the choice, Lady, whether thou wilt go with us and be made Empress of Rome, or that Maxen the Emperor come hither and take thee for his wife?" The maiden said: "I will not deny what ye say, neither will I believe it too well. If the Emperor love me, let him come here to seek me."

By day and night the messengers hied them back to Rome. And when they came to Rome and into the palace, they saluted the Emperor, and they said unto him: "We will be thy guides, Lord, over sea and over land, to the place where is the woman whom thou best lovest, for we know her name, and her kindred, and her race."

And immediately the Emperor set forth with soldiers and with the thirteen messengers for his guides. Towards the Island of Britain they went, over the sea and the ocean. The Emperor knew the land when he saw it. And when he beheld the castle he said: "Look yonder, there is the castle wherein I saw the maiden whom I best love." And he went forward into the castle, and there he saw Eudav, the son of Caradog, sitting on a chair of ivory carving chess-men. And the maiden whom he beheld in his sleep, he saw sitting on a chair of gold. "Empress of Rome," said he, "all hail!" And the Emperor threw his arms around her neck. Then Helen, the daughter of Eudav, became the bride of Maxen, the Emperor of Rome.

He stayed at Eudav's castle, and he conquered the Island from Beli, the son of Manogan, and his sons, and drove them to the sea. And he gave the Island of Britain to Helen for her father, from the Channel to the Irish Sea. And he had three castles made for her in the places that she herself chose. And she chose to have the highest castle made at Arvon. After that two other castles were made for her, one the castle of Caerleon, and the other the castle of Caermarthen.

Seven years did Maxen the Emperor tarry in the Island of the Mighty. Now, at that time the men of Rome had a custom, that whatsoever Emperor should remain in other lands more than seven years should remain to his own overthrow, and should never be permitted to return to Rome again.

So the men of Rome made a new Emperor. And this one wrote a letter of threat to Maxen in Britain. There was nought in the letter but only this: "If thou comest, and if thou ever comest to Rome." Then sent Maxen a letter to the man who styled himself Emperor in Rome. There was nought in the letter but only this: "If I come to Rome, and if I come."

Thereupon Maxen set forth towards Rome with his soldiers. He conquered all lands that were on his way, and he came before the city and he was sure that he could take Rome from the one who styled himself Emperor.

But for a year he stayed before the city, and he was no nearer taking it than on the first day. And then there came to join him Helen's brothers from the Island of Britain. A small army was with them, but better warriors were in that small army than twice as many Romans. Helen went to see the armies that were encamped, and she knew the standards of her brothers. And she brought them, Kynan and Adeon, the sons of Eudav, to Maxen. And the Emperor was glad because of their coming, and he embraced them.

Then Helen's brothers watched Maxen's Roman army attack the city. And after they had watched the attack Kynan said to his brother: "We will try to attack the city more expertly than this." So they measured by night the height of the wall, and they sent their carpenters to the wood, and they had ladders made for every four men of their army. Now every day, at mid-day, the

Emperor in the camp and the Emperor in the city went to eat, and they ceased to fight on both sides till all had finished eating. In the morning the men of Britain were wont to take their food. Now, while the two Emperors were at meat, Kynan and Adeon and their army came to the city, and placed ladders against the wall, and forthwith they came in through the city.

The new Emperor had no time to arm himself when they fell upon him, and slew him, and many others with him. And three days and three nights were they subduing the men that were in the city. While some of the men of Britain fought, others kept the walls, lest any of the host of Maxen should come therein, until they had subjected the whole of Rome to their will.

Maxen the Emperor said to Helen: "I marvel, Lady, that thy brothers with their army have been able to do so little for me." "Lord," answered Helen, "the wisest youths in the world are my brothers. Go thou to them and ask them to take the city for thee." So the Emperor and Helen went forward. And then they saw that the gates of the city of Rome were opened, and they were told that none had taken the city, and that none could give it to Maxen, but the men of the Island of Britain.

Then Maxen sat on his throne with Helen beside him, and all the men of Rome submitted themselves unto them. Then the Emperor said to Kynan and Adeon: "Lords, I have now possession of the whole of my empire. And the army that is here I give unto ye to vanquish whatever region ye may desire in the world."

So Kynan and Adeon set forth and they conquered lands, and castles, and cities. And thus they continued until the young men that had come with them were grown grey-headed, from the length of time they were upon this conquest. Then Kynan said unto Adeon, his brother: "Whether wilt thou rather tarry in this far land, or go back to the land whence thou didst come forth?" Adeon chose to go back to his own land, and many went with him. And Mabon, the son of Modron, was one who was with Kynan in that time far back, and who remembers what it was that brought the men of Britain out from their own land, and brought certain of them back again.

VI

HOW KING ARTHUR MET
THE JET BLACK SORCERESS

The story was no more than finished when messengers came to Arthur to tell him that the boar Truith was nigh with his seven pigs. Arthur arose; with his household and his hounds he went to the chase.

All wasted was the country that Truith and his seven pigs had gone through. They came upon the seven pigs. Two of the huntsmen went against them and they were killed by the pigs. Then Arthur came up to where two of the pigs were, and he let loose the whole pack of his dogs upon them. The shouting of the men, and the barking of the dogs, and the grunting of the pigs brought the boar Truith to the help of the pigs.

From the time that Truith had crossed the Irish Sea, Arthur had not looked upon the boar until then. He set his men and his dogs upon the great-tusked, fiery-eyed boar. Thereupon Truith started off, his seven pigs with him. They went on, with the great company of men and dogs keeping them in chase. At the next place where they made a stand one of the pigs was killed. Again the chase went on. Where they made a stand next, Lawin and Gwis, two of the pigs, were killed. Again the chase went on. They made a stand at another place, and there two pigs more, Banu and Benwig, were killed by the dogs and the men. And the two pigs that were left parted from Truith there.

And of these two pigs, one went to Garth Gregin, and there he slew many men. And the other went on until he was met by the men of Armorica. In that encounter the pig slew the King of Armorica, and slew King Arthur's two uncles, and there the pig was slain.

But the boar Truith kept southward, and southward, too, went Arthur and his men in pursuit of him. The King summoned all Cornwall and Devon to meet him. To the estuary of the River Severn they came, and Arthur, looking on the warriors of the Island of the Mighty, said, "The boar Truith has slain many of my men, but, by the valour of warriors, while I live he shall not go into Cornwall. I will not follow him any longer; I will bring him to bay, and oppose him life to life." Then the warriors of the Island of the Mighty said that all of them would oppose their lives to the boar.

Arthur then sent a body of men with dogs to a certain place, instructing them to return thence to the Severn, and he sent tried warriors to traverse the Island, and force the boar into the River Severn.

Kilhuch was with the men who went to do this. Mabon, the son of Modron, was there, mounted on the horse that was swift as the wave. Kilhuch with four others, all mighty warriors, dashed upon the great-tusked, fiery-eyed boar; they seized hold of him; catching him by the feet they plunged him into the Severn. Its waters overwhelmed him. On one side Mabon, the son of Modron, spurred up his steed, and snatched the razor from between the boar's ears. Kilhuch snatched the scissors. But before they could obtain the comb, Truith had regained the ground. From the moment that he reached the shore, neither dog, nor man, nor horse could overtake him until he entered Cornwall.

Then Arthur and his men went through Cornwall seeking the boar that still had the comb between his ears. And then Kilhuch came upon him. And Kilhuch was holding Drudwin, the Little Dog of Greit, by the leash that had been made out of the beard of Dillus the Robber. He unloosed the dog. The boar flung off the comb that was between his ears. The Little Dog of Greit rushed at him and drove him straight forward and into the deep sea. All the warriors watched Truith plunge into the sea. Thenceforward it was never known where he went. But wherever he went, Drudwin, the Little Dog of Greit, went too.

So Kilhuch gained the comb, the last of the precious things that was between Truith's ears; he had the scissors, and the razor that Mabon, the son of Modron, had taken was given him. He had, too, the tusk of the lesser boar. Then with Arthur and his companions, and Goreu, the son of Custennin the Herdsman, he went to the castle of Yspaddaden, Chief of Giants.

Olwen was in the hall when the porter let them in. She was there and Kilhuch looked upon her, but her father drove her out of the hall. "Have you brought all that is needful for the washing of my head and the shaving of my beard?" he asked roughly, when he saw them before him.

Then Kilhuch showed him the tusk of Yskithyrwyn; he showed him the comb, and the razor, and the scissors that had been between the ears of the boar Truith. Yspaddaden looked on all of them. "To-morrow," he said, "we will examine all of these things and see if it is fitting that you should have my daughter for your wife." And then he said, "To-night I would have you join in revelry in my hall." So Yspaddaden feasted King Arthur and his companions and feasted Kilhuch, the youth who had come to claim his daughter for wife. After they had feasted they all went to rest.

The next morning when they came together again Yspaddaden said, "The tusk of Yskithyrwyn you have brought me, and the comb and scissors and razor that were between the ears of the boar Truith. But I must spread out my hair in order to have it shaved, and it will never be spread out unless I have the blood of the Jet Black Sorceress, the daughter of the Pure White Sorceress from the Source of the Stream of Sorrow at the confines of Hell. This you have not brought me. And I declare before all of you that I will not let myself be cheated in this way."

Then it seemed to Kilhuch that in spite of all the labours that had been done he would not gain Olwen for his wife. But King Arthur rose up, and he declared by his confession to Heaven, that he would bring the blood of the Jet Black Sorceress to them, and that he would force Yspaddaden, Chief of Giants, to give Olwen to Kilhuch for his wife.

King Arthur went without. And there was Gwyn ab Nudd who had come with Arthur's companions. He asked Gwyn to give him counsel as to how he might come to where the Jet Black Sorceress, the daughter of the Pure White Sorceress, was.

And Gwyn advised the King to mount his mare Lamrei and to ride to the cave that he would guide him to, the cave that opened to where was the Source of the Stream of Sorrow. When they came to that cave, Gwyn advised Arthur to send his two servants in, "For it would not be fitting or seemly," he said, "to have you, King Arthur, struggle with a sorceress."

The two servants went within the cave. But no sooner did they go within than they became rooted to the ground. "What has happened to my servants?" said Arthur. "I know now," said Gwyn, "that your servants cannot move backward or forward, and neither can anyone else unless he is mounted on your mare Lamrei." Arthur, hearing this, rode into the cave. He lifted up his servants on Lamrei, his mare. As he did, the Sorceress dashed at him. With his dagger he struck at her, and she fell in two halves. Then Gwyn ab Nudd took the blood of the Sorceress and kept it.

Arthur with Gwyn came into the castle of Yspaddaden. The hair of the Chief of the Giants was spread out, and Goreu, Custennin's son, went to him. And Goreu shaved his beard, and cut him from ear to ear. "Art thou shaved, man?" said Goreu. But the Chief of Giants did not answer; terror at seeing Goreu whose brothers he had slain, at seeing Goreu come to him with the sharp things in his hands, made Yspaddaden die.

Then Arthur and those who were with him took possession of that vast castle and all the treasures that were in it. Goreu, the son of Custennin the Herdsman, lived in it henceforth. Olwen became the bride of Kilhuch, and she and he were happy together for as long as they lived. Those who were with Arthur left the castle then, each man going to his own place. And thus did Kilhuch obtain Olwen, the daughter of Yspaddaden, Chief of Giants.

THE COMPANIONS OF ARTHUR

THE KNIGHT OWEN
AND THE LADY OF THE FOUNTAIN

I

One day King Arthur spoke to those who were around him, saying: "If I thought you would not disparage me while I was not listening to you, I would sleep for a little. And as for the rest of you, you can obtain a flagon of mead and some meat from Kai, and entertain one another with relating tales." And when he had said this, King Arthur went to sleep.

Arthur was in a chamber of his palace in Caerleon, and Owen, the son of Urien, and Kynon, and Kai were with him, and Queen Gwenhuivar and her maidens were there also. In the centre of the chamber King Arthur sat upon a seat of green rushes, over which was spread a covering of flame-coloured satin, and a cushion of red satin was under his elbow. And when he turned to sleep, Kai went to the kitchen and to the mead-cellar, and returned bearing a flagon of mead and a golden goblet, and broiled collops of meat. They ate, and they began to drink the mead out of the golden goblet.

Then said Kai: "It is time I should get paid by being told a story." "Kynon," said Owen to the other knight who was there, "do thou pay Kai the tale that is his due." "Truly," said Kynon, "thou art older, Owen, and art a better teller of tales than I, and hast seen more marvellous things; do thou, therefore, pay Kai his tale." "Begin thyself," said Owen, "with the best tale thou knowest." "I will do so," said Kynon. Then he began:

"I was the oldest son of my mother and father, and I was exceedingly aspiring, and my daring was very great. I thought there was no enterprise in the world too mighty for me, and after I had achieved all the adventures that were to achieve in my own country, I equipped myself, and set forth to journey through deserts and distant regions. And at length it chanced that I came to the fairest valley in the world.

"In that valley there were trees of equal growth, and a river ran through it, and a path was by the side of the river. I followed the path until mid-day, and continued my journey along the remainder of the valley until the evening; and at the end of the plain I came to a great castle, at the foot of which was a torrent. I approached the castle, and there I beheld two youths with yellow curling hair, each with a frontlet of gold upon his head, and clad in a garment of yellow satin, and they had gold clasps upon their insteps. In the hand of each of them was an ivory bow, strung with the sinews of the stag; and their arrows had shafts of the bone of the whale, and were winged with peacock's feathers; their shafts also had golden heads. And they had daggers with blades of gold, and with hilts of the bone of the whale. The two youths were throwing their daggers.

"And a little way from them I saw a man clad in a robe and mantle of yellow satin; and round the top of his mantle was a band of gold lace. On his feet were shoes of variegated leather, fastened by two bosses of gold. When I saw this man, I went towards him and saluted him, and such was his courtesy that he no sooner received my greeting than he returned it. And he went with me towards the castle.

"In the hall of the castle I saw four and twenty maidens embroidering satin at a window. And this I tell thee, Kai, that the least fair of them was fairer than the fairest maid that thou hast ever beheld in the Island of Britain, and the least lovely of them was more lovely than Gwenhuivar when she appears at the Offering on the day of the Nativity, or at the feast of Easter. The maidens rose up at my coming, and six of them took my horse and divested me of my armour; and six others took my arms, and washed them in a vessel until they were perfectly bright. And the third six spread cloths upon the tables and prepared meat. And the fourth six took off my soiled garments, and placed others upon me; namely, an under-vest and doublet of fine linen, and a robe, and a surcoat, and a mantle of yellow satin with a broad gold band upon the mantle. They placed cushions both beneath and around me, with coverings of red linen; and I sat down.

"Now the six maidens who had taken my horse unharnessed him, as well as if they had been the best squires in the Island of Britain. Then, behold, they brought bowls of silver wherein was water to wash, and towels of linen, and I washed. Then, in a little while, the man who had brought me into the hall sat down to the table. I sat next to him, and below me sat all the maidens, except those who waited on us. And the table was of silver, and the cloths upon the table were of linen; and no vessel was served upon the table that was not either of gold or of silver, or of buffalo-horn. And verily, Kai, I saw there every sort of meat and every sort of liquor that I have ever seen elsewhere; but the meat and liquor were better served there than I have ever seen them in any other place.

"Until the repast was half over, neither the man nor any one of the maidens spoke a single word to me; but when the man perceived it would be more agreeable to me to converse than to eat any more, he began to inquire of me who I was and where I had come from. I said I was glad to find that there was some one who would discourse with me. 'Chieftain,' said the man, 'we would have talked with thee sooner, but we feared to disturb thee during thy repast; now, however, we will discourse.'

"Then I told the man who I was, and what was the cause of my journey; and said that I was seeking whether anyone was superior to me, or whether I could gain the mastery over all. The man looked upon me, and he smiled and said, 'If I did not fear to distress thee too much, I would show thee that which thou seekest.' Upon this I became anxious and sorrowful, and when the man perceived it, he said, 'If thou wouldst rather that I should show thee thy disadvantage than thine advantage, I will do so. Sleep here to-night, and in the morning arise early, and take the road upwards through the valley until thou reachest the wood through which thou camest hither. A little way within the wood thou wilt meet with a road branching off to the right, by which thou must proceed, until thou comest to a large sheltered glade with a mound in the centre. And thou wilt see a Black Man of great stature on the top of the mound. He is not smaller in size than two men of this world. And he has a club of iron, and it is certain that there are no two men in the world who would not find their burden in that club. He has but one foot, and there is but one eye in the middle of his forehead. He is the guardian of the wood. And thou wilt see a thousand wild animals grazing around him. Inquire of him the way out of the glade, and he will reply to thee briefly, and will point out the road by which thou shalt find that which thou art in quest of.'

"The next morning I arose and equipped myself, and mounted my horse, and proceeded straight through the valley to the wood; and I followed the crossroad which the man had pointed out to me, till at length I arrived at the glade. And there I was three times more astonished at the number of wild animals I beheld than the man had said I should be. And the Black Man was there, sitting on the top of the mound. Huge of stature as the man had told me he was, I found him to exceed by far the description he had given me of him. As for the iron club which the man had told me was a burden for two men, I am certain, Kai, that it would be a heavy weight for four warriors to lift; and this was in the Black Man's hand.

"He only spoke to me in answer to my questions. I asked him what power he held over the wild animals that were around. 'I will show thee, little man,' said he. And he took his club in his hand, and with it he struck a stag a great blow so that he brayed vehemently, and at his braying the animals came together, as numerous as the stars in the sky, so that it was difficult for me to find room in the glade to stand among them. There were serpents, and dragons, and divers sorts of animals. And the Black Man looked at them, and bade them go and feed; and they bowed their heads, and did him homage as vassals to their lord.

"Then the Black Man said to me, 'Seest thou now, little man, what power I hold over these animals?' Then I inquired of him the way, and he became very rough in his manner to me; however, he asked me whither I would go. And when I told him who I was and what I sought, he directed me. 'Take,' said he, 'that path that leads towards the head of the glade, and ascend the wooded steep until thou comest to its summit; and there thou wilt find an open space like to a large valley, and in the midst of

"Seest thou now, little man, what power I hold over these animals?"

it a tall tree, whose branches are greener than the greenest pine trees. Under this tree is a fountain, and by the side of the fountain a marble slab, and on the marble slab a silver bowl, attached by a chain of silver, so that it may not be carried away. Take the bowl, and throw a bowlful of water upon the slab, and thou wilt hear a mighty peal of thunder, so that thou wilt think that heaven and earth are trembling with its fury. With the thunder there will come a shower so severe that it will be scarce possible for thee to endure it and live. And the shower will be of hailstones; and after the shower the weather will become fair, but every leaf that was upon the tree will have been carried away by the shower. Then a flight of birds will come and alight upon the tree; and in thine own country thou didst never hear a strain so sweet as that which they will sing. And at the moment thou art most delighted with the song of the birds, thou wilt hear a murmuring and complaining coming towards thee along the valley. And thou wilt see a knight upon a coal-black horse, clothed in black velvet, and with a pennon of black linen upon his lance; and he will ride unto thee to encounter thee with the utmost speed. If thou fleest from him he will overtake thee, and if thou abidest there, as sure as thou art a mounted knight, he will leave thee on foot. And if thou dost not find trouble in that adventure, thou needst not seek it during the rest of thy life.'

"Then I journeyed on until I reached the summit of the steep, and there I found everything as the Black Man had described it to me. And I went up to the tree, and beneath it I saw the fountain, and by its side the marble slab, and the silver bowl fastened by the chain. Then I took the bowl, and cast a bowlful of water upon the slab; and thereupon, behold, the thunder came, much more violent than the Black Man had led me to expect; and after the thunder came the shower; and of a truth I tell thee, Kai, that there is neither man nor beast that can endure that shower and live. For not one of those hailstones would be stopped, either by the flesh or by the skin, until it had reached the bone. I turned my horse's flank towards the shower, and placed the beak of my shield over his head and neck, while I held the upper part of it over my own head. And thus I withstood the shower. When I looked on the tree there was not a single leaf upon it, and then the sky became clear, and with that, behold, the birds lighted upon the tree, and sang. And truly, Kai, I never heard any melody equal to that, either before or since.

"Then, when I was most charmed with listening to the birds, lo, a murmuring voice was heard through the valley, approaching me and saying, 'O Knight, what has brought thee hither? What evil have I done to thee, that thou shouldst act towards me and my possessions as thou hast this day? Dost thou not know that the shower to-day has left in my dominions neither man nor beast alive that was exposed to it?' And thereupon, behold, a knight on a black horse appeared, clothed in jet-black velvet, and with a tabard of black linen about him. We charged each other, and, as the onset was furious, it was not long before I was overthrown. Then the knight passed the shaft of his lance through the bridle rein of my horse, and rode off with the two horses, leaving me where I was. And he did not even bestow so much notice upon me as either to take me prisoner or to despoil me of my arms.

"So I returned along the road by which I had come. And when I reached the glade where the Black Man was, I confess to thee, Kai, it is a marvel that I did not melt down into a liquid pool, through the shame that I felt at the Black Man's derision. I returned to the castle where I had spent the night preceding. And I was more agreeably entertained that night than I had been the night before; and I was better feasted, and I conversed freely with the inmates of the castle, and none of them alluded to my expedition to the fountain, neither did I mention it to any; and I remained there that night. When I arose in the morning, I found, ready saddled, a dark bay horse, with nostrils as red as scarlet; and after putting on my armour, and leaving there my blessing, I returned to my own court. And that horse I still possess, and he is in the stable yonder, and I declare that I would not part with him for the best horse in the Island of Britain.

"Now of a truth, Kai, no man ever before confessed to an adventure so much to his own discredit, and verily it seems strange to me, that neither before nor since have I heard of any person besides myself who knew of this adventure, and that the

place of its happening should be within King Arthur's dominions, without any other person lighting upon it."

"Now," said Owen, "would it not be well to go and endeavour
to discover that place?"

"By the hand of my friend," said Kai, "often dost thou utter
things with thy tongue which thou wouldst not make good with
thy deeds."

"In very truth," said Gwenhuivar, "it were better thou wert
hanged, Kai, than to use such uncourteous speech towards a
man like Owen."

"By the hand of my friend, good lady," said Kai, "thy praise of
Owen is not greater than mine."

With that Arthur awoke, and asked if he had not been sleeping a little.

"Yes, Lord," said Owen, "thou hast slept a while."

"Is it time for us to go to meat?"

"It is, Lord," said Owen.

Then the horn for washing was sounded, and the King and all
his household washed, and then sat down to eat. And when the
meal was finished Owen withdrew to his lodging, and there he
made ready his horse and his arms.

II

On the morrow, with the dawn of day, Owen put on his armour, and mounted his horse, and travelled through distant lands and over desert mountains. And at length he arrived in the valley which Kynon had described to him. Journeying along the valley by the side of the river, he followed its course till he came to the plain and within sight of the castle. When he approached the castle, he saw the youths throwing their daggers in the place where Kynon had seen them, and the man in yellow standing by. And no sooner had Owen saluted the man than he was saluted by him in return.

He went within the castle, and when he had entered the hall he beheld the maidens working at satin embroidery, in chairs of gold. And their beauty seemed to Owen far greater than Kynon had represented to him. They rose to wait upon Owen as they had done to Kynon. Then, about the middle of the repast, the man in yellow asked Owen about the object of his journey. Owen said: "I am in quest of the knight who guards the fountain." Upon this the man in yellow said that he was as loth to show that adventure to him as he had been to the knight who had come before. However, he described the place to Owen, and they retired to rest.

The next morning Owen found his horse made ready for him by the maidens, and he set forward and came to the glade where the Black Man was. The stature of the Black Man seemed more wonderful to Owen than Kynon had described it to him. Owen asked of him his road, and the Black Man showed it to him. He followed the road till he came to the green tree; he beheld the fountain and the slab beside the fountain with the bowl upon it. Owen took the bowl, and threw a bowlful of water upon the slab. And, lo, the thunder was heard, and after the thunder came the shower, much more violent than Kynon had described it, and after the shower the sky became bright. When Owen looked at the tree, there was not one leaf upon it. And immediately the birds came, and settled upon the tree, and sang. And when their song was most pleasing to Owen he beheld a knight coming towards him through the valley.

The knight and Owen encountered each other violently. Having broken both their lances, they drew their swords, and fought blade to blade. Then Owen struck the knight a blow through the helmet, head-piece and visor, and through the skin and the flesh, and the bone. Then the Black Knight felt that he had received a mortal wound, upon which he turned his horse's head, and fled. Owen followed close upon him, and they came to the gate of a vast and resplendent castle.

The Black Knight was allowed to enter, and the portcullis was let fall upon Owen as he followed; it struck his horse behind the saddle, and cut the horse in two, and carried away the rowels of the spurs that were upon Owen's heels. And the rowels of the spurs and part of the horse were without, and Owen with the other part of the horse remained between the two gates, and the inner gate was closed, so that Owen could not go hence.

He could see through an aperture in the gate a street facing him, with a row of houses on each side. And he beheld a maiden, with yellow curling hair, and a frontlet of gold upon her head; she was clad in a dress of yellow satin, and on her feet were shoes of variegated leather. She approached the gate, and tried to have it opened.

Then said Owen to the maiden: "Heaven knows it is no more possible for me to open to thee from hence, than it is for thee to set me free." "Truly," said the maiden, "it is very sad that thou canst not be released, and every woman ought to succour thee, for I think thou art most faithful in the service of ladies. Therefore," said she, "whatever is in my power to do for thy release, I will do it. Take this ring and put it on thy finger, with the stone inside thy hand; and close thy hand upon the stone. As long as thou concealest it, it will conceal thee. When they have consulted together, they will come forth to fetch thee, in order to put thee to death; and they will be much grieved that they cannot find thee. I will await thee on the horse-block yonder; and thou wilt be able to see me, though I cannot see thee; therefore come and place thy hand upon my shoulder, that I may know that thou art near me."

Then she went away from him, and Owen did all that the maiden had told him. The people of the castle came to seek Owen, to put him to death, and when they found nothing but the half of his horse, they were sorely grieved.

Owen went to the maiden, and placed his hand upon her shoulder; whereupon she set off, and he followed her, until they came to the door of a large and beautiful chamber, and the maiden opened it, and they went in, and closed the door. And Owen looked around the chamber while the maiden kindled a fire, and took water in a silver bowl, and put a towel of linen on her shoulder, and gave him water to wash. Then she placed before him a silver table, upon which was a cloth of yellow linen; and she brought him food. Owen ate and drank, and then late in the afternoon they heard a mighty clamour in the castle, and he asked the maiden what the outcry was. "They are administering extreme unction," she said, "to the lord who owns the castle."

The couch which the maiden prepared for him was meet for Arthur himself; it was of scarlet and fur, and satin, and sendal, and fine linen. In the middle of the night they heard a woeful cry. "What outcry again is this?" said Owen. "The lord who owned the castle is now dead," said the maiden. And a little after daybreak, they heard an exceeding loud clamour and wailing. Owen asked the maiden what was the cause of it. "They are bearing to the church the body of the lord who owned the castle," she said.

Then Owen rose up, and opened a window of the chamber, and looked towards the castle. In the midst of a throng, he beheld a bier, over which was a veil of white linen. And following the bier he beheld a lady with yellow hair falling over her shoulders, and about her a dress of yellow satin, which was torn. Truly she would have been the fairest lady Owen ever saw, had she been in her proper attire.

He inquired of the maiden who the lady was. "She is the

fairest and the wisest of women," the maiden said. "She is the Lady of the Fountain, the wife of him whom thou didst slay yesterday." "Verily," said Owen, "she is the woman that, in the whole world, I love best."

When he had said this, the maiden whose name was Luned went from the chamber, shutting the door after her and leaving Owen within, and went towards the castle. She found the Lady of the Fountain and saluted her, but the lady answered her not. Luned bent down towards her, and said, "What aileth thee, that thou answerest no one to-day?" "Luned," said the lady, "what change hath befallen thee, that thou hast not come to visit me in my grief? It was wrong in thee." "Truly," said Luned, "I thought thy good sense was greater than I find it to be. Is it well for thee to mourn after thy lord, or for anything else, that thou canst not have?" "I declare to Heaven," said the lady, "that in the whole world there is not one to take his place." "An ugly man would be as good as he, or better than he," said Luned. "I declare to Heaven," said the lady to her, "that were it not repugnant to me to cause to be put to death one whom I have brought up, I would have thee executed, for saying such a thing to me. As it is, I will banish thee." "I am glad," said Luned, "that thou hast no other cause to do so, than that I would have been of service to thee. And henceforth evil betide whichever of us shall make the first advance towards reconciliation to the other; whether I should seek an invitation from thee, or thou of thine own accord shouldst send to invite me."

With that Luned went forth, but the lady arose and followed her to the door of the chamber. "In truth," said the lady, "evil is thy temper, Luned, but if thou knowest what is to my advantage, declare it to me." "I will do so," said Luned.

"Thou knowest," she said to the Lady of the Fountain, "that except by warfare and arms it is impossible for thee to preserve thy possessions; delay not, therefore, to seek some one who can defend them." "How can I do that?" the Lady of the Fountain asked. "I will tell thee," said the maiden Luned. "Unless thou canst defend the Fountain, thou canst not maintain thy dominions; and no one can defend the Fountain, except it be a knight of Arthur's household. I will go to Arthur's Court, and I will not

return thence without a warrior who can guard the Fountain."
"Go," said the lady, "and make proof of that which thou hast
promised."

Then Luned went back to the chamber where she had left
Owen, and she tarried as long as it might have taken her to have
travelled to the Court of King Arthur. And at the end of that
time, she apparelled herself and went to visit the Lady of the
Fountain. The lady was much rejoiced when she saw her, and
inquired what news she brought from Arthur's Court. "I bring
thee the best of news," said Luned, "for I have brought back one
who can defend the Fountain." "Bring him here to visit me to-
morrow, at mid-day," said the Lady of the Fountain.

Right glad was the lady of the coming of Owen and Luned
when she saw them before her next day. She gazed steadfastly
upon Owen, and said, "Luned, this knight has not the look of a
traveller." "What harm is there in that, lady?" asked Luned. "Go
back to thine abode," said the lady, "and I will take counsel."

The next day the lady took Owen for her husband, and thereafter he defended the Fountain with lance and sword. Whenso-
ever a knight came there he overthrew him. And it was thus for
the space of three years.

But there was grief in Arthur's Court because Owen did not
return. And it befell that as Gwalchmai went forth one day with
King Arthur, he perceived him to be very sad and sorrowful.
And Gwalchmai was much grieved to see Arthur in this state;
and he questioned him, saying, "Oh, my Lord! what has befall-
en thee?" "I am grieved concerning Owen, whom I have lost
these three years," said Arthur, "and I shall certainly die if the
fourth year passes without my seeing him. And I am sure that it
is through the tale which Kynon related that I have lost Owen."
Then said Gwalchmai: "Thou thyself and the men of thy household will be able to avenge Owen, if he be slain; or to set him
free, if he be in prison; and, if alive, to bring him back with
thee." It was settled according to what Gwalchmai said: that
Arthur and his household should go in search of Owen.

They went, and Kynon acted as their guide. And Arthur came
to the castle where Kynon had been before, and when he came
there the youths were throwing the daggers in the same place,

"Luned, this knight has not the look of a traveller."

and the man in yellow was standing hard by. When he saw Arthur he greeted him, and invited him to the castle; and Arthur accepted his invitation, and they entered the castle together. The maidens rose up to wait on them, and the service of the maidens appeared to them all to excel any attendance they had ever met with.

The next morning Arthur set out thence, with Kynon for his guide, and they came to the place where the Black Man was. And the stature of the Black Man was more surprising to Arthur than it had been represented to him. Then they came to the top of the wooded steep, and traversed the valley till they reached the green tree, where they saw the Fountain, and the bowl, and the slab. And upon that, Kai came to Arthur and spoke to him. "My Lord," said he, "I know the meaning of all this, and my request is, that thou wilt permit me to throw the water on the slab, and to receive the first adventure that may befall." Arthur gave him leave.

Then Kai threw a bowlful of water upon the slab, and immediately there came the thunder, and after the thunder the shower. Such a thunder-storm they had never known before, and many of the attendants who were in Arthur's train were killed by the shower. Then the sky became clear; and on looking at the tree they beheld it completely leafless. The birds descended on the tree, and the song of the birds was far sweeter than any strain they had ever heard before. Then they beheld a knight on a coal-black horse, clothed in black satin, coming rapidly towards them. Kai met him and encountered him, and it was not long before Kai was overthrown. The knight withdrew, and Arthur and his host encamped for the night.

When they arose in the morning they perceived that the knight was near them, and that the signal of combat was upon his lance. Arthur armed himself to encounter the knight. "Oh, my Lord," said Gwalchmai, "permit me to fight with him first." Arthur permitted him. And Gwalchmai went forth to meet the knight, having over himself and his horse a robe of honour which had been given him by the daughter of an earl, and in this dress he was not known by any of the host. The two charged each other, and fought all that day until evening, and neither of them was able to unhorse the other.

The next day they fought with strong lances, and neither of them could obtain the mastery.

And the third day they fought with exceeding strong lances. They fought furiously, even until noon. And they gave each other such a shock that the girths of their horses were broken, so that they fell over their horses' cruppers to the ground. They rose up speedily, and drew their swords, and resumed the combat; and the multitude that witnessed their encounter felt assured that they had never before seen two men so valiant and so powerful.

The knight in black gave Gwalchmai a blow that turned his helmet from off his face, so that the knight saw him and knew that he was Gwalchmai. Then the knight said: "My Lord Gwalchmai, I did not know thee for my cousin, owing to the robe of honour that enveloped thee; take my sword and my arms." Said Gwalchmai: "Thou, Owen, art the victor; take thou my sword." With that Arthur saw that they were conversing, and advanced towards them. "My Lord Arthur," said Gwalchmai, "here is Owen, who has vanquished me, and will not take my arms." "My Lord," said Owen, "it is he that has vanquished me, and he will not take my sword." "Give me your swords," said Arthur, "and then neither of you has vanquished the other." Then Owen put his arms around Arthur's neck, and they embraced.

They retired that night, and the next day Arthur prepared to depart. "My Lord," said Owen, "this is not well of thee; for I have been absent from thee these three years, and during all that time, up to this very day, I have been preparing a banquet for thee, knowing that thou wouldst come to seek me. Tarry with me, therefore, until thou and thy attendants have recovered the fatigues of the journey."

Then they all proceeded to the castle of the Lady of the Fountain, and the banquet which had been three years preparing was consumed in three months. Never had they a more delicious or agreeable banquet. Afterwards Arthur prepared to depart. And he begged the Lady of the Fountain to permit

Owen to go with him for the space of three months, so that he might show him to the nobles and the fair ladies of the Island of Britain. At first the Lady of the Fountain would not let him go, for she saw that his going would bring sorrow to them both. But at last she gave her consent, although it was very painful to her. So Owen came with Arthur to the Island of Britain. But when he was once more with his friends and amongst his kindred, forgetfulness of the Lady of the Fountain came over him.

III

Now one day when Owen sat in his hall in the city of Caerleon, there came towards him a maiden upon a bay horse, with a curling mane and covered with foam, and the bridle and so much as was seen of the saddle were of gold. The maiden was arrayed in a dress of yellow satin. And she came up to Owen, and she took the ring from off his hand. "Thus," said she, "shall be treated the deceiver, the traitor, the faithless, and the disgraced."

And when she said that and went her way, Owen remembered the Lady of the Fountain, and he was sorrowful; and having finished eating he went to his own abode and made preparations that night. And the next day he arose but did not go to Arthur's Court; he wandered to the distant parts of the earth and to uncultivated mountains. He remained there until all his apparel was worn out, and his body was wasted away, and his hair was grown long. And he wandered about with the wild beasts and fed with them, until they became familiar with him.

One day as he journeyed, he heard a loud yelling in a wood. It was repeated a second and a third time. And Owen went towards the spot, and beheld a huge, craggy mound in the middle of the wood, on the side of which was a grey rock. There was a cleft in the rock, and a serpent was within the cleft. Near the rock stood a black lion, and every time the lion sought to go thence, the serpent darted towards him to attack him. Owen unsheathed his sword and drew near to the rock, and as the serpent sprang out, he struck him with his sword, and cut him in two. Then he went on his way as before. But behold, the lion followed him, and played about him, as though he had been a greyhound that he had reared.

He struck him with his sword.

They proceeded thus throughout the day, until the evening. And when it was time for Owen to take his rest, he dismounted, and turned his horse loose in a flat and wooded meadow. He struck fire, and when the fire was kindled, the lion brought him fuel enough to last for three nights. Then the lion disappeared. And presently he returned, bearing a large roebuck. The lion threw it down before Owen.

Then Owen took the roebuck, and skinned it, and placed collops of its flesh upon skewers, around the fire. The rest of the buck he gave to the lion to devour.

Just as he was turning to rest in the wooded meadow he heard a deep sigh near him, and a second, and a third. Owen called out to know whether the sigh he heard came from a mortal, and he received answer that it did. "Who art thou?" said Owen. "Truly," said the voice, "I am Luned, the handmaiden of the Lady of the Fountain." "And what dost thou here?" said Owen. "I am imprisoned," said she, "on account of the knight who came from Arthur's Court, and wed the Lady of the Fountain. He afterwards departed from her, and has not returned since. They have imprisoned me in a stone vault, and they say that I shall be put to death, unless he comes himself to deliver me, by a certain day, and that is no further off than to-morrow. I have no one to send to seek him for me. His name is Owen, the son of Urien." "And art thou certain that if that knight knew all this, he would come to thy rescue?" "I am most certain of it," said she.

The next morning he was awakened by his lion, and he saw that two men had come, and that they had taken the maiden Luned out of the stone vault, and were leading her away. Owen went to rescue her, and the men attacked him, and he was hard beset by them. The lion came to Owen's assistance, and the man and beast got the better of the two men. "Chieftain," said they, "it is harder for us to contend with yonder animal than with thee." Owen put the lion in the place where the maiden had been imprisoned, and blocked up the door with stones, and he went to fight with the men, as before. But Owen had not his usual strength, and the men pressed hard upon him. The lion roared incessantly at seeing Owen in trouble, and he dashed at the wall until he found a way out, and he rushed upon the men, and instantly slew them. So Luned was saved.

Then Owen revealed to her who he was, and the maiden guided him to the dominions of the Lady of the Fountain. He dwelt there greatly beloved until he went away with his followers. His followers were the army of three hundred ravens which Kenverchyn had left him. And wherever Owen went with these he was victorious.

And this is the tale of "The Knight Owen and the Lady of the Fountain."

PEREDUR AND THE CASTLE
OF WONDERS

I

There was once one who owned the Earldom of the North. And this earl supported himself, not so much by his own possessions, as by taking part in battles and tournaments by which he won much in prizes and spoils. He had seven sons. And, as often befalls those who join in encounters and wars, he was slain, and six of his sons were slain likewise.

His seventh son was not of an age to go to wars and encounters, otherwise he might have been slain as were his father and his six brothers. Peredur was this boy's name. Now his mother, who was a very thoughtful woman, to save the last of her sons, decided to leave the inhabited country with him, and to rear him in a place where he should know nothing of fighting and feats of arms. She went into the deserts and unfrequented wildernesses, and she permitted none to go with her son and herself except women and boys and spiritless old men who were unequal to wars and fighting. She permitted none to bring horses and arms near the place where her son was, lest he should set his mind upon them.

Peredur, when he had grown up, used often to go into the forest and divert himself by flinging sticks and staves. One day he saw his mother's flock of goats, and near the goats he saw two deer standing. He marvelled greatly that they should be without horns, while the goats had horns. He thought that these deer were goats that had run wild and had lost their horns. Peredur went after them, and by his activity and swiftness he drove the deer and the goats into the shed which was for the goats. Then he returned to his mother. "Ah, mother," said he, "a marvellous thing have I seen in the wood; two of thy goats have run wild, and lost their horns through their having been so long missing in the wood. And no man had ever more trouble than I have had in driving them in." All within the house rose to see what the youth had done. And when they beheld the deer in the same shelter as the goats they were greatly astonished.

Some time after that Peredur saw three knights riding along the borders of the forest. "Mother," said he, "what are those yonder?" And his mother, fearful lest he should want to join the knights, said, "They are angels, my son." "By my faith," said Peredur, "I will go and become an angel with them."

So he went through the ways of the forest until he came to a place where he met the three knights. "Tell me, good soul," said Owen who was one of the knights, "sawest thou a knight pass this way?" "I know not," said Peredur, "what a knight is." "Such a one as I am," said Owen. Then said Peredur, "What is this?" touching the saddle. "It is a saddle," said Owen. Then the youth asked him about the accoutrements which he saw upon the men, and the horses, and the arms, and what they were for, and how they were used. And Owen showed him all these things fully, and told him what use was made of each of them.

Then Peredur returned to his mother and her company, and he said to her, "Mother, these were not angels, but honourable knights." Then his mother swooned away, for she knew that, having spoken with the knights, he would be drawn away from her.

Peredur then went to the place where they kept the old horses that carried firewood from the forest and brought provisions from the inhabited country, and he took a bony piebald horse, and he pressed a pack into the form of a saddle, and with twisted twigs he imitated the trappings which he had seen upon the horses. And when he came before his mother again she had recovered from her swoon and she said to him, "My son, desirest thou to ride forth?" "Yes, with thy leave," said he. "Wait, then, that I may counsel thee before thou goest." "Willingly," he answered. "Go forward, then," said she, "to the Court of Arthur, where there are the best, and the boldest, and the most bountiful of men."

Peredur thanked his mother for her counsel; he bade goodbye to her, mounted the horse, and, taking a handful of sharp pointed forks in his hand, he rode forth. And he journeyed for two days and two nights in the woody wildernesses and in desert places, without food and without drink. Then he came to a vast, wild wood, and far within the wood he saw a fair, even glade. From that even glade he journeyed on until he came to Arthur's Court.

It happened that before Peredur reached the Court a stranger knight had arrived, and this knight had gone into the hall where Arthur and his household, with Gwenhuivar and her maidens, were assembled. The page of the chamber was serving the Queen with a golden goblet. As she was taking it, the stranger knight dashed the liquor that was in the goblet into Gwenhuivar's face, saying aloud, "If any have the boldness to dispute this goblet with me, and to avenge the insult to Gwenhuivar, let him follow me to the meadow, and there I will await him." And the knight had gone out of the hall.

The household was standing, their heads down, lest any of them should be requested to go and avenge the insult to Gwenhuivar. For it seemed to them that no one would have ventured on so daring an outrage unless he possessed such powers, through magic or charms, that none would be able to take vengeance upon him. Then, behold, Peredur came in upon the bony piebald horse, with the uncouth trappings upon it. In the centre of the hall stood Kai. "Tell me, tall man," said Peredur to him, "is that Arthur yonder?" "What wouldst thou with Arthur?" said Kai. "My mother told me to go to Arthur and receive from him the honour of knighthood." "By my faith," said Kai, "thou art all too meanly equipped with horse and arms to receive such honour." As he said that a dwarf came forward into the middle of the hall.

Now this dwarf had been a year at Arthur's Court, both he and a female dwarf. They had craved harbourage of Arthur, and had obtained it; and during the whole year, neither of them had spoken a single word to anyone. But now that he beheld Peredur he cried out, "Haha! the welcome of Heaven be unto thee, goodly Peredur, the chief of warriors, and flower of knighthood." "Truly," said Kai, "thou art ill-taught to remain a year mute at Arthur's Court, with choice of company, and now, before the face of Arthur and all his household, to call out, and declare such a man as this the chief of warriors, and the flower of knighthood." And he gave him such a box on the ear that the dwarf fell senseless on the ground.

Then exclaimed the female dwarf, "Haha! goodly Peredur; the welcome of Heaven be unto thee, flower of knights, and light of chivalry." "Of a truth," said Kai, "thou art ill-bred to remain mute at the Court of Arthur for a year, and then to speak as thou dost of such a man as this." And Kai gave the female dwarf a box on the ear.

"Tall man," said Peredur, "show me which is Arthur." "Hold thy peace," said Kai to him, "and go after the knight who went hence to the meadow, and take from him the goblet, and over-throw him, and possess thyself of his horse and arms, and then thou shalt receive the honour of knighthood." "I will do so, tall man," said Peredur. And saying this he turned his horse's head towards the meadow.

When he came to the meadow he found the knight riding up and down, proud of his strength, and valour, and noble mien. "Tell me," said the knight, "didst thou see anyone coming after me from the Court?" "The tall man desired me to come, and overthrow thee, and to take from thee the goblet, and thy horse and thy armour for myself," said Peredur. "Silence!" said the knight. "Go back to the Court, and tell Arthur, from me, either to come himself, or to send some other to fight with me, and unless he do so quickly, I will not wait for him." "By my faith," said Peredur, "choose thou whether it shall be willingly or unwillingly, but I will have the horse, and the arms, and the goblet."

When he said this the knight ran at him furiously, and struck him a violent blow with the shaft of his lance between the neck and the shoulder. "Haha! lad," said Peredur, "my mother's ser-vants were not used to play with me in this wise; therefore, thus will I play with thee." And thereupon he struck him with a sharp pointed fork; it went through him, and the knight fell down lifeless.

Just at that time Owen was speaking to Kai. "Verily," said he,

Peredur struck him with a sharp pointed fork.

"thou wert ill-advised, Kai, when thou didst send that madman after the knight. He must be either overthrown or slain. If he is overthrown by the knight, an eternal disgrace will it be to Arthur and his warriors. And if he is slain, the disgrace will be the same, and moreover, his sin will be upon him; therefore will I go to see what has befallen him." So Owen went to the meadow, and he found Peredur dragging a man about. "What art thou doing?" said Owen. "This iron coat," said Peredur, "will never come off him; not by my efforts at any rate." Then Owen unfastened the knight's armour, and he saw that the knight was dead. "Here," said he to Peredur, "here, my good soul, is a horse and armour better than thine. Take them joyfully, and come with me to Arthur, to receive the order of knighthood, for thou dost merit it." "May I never show my face again if I go," said Peredur, "but take thou the goblet to the Queen, and tell Arthur that, wherever I am, I will be his vassal, and will do him what profit and service I am able. And say that I will not come to his Court until I have encountered the tall man who is there, to avenge the injury he did to the dwarf and dwarfess." And Owen went back to the Court, and related all these things to Arthur and Gwenhuivar, and to all the household.

Then Peredur rode forward. He was mounted on the knight's horse and he had on the knight's armour. As he proceeded, behold a knight met him. "Whence comest thou?" said the knight. "I come from Arthur's Court," said Peredur. "I have always been Arthur's enemy," said the knight, "and all such of his men as I have ever encountered I have slain." Then, without further parlance they fought, and it was not long before Peredur brought him to the ground, over his horse's crupper. Then the knight besought his mercy. "Mercy thou shalt have," said Peredur, "if thou wilt take oath to me that thou wilt go to Arthur's Court, and tell him that it was I who overthrew thee, for the honour of his service; and say that I will never come to the court until I have avenged the insult offered to the dwarf and dwarfess." The knight pledged him his faith of this, and proceeded to the Court of Arthur, and said as he had promised, and conveyed the threat to Kai.

And Peredur rode forward. And within that week he encountered sixteen knights, and he overthrew them all. And they all went to Arthur's Court, taking with them the same message which the first knight had conveyed from Peredur, and the same threat which he had sent to Kai. And thereupon Kai was reproved by Arthur; and Kai was greatly grieved thereat.

Still Peredur rode forward. And he came to a vast and desert wood, on the confines of which was a lake. And on the other side was a fair castle. Peredur rode to the castle, and the door was open, and he entered the hall. And there was a hoary-headed man sitting on a cushion, and a large blazing fire burning before him. The household and the company arose to meet Peredur, and helped him to doff his armour. The man asked him to sit on the cushion; he sat with him, and they conversed together. When it was time, the tables were laid, and they went to meat. And when they had finished their meal, the man inquired of Peredur if he knew well how to fight with the sword. "I know not," said Peredur, "but were I to be taught, doubtless I should." "Whoever can play well with cudgel and shield, will also be able to fight with a sword." The man had two sons; the one had yellow hair, and the other auburn hair. "Arise, youths," said he, "and play with the cudgel and the shield." And so they did.

"Tell me, my soul," said the man to Peredur, "which of the youths, thinkest thou, plays best?" "I think," said Peredur, "that the yellow-haired youth could draw blood from the other, if he chose." "Arise thou, my life, and take the cudgel and the shield from the hand of the youth with the auburn hair, and draw blood from the yellow-haired youth if thou canst." So Peredur arose, and went to play with the yellow-haired youth, and he struck him such a blow that the blood flowed. "Ah, my life," said the man, "come now, and sit down, for thou wilt become the best fighter with the sword of any in this island; and I am thy uncle, thy mother's brother. And with me shalt thou remain a space, in order to learn the manners and customs of different countries, and courtesy, and gentleness, and noble bearing. I will be thy teacher; and I will raise thee to the rank of knight from this time forward."

Now there was on the floor of the hall a huge staple to which horses were tied. And after he had trained him the hoary-headed man said to Peredur: "Take yonder sword and strike the iron staple." So Peredur arose and struck the staple, so that he cut it in two; and the sword broke in two parts also. "Place the two parts together, and reunite them." And Peredur placed them together, and they became entire as they were before.

A second time he struck upon the staple, so that both it and the sword broke in two, and as before, they reunited. And the third time he gave a like blow, and placed the broken parts together, and neither the staple nor the sword would unite as before. "Youth," said the hoary-headed man, "come now, and sit down, and my blessing be upon thee. Thou fightest best with the sword of any man in this kingdom. Thou hast arrived at two thirds of thy strength, and the other third thou hast not yet obtained; and when thou attainest to thy full power, none will be able to contend with thee."

About this time, Owen, the son of Urien, said: "The youth will never come into the Court until Kai has gone forth from it." "By my faith," said Arthur, "I will search all the deserts in the Island of Britain until I find Peredur, and then let him and his adversary do their utmost to each other."

Afterwards Peredur rode forward. He came to a wood, where he saw not the track either of men or of beasts, and where there was nothing but bushes and weeds. And at the upper end of the wood he saw a castle; and when he came near the gate, he found the weeds taller than he had seen elsewhere. He struck the gate with the shaft of his lance, and thereupon a lean, auburn-haired youth came to an opening in the battlements. "Say that I am here," said Peredur, "and if it is desired that I should enter, I will go in." The youth came back, and opened the gate for him, and Peredur went in.

He beheld eighteen youths, lean and red-headed, of the same height, and of the same aspect, and of the same dress, and of the same age as the one who had opened the gate for him. They were well skilled in courtesy and in service. They disarrayed him. Then they sat down to discourse. Thereupon, behold, five maidens came from the chamber into the hall. And Peredur was certain that he had never seen another of so fair an aspect as the chief of the maidens. She had an old garment of satin upon her, which had once been handsome, but was then so tattered that her skin could be seen through it. Whiter was her skin than the bloom of crystal, and her hair and her two eyebrows were blacker than jet, and on her cheeks were two red spots, redder than whatever is reddest. The maiden welcomed Peredur, and made him sit down beside her.

Not long after this he saw two nuns enter, and a flask full of wine was borne by one, and six loaves of white bread by the other. "Lady," said the nuns to the maiden, "Heaven is witness that there is not so much of food and liquor as this left in the convent this night." Then they went to eat, and Peredur observed that the maiden wished to give more of the food and of the liquor to him than to any of the others. "My sister," said Peredur, "I will share out the food and the liquor." "Not so, my soul," said she. "By my faith but I will." So Peredur took the bread, and he gave an equal portion of it to each alike, as well as a cup full of wine. And when it was time for them to sleep, a chamber was prepared for Peredur, and he went to rest.

And when he had gone the youths spoke to the fairest and the most exalted of the maidens. "Behold, sister," they said, "we have counsel for thee." "What may it be?" she inquired. "Go to the youth who is in the upper chamber, and offer to become his wife, or the lady of his love, if it seem well to him." "That were indeed unfitting," said she. "Hitherto I have not been the lady-love of any knight, and to make him such an offer before I am wooed by him, that, truly, can I not do." "By our confession to Heaven," said they, "unless thou actest thus, we will leave thee here to thy enemies, to do as they will with thee."

Through fear that the youths would do as they said, the maiden went forth; and shedding tears, she proceeded to the chamber. With the noise of the door opening, Peredur awoke; and the maiden was weeping and lamenting. "Tell me, my sister," said Peredur, "wherefore dost thou weep?" "I will tell thee, Lord," said she. And then she said:

"My father possessed these dominions as their chief, and this castle was his, and with it he held the best earldom in the kingdom; then the son of another earl sought me of my father, and I was not willing to be given unto him, and my father would not give me against my will, either to him or any earl in the world. And my father had no child except myself. After my father's death, these dominions came into my own hands, and then was I less willing to accept him than before. So he made war upon me, and conquered all my possessions, except this one castle. Through the valour of the men whom thou hast seen, who are my foster-brothers, and the strength of the castle, it can never be taken while food and drink remain. But now our provisions are exhausted; as thou hast seen, we have been fed by the nuns, to whom the country is free. And at length they also are without supply of food or liquor. At no later date than to-morrow, the earl will come against this place with all his forces; and if I fall into his power, my fate will be no better than to be given over to the grooms of his horses. Therefore, Lord, I am come to offer to place myself in thy hands, that thou mayest succour me, either by taking me hence, or by defending me here, whichever may seem best unto thee." "Go, my sister," said Peredur, "and sleep; nor will I depart from thee until I do that which thou requirest, or prove whether I can assist thee or not."

Then the maiden went to rest; and the next morning she came to Peredur, and saluted him. "Heaven prosper thee, my soul, and what tidings dost thou bring?" "None other than that the earl and all his forces have alighted at the gate, and I never beheld any place so covered with tents, and thronged with knights." "Truly," said Peredur, "let my horse be made ready." So his horse was accoutred, and he rose and sallied forth to the meadow.

There was a knight riding proudly along the meadow, having raised the signal for battle. He and Peredur encountered, and Peredur threw the knight over his horse's crupper to the ground. At the close of the day, one of the chief knights came to fight with him, and he overthrew him also, so that he besought his mercy. "Who art thou?" said Peredur. "Verily," said he, "I am Master of the Household to the earl." "And how much of the lady's possessions is there in thy power?" "The third part, verily," answered he. "Then," said Peredur, "restore to her the third of her possessions in full, and all the profit thou hast made by them, and bring meat and drink for a hundred men, with their horses and arms, to her court this night. And thou shalt remain her captive, unless she wish to take thy life." And this the man did forthwith. That night the maiden was right joyful, and all in the castle fared plenteously.

The next day Peredur rode forth to the meadow; and that day he vanquished a multitude of the host. And at the close of the day, there came a proud and stately knight, and Peredur overthrew him, and he besought his mercy. "Who art thou?" said Peredur. "I am Steward of the Palace," said he. "And how much of the lady's possessions are under thy control?" "One third part," answered he. "Verily," said Peredur, "thou shalt fully restore to the maiden her possessions, and, moreover, thou shalt give her meat and drink for two hundred men, and their horses and their arms. And for thyself, thou shalt be her captive." And immediately it was so done.

The third day Peredur rode forth to the meadow; and he vanquished more that day than on either of the days preceding. And at the close of the day, an earl came to encounter him, and he overthrew him, and the earl besought his mercy. "Who are thou?" said Peredur. "I am the Earl," said he, "I will not conceal it from thee." "Verily," said Peredur, "thou shalt restore the whole of the maiden's earldom, and thou shalt give her thine own earldom in addition thereto, and meat and drink for three hundred men, and their horses and arms, and thou thyself shalt remain in her power." And as Peredur said, so it was.

He tarried three weeks in the country, causing tribute and obedience to be paid to the maiden of the castle, and the government to be placed in her hands. "With thy leave," said Peredur, "I will go hence." "Verily, my brother," said she, "desirest thou this?" "Yes, by my faith; and had it not been for love of thee, I should not have been here thus long." "My soul," said she, "who art thou?" "I am Peredur, and if ever thou art in trouble or danger, acquaint me therewith, and if I can, I will protect thee."

Then Peredur rode forward. In the evening he entered a valley, and at the head of the valley he came to a hermit's cell, and the hermit welcomed him gladly, and there he spent the night.

And in the morning he arose, and when he went forth, behold a shower of snow had fallen the night before, and a hawk had killed a wild fowl in front of the cell. And the noise of the horse scared the hawk away, and a raven alighted upon the bird. Peredur stood, and compared the blackness of the raven and the whiteness of the snow, and the redness of the blood, to the hair of the lady that best he loved, which was blacker than jet, and to her skin which was whiter than snow, and to the two red spots upon her cheeks, which were redder than the blood upon the snow appeared to be.

At that time Arthur and his household were in search of Peredur. "Know ye," said Arthur, "who is the knight with the long spear who stands by the brook up yonder?" "Lord," said one of his companions, "I will go and learn who he is." So the youth came to the place where Peredur was, and asked him what he did thus, and who he was. And from the intensity with which he thought upon the lady whom best he loved, Peredur gave him no answer. Then the youth thrust at him with his lance, and Peredur turned upon him, and struck him over his horse's crupper to the ground. After this, four and twenty youths came to him, and he did not answer one more than another, but gave the same reception to all, bringing them with one single thrust to the ground. And then came Kai, and spoke to Peredur rudely and angrily; and Peredur cast him from him with a thrust of his spear. And while Kai lay thus, his horse returned at a wild and prancing pace. The household, when they saw the horse come back without his rider, rode forth in haste to the place where the encounter had been. And Peredur moved not from his meditation on seeing the concourse that came around Kai. Kai was brought to Arthur's tent, and Arthur was grieved that he had met with this reverse, for he loved Kai greatly.

"Then," said Gwalchmai, "it is not fitting that any should disturb an honourable knight from his thought unadvisedly; for either he is pondering some damage that he has sustained, or he is thinking of the lady whom best he loves. And through such ill-advised proceeding, perchance this misadventure has befallen Kai. If it seem well to thee, Lord, I will go and see if this knight hath changed from his thought; and if he has, I will ask him courteously to come and visit thee." Said Arthur to Gwalchmai, "Thou speakest like a wise and prudent man; go, and take enough of armour about thee, and choose thy horse." And Gwalchmai accoutred himself, and rode forward hastily to the place where Peredur was.

Peredur was resting on the shaft of his spear, pondering the same thought, and Gwalchmai came to him without any signs of hostility, and said to him, "If I thought it would be as agreeable to thee as it would be to me, I would converse with thee. I have also a message from Arthur unto thee, to pray thee to come and visit him. Two men have been here before on this errand." "That is true," said Peredur, "and uncourteously they came. They attacked me, and I was annoyed thereat, for it was not pleasing to me to be drawn from the thought that I was in, for I was thinking of the lady whom best I love." Said Gwalchmai, "This was not an ungentle thought, and I should marvel if it were pleasant to thee to be drawn from it." "Tell me," said Peredur, "is Kai in Arthur's Court?" "He is," said Gwalchmai, "and behold he is the knight who fought with thee last; and it would have been better for him had he not come, for his arm was broken with the fall which he had from thy spear." "Verily," said Peredur, "I am not sorry to have thus begun to avenge the insult to the dwarf and dwarfess." Gwalchmai marvelled to hear him speak of the dwarf and dwarfess; and he approached him, and threw his arms around his neck, and asked him what was his name. "Peredur, I am called," said he, "and thou, who art thou?" "I am called Gwalchmai," he replied. "I am right glad to meet with thee," said Peredur, "for in every country where I have been I have heard of thy fame for prowess and uprightness, and I solicit thy fellowship." "Thou shalt have it, by my faith, and grant me thine," said Gwalchmai. "Gladly will I do so," answered Peredur.

So they rode forth together joyfully towards the place where Arthur was, and when Kai saw them coming, he said, "I knew Gwalchmai needed not to fight the knight. And it is no wonder that he should gain fame; more can he do by his fair words than I by the strength of my arm." Peredur went with Gwalchmai to his tent, and they took off their armour. Peredur put on garments like those that Gwalchmai wore, and they went together unto Arthur, and saluted him. "Behold, Lord," said Gwalchmai, "him whom thou hast sought so long." "Welcome unto thee, Chieftain," said Arthur. "With me thou shalt remain; and had I known thy valour had been such, thou shouldst not have left me as thou didst; nevertheless, this was predicted of thee by the dwarf and dwarfess, whom Kai ill-treated and whom thou hast avenged." And thereupon, behold, there came the Queen and her maidens, and Peredur saluted them. And Arthur did him great honour and respect, and they returned towards Caerleon.

II

One day after Peredur came to Arthur's Court, as he walked in the city after his repast, behold there met him the lady who was called Angarrad of the Golden Hand. "By my faith, sister," said Peredur to her, "thou art a beauteous and lovely maiden; and, were it pleasing to thee, I could love thee above all women." "I pledge my faith," said she, "that I do not love thee, nor will I ever do so." "I also pledge my faith," said Peredur, "that I will never speak a word to any Christian again, until thou come to love me above all men."

The next day Peredur went forth by the high road, along a mountain ridge, and above him he beheld a castle, and thitherward he went. And he struck upon the gate with his lance, and then, behold, a comely auburn-haired youth opened the gate, and he had the stature of a warrior, and the years of a boy. And when Peredur came into the hall, there was a tall and stately lady sitting in a chair, and many maidens around her; and the lady rejoiced at his coming. When it was time they went to meat. And after the repast was finished the lady said, "It were well for thee, Chieftain, to go elsewhere to sleep. Nine sorceresses are here, of the witches of Gloucester, and unless we can make our escape before daybreak, we shall be slain; for already they have conquered and laid waste all the country, except this one dwelling." Peredur said no word, but he showed them that he would stay. Then they all went to rest.

With the break of day Peredur heard a dreadful outcry. Hastily he arose, and went forth in his vest and his doublet, with his sword about his neck, and he saw a sorceress overtake one of the watch, who cried out violently. Peredur attacked the sorceress, and struck her upon the head with his sword, so that he flattened her helmet and her head-piece like a dish upon her head.

"Thy mercy, goodly Peredur," said the un-Christian sorceress. "How knowest thou, hag, that I am Peredur?" "By destiny, and the foreknowledge that I should suffer harm from thee. Thou shalt take a horse and armour of me; and with me thou shalt go to learn chivalry and the use of thy arms." Said Peredur, "Thou shalt have mercy, if thou pledge thy faith thou wilt never more injure the dominions of the Lady of the Castle." The sorceress pledged her faith, and Peredur took surety of her, and with the permission of the Lady of the Castle he went forth with the sorceress to the Palace of the Sorceresses. And there he remained for three weeks, and then he made choice of a horse and arms, and went his way.

And after he had left the Palace of the Sorceresses, Peredur came to that castle that he afterwards called the Castle of Wonders. First he came to a vast desert wood, and at the further end of the wood was a meadow, and at the other side of the meadow he saw a great castle. Thitherward Peredur bent his way. On the border of a lake he saw a nobleman, sitting upon a velvet cushion, and having a garment of velvet upon him. His attendants were fishing in the lake. When the hoary-headed nobleman beheld Peredur approaching, he arose and went towards the castle. Peredur saw that he was old and lame.

Peredur rode to the castle, and the door was open, and he entered the hall. And there was the hoary-headed man sitting on a cushion, and a large blazing fire was burning before him. And the household and the company arose to meet Peredur, and disarrayed him.

They placed him beside the owner of the castle, and when it was time to eat, they caused him to sit beside him during the repast. Afterwards he beheld two youths enter the hall, and proceed up to the chamber, bearing a spear of mighty size, with three streams of blood flowing from the point to the ground. And when all the company saw this, they began wailing and lamenting. But Peredur spoke no word and asked no question. And when the clamour had a little subsided, behold two maidens entered, with a large salver between them, in which was a man's head, surrounded by a profusion of blood. Thereupon the company of the court made so great an outcry that it was

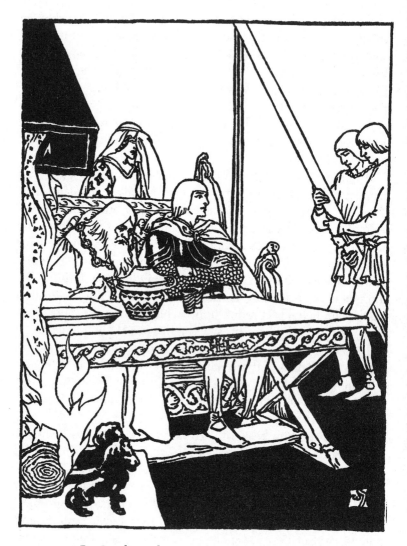

But Peredur spoke no word and asked no question.

irksome to be in the same hall with them. At length they were silent. And still Peredur said no word. When the time came that they should sleep, Peredur was brought into a fair chamber in that strange castle.

Peredur rode forward next day, and he traversed a vast tract of desert, in which no dwellings were. At length he came to a habitation, mean and small. And there he heard that there was a serpent that lay upon a gold ring, and suffered none to inhabit the country for seven miles around. Peredur came to the place where he heard the serpent was. And angrily, furiously, and desperately fought he with the serpent; and at last he killed it, and took away the ring.

Thus he was for a long time without speaking a word to any Christian. Therefore he lost his colour and his aspect, through extreme longing after the Court of Arthur, and the society of the lady whom best he loved, and of his companions. Then he proceeded towards Arthur's Court, and on the road there met him Arthur's household going on a particular errand, with Kai at their head. And Peredur knew them all, but none of the household recognized him. "Whence comest thou, Chieftain?" asked Kai. And this he asked him twice and three times, and he answered him not. And Kai thrust him through the thigh with his lance. Then, lest he should be compelled to speak, and to break his vow, Peredur rode on without stopping. "Then," said Gwalchmai, "I declare to Heaven, Kai, that thou hast acted ill in committing such an outrage on a youth like this, who cannot speak." And Gwalchmai turned back to Arthur's Court. "Lady," said he to the Queen, "seest thou how wicked an outrage Kai has committed upon this youth who cannot speak; for Heaven's sake, and for mine, cause him to have medical care before I come back, and I will repay thee the charge."

Afterwards Arthur and his household were going to mass, and they beheld a knight who had raised the signal for combat. "Verily," said Arthur, "by the valour of men, I will not go hence until I have my horse and my arms to overthrow yonder boor who has raised the signal for combat on a holy day." Then went the attendants to fetch Arthur's horse and arms. Peredur met them as they were going back, and he took the horse and arms from them, and proceeded to the meadow; and all those who saw him arise and go to do battle with the knight, went upon the tops of the houses, and the mounds, and the high places, to behold the combat.

Peredur beckoned with his hand to the knight to commence the fight. The knight thrust at him. And Peredur spurred his horse, and ran at him wrathfully, furiously, fiercely, desperately, and with mighty rage, and he gave him a thrust, deadly-wounding, severe, furious, adroit, and strong, under his jaw, and raised him out of his saddle, and cast him a long way from him. Then Peredur went back, and left the horse and the arms with the attendant as before, and he went on foot to Arthur's Court.

Then Peredur went by the name of the Dumb Youth. And behold, one day, Angarrad of the Golden Hand met him. "I declare to Heaven, Chieftain," she said, "woeful is it that thou canst not speak; for couldst thou speak, I would love thee best of all men; and by my faith, although thou canst not, I do love thee above all." "Heaven reward thee, my sister," said Peredur, "by my faith I also do love thee." Thereupon it was known that he was Peredur. And then he held fellowship with Gwalchmai, and Owen, the son of Urien, and all the household, and he remained in Arthur's Court.

III

Arthur was in Caerleon upon the River Usk; and he went to hunt, and Peredur went with him. And Peredur let loose his dog upon a stag, and the dog killed the stag in a desert place. Peredur rode hence, and he came to the fairest valley he had ever seen, through which ran a river; and there he beheld many tents of various colours. And he marvelled still more at the number of water-mills and of wind-mills that he saw. There rode up to him a tall auburn-haired man, in a workman's garb, and Peredur inquired of him who he was.

"I am the chief miller," said he, "of all the mills yonder." "Wilt thou give me a lodging?" said Peredur. "I will, gladly," he answered. And Peredur came to the miller's house, and the miller had a fair and pleasant dwelling. Peredur asked money as a loan from the miller, that he might buy meat and liquor for himself and for the household, and he promised that he would pay him again ere he went thence. He inquired of the miller wherefore such a multitude was there assembled. And the miller said, "One thing is certain: either thou art a man from afar, or thou art not sensible. The Empress of Cristinobyl the Great is here; and she will have no one but the man who is most valiant; for riches she does not require. And it was impossible to bring food for so many thousands as are here, therefore were all these mills constructed." That night Peredur took his rest in the miller's house.

The next day Peredur arose, and he equipped himself and his horse for the tournament. Amongst the other tents he beheld one, which was the fairest he had ever seen. And he saw a beauteous maiden leaning her head out of the window of the tent, and he had never seen a maiden more lovely than she. Upon her was a garment of satin. He gazed fixedly on her, and he began to love her greatly. He remained there from morning until mid-day, and from mid-day until evening; and then the tournament was ended and he went to his lodging and drew off his armour.

He asked money of the miller, as a loan, and the miller's wife was wroth with Peredur; nevertheless, the miller lent him the money. The next day he did in like manner as he had done the day before. And at night he came to his lodging, and took money as a loan from the miller. And the third day, as he was in the same place, gazing upon the maiden, he felt a hard blow between the neck and the shoulder, from the edge of an axe. When he looked behind him he saw that it was the miller; and the miller said to him, "Do one of two things, either turn thy head from hence, or go to the tournament." Peredur smiled on the miller and went to the tournament.

At the tournament, all that encountered him that day he over-threw. And as many as he vanquished he sent as a gift to the Empress, and their horses and arms he sent as a gift to the wife of the miller, in payment of the borrowed money. Peredur stayed at the tournament until all were overthrown, and he sent all the men to the Empress, and the horses and arms to the wife of the miller, in payment of the borrowed money. The Empress sent to the Knight of the Mill to ask him to come and visit her. But Peredur went not for the first nor for the second message.

The third time she sent a hundred knights to bring him against his will, and they went to him and told him their mission from the Empress. Peredur fought with them, and caused them to be bound like stags. Then the Empress sought the advice of a wise man who was in her counsel; and he said to her: "With thy permission, I will go to him myself." So he came to Peredur, and saluted him, and besought him, for the sake of the lady of his love, to come and visit the Empress. They went together. And Peredur went and sat down in the outer chamber of the tent, and she came and placed herself by his side. There was but lit-tle discourse between them. And Peredur took his leave, and went to his lodging.

The next day he came to visit her, and when he came into the tent there was no one chamber less decorated than the others. They knew not where he would sit. Peredur went and sat beside the Empress, and discoursed with her courteously. And while they were thus, they beheld a black man enter with a goblet full of wine in his hand. He dropped upon his knee before the Empress, and besought her to give it to no one who would not fight with him for it. The Empress looked upon Peredur. "Lady," said he, "bestow on me the goblet." Peredur drank the wine, and sent the goblet to the miller's wife.

And while they were thus, behold there entered a black man of larger stature than the other, with a wild beast's claw in his hand, wrought into the form of a goblet and filled with wine. He presented it to the Empress, and besought her to give it to no one but the man who would fight with him. "Lady," said Peredur, "bestow it on me." And she gave it to him. Peredur drank the wine, and sent the goblet to the wife of the miller.

While they were thus, behold a rough-looking, crisp-haired man, taller than either of the others, came in with a bowl in his hand full of wine; and he bent upon his knee, and gave it into the hands of the Empress, and besought her to give it to none but him who would fight with him for it. She gave it to Peredur, and he sent it to the miller's wife. That night Peredur returned to his lodging; and the next day he accoutred himself and his horse, and went to the meadow and fought with and slew the three men, one after the other. Then Peredur proceeded to the tent, and the Empress put her arms around his neck and welcomed him. And Peredur was entertained there by the Empress, as the story relates, for fourteen years.

IV

Arthur was in Caerleon upon the River Usk, his principal palace; and in the centre of the floor of the hall were four men sitting on a carpet of velvet—Owen, Gwalchmai, Howel, and Peredur of the Long Lance. And they saw a black curly-headed maiden enter, riding upon a yellow mule, with jagged thongs in her hand to urge it on, and having a rough and hideous aspect. Blacker were her face and her two hands than the blackest iron covered with pitch; and her hue was not more frightful than her form. High cheeks had she, and a face lengthened downwards, and a short nose with distended nostrils. One eye was of piercing mottled grey, and the other was black as jet, deep-sunk in her head. And her teeth were long and yellow, more yellow were they than the flower of the broom. Her back was the shape of a crook, and her legs were large and bony. And her figure was very thin and spare, except her feet and her legs, which were of huge size.

She greeted Arthur and all his household except Peredur. And to him she spoke harsh and angry words. "Peredur, I greet thee not," she said, "seeing that thou dost not merit it. Blind was fate in giving thee fame and favour. When thou wast in the court of the Lame King, and didst see there the youth bearing the streaming spear, from the points of which were drops of blood flowing in streams even to the hand of the youth, and many other wonders likewise, thou didst not inquire their meaning nor their cause. Hadst thou done so, the King would have been restored to health, and his dominions to peace. Whereas from henceforth, he will have to endure battles and conflicts, and his knights will perish, and wives will be widowed, and maidens will be left portionless, and all this is because of thee." Then she said unto Arthur, "May it please thee, Lord, my dwelling is far hence, in the stately castle of which thou hast heard, and therein are five hundred and sixty-six knights of the order of chivalry, and the lady whom best he loves with each; and whoever would acquire fame in arms, and encounters, and conflicts, he will gain it there, if he deserve it. And whoso would reach the summit of fame and of honour, I know where he may find it. There is a castle on a lofty mountain, and there is a maiden therein, and she is detained a prisoner there, and whoever shall set her free will attain the summit of the fame of the world." And thereupon she rode away.

Then Peredur said, "By my faith, I will not rest tranquilly until I know the story and the meaning of the lance whereof the black maiden spoke." Then he rode forward. And he wandered over the whole island, seeking tidings of the black maiden, and he could meet with none. And he came to an unknown land, in the centre of a valley, watered by a river. As he traversed the valley he beheld a horseman coming towards him, and wearing the garments of a priest; Peredur besought his blessing. "Wretched man," said the priest, "thou meritest no blessing, and thou wouldst not be profited by one, seeing that thou art clad in armour on such a day as this." "And what day is to-day?" asked Peredur. "To-day is Good Friday." "Chide me not that I knew not this, seeing that it is a year to-day since I journeyed forth from my country." Then Peredur dismounted, and led his horse.

He had not proceeded far along the high road before he came to a crossroad, and the crossroad traversed a wood. On the other side of the wood he saw an unfortified castle, which appeared to be inhabited. At the gate of the castle there met him the priest whom he had seen before, and he asked his blessing. "The blessing of Heaven be unto thee," said the priest, "it is more fitting to travel in thy present guise than as thou wast erewhile; and this night thou shalt tarry with me." So Peredur remained there that night.

The next day Peredur sought to go forth. "To-day may no one journey," said the priest. "Thou shalt remain with me to-day and to-morrow, and the day following, and I will direct thee as best I may to the place which thou art seeking." And the fourth day

Peredur sought to go forth, and he entreated the priest to tell him how he should find the Castle of Wonders. "What I know thereof I will tell thee," he replied. "Go over yonder mountain, and on the other side of the mountain thou wilt come to a river, and in the valley wherein the river runs is a King's palace, therein the King sojourned during Easter. And if thou mayest have tidings anywhere of the Castle of Wonders, thou wilt have them there."

Then Peredur again rode forward. And he came to the valley in which was the river. And a short space from him he saw signs of a dwelling, and towards the dwelling he went, and he beheld a hall, and at the door of the hall he found four swarthy youths playing at chess. And when he entered, he beheld three maidens sitting on a bench, and they were all clothed alike, as became persons of high rank. And he came, and sat by them on the bench, and one of the maidens looked steadfastly upon Peredur, and wept. Peredur asked her wherefore she was weeping. "Through grief, that I should see so fair a youth as thou art slain." "Who will slay me?" inquired Peredur. "If thou art so daring as to remain here to-night, I will tell thee." "Howsoever great my danger may be from remaining here, I will listen unto thee." "This place is owned by him who is my father," said the maiden, "and he slays everyone who comes hither without his leave." "What sort of a man is thy father, that he is able to slay everyone thus?" "A man who does violence and wrong unto his neighbours, and who renders justice unto none."

Thereupon Peredur saw the youths arise and clear the chessmen from the board. He heard a great tumult; and after the tumult there came in a huge, black, one-eyed man, and the maidens rose to meet him. And they disarrayed him, and he went and sat down; and after he had rested and pondered awhile, he looked at Peredur, and asked who he was. "Lord," said one of the maidens, "he is the fairest and gentlest youth that ever thou didst see. And for the sake of Heaven, and of thine own dignity, have patience with him." "For thy sake I will have patience, and I will grant him his life this night."

Then Peredur came towards the fire, and partook of food and liquor, and entered into discourse with the maidens. And he said to the Black Man, "It is a marvel to me, so mighty as thou art, who could have put out thine eye." "It is one of my habits," said the Black Man, "that whosoever puts to me the question which thou hast asked, shall not escape with his life, either as a free gift or for a price." "Lord," said the maiden, "whatsoever he may say to thee in jest, make good that which thou saidst, and didst promise me just now." "I will do so, gladly, for thy sake," said he. "Willingly will I grant him his life this night." And that night they were at peace.

The next day the Black Man got up, and put on his armour, and said to Peredur, "Arise, man, and suffer death." And Peredur said unto him, "Do one of two things, Black Man; if thou wilt fight with me, either throw off thy own armour, or give arms to me, that I may encounter thee." "Ha, man," said he, "couldst thou fight if thou hadst arms? Take, then, what arms thou dost choose."

Thereupon one of the maidens came to Peredur with such arms as pleased him; and he fought with the Black Man, and forced him to crave his mercy. "Black Man," said Peredur, "thou shalt have mercy, provided thou tell me who thou art, and who put out thine eye." "Lord, I will tell thee; I lost it in fighting with the Black Serpent of the Cairn. There is a mound, which is called the Mound of Mourning, and on the mound there is a cairn, and in the cairn there is a serpent, and on the tail of the serpent there is a stone, and the virtues of the stone are such, that whosoever should hold it in one hand, in the other he will have as much gold as he may desire. And in fighting with this serpent was it that I lost my eye. The Black Oppressor I am called." "Tell me," said Peredur, "how far hence is the Mound of Mourning?" "The same day that thou settest forth thou wilt come to it."

Then Peredur rode forward. He came to a mound, whereon sat the fairest lady he had ever beheld. "I know thy quest," said she, "thou art going to encounter the Black Serpent that is called the Addanc. He will slay thee, and that not by courage, but by craft. He has a cave, and at the entrance of the cave there is a stone pillar, and he sees everyone who enters, and none sees him; and from behind the pillar he slays everyone with a poiso-

The Black Man said, "Arise, man, and suffer death."

nous dart. But I will give thee a stone by which thou shalt see
him when thou goest in, and he shall not see thee." Then when
Peredur looked on her he saw that she was his love, the
Empress of Cristinobyl the Great. "When thou seekest me, seek
towards India," she said. And then she vanished, after placing
the stone in his hand.

He came towards a valley, through which ran a river; and the
borders of the valley were wooded, and on each side of the river
were level meadows. On one side of the river he saw a flock of
white sheep, and on the other a flock of black sheep. And whenever one of the white sheep bleated, one of the black sheep
would cross over and become white; and when one of the black
sheep bleated, one of the white sheep would cross over and
become black. And he saw a tall tree by the side of the river, one
half of which was in flames from the root to the top, and the
other half was green and in full leaf. Nigh thereto he saw a youth
sitting upon a mound, and two grey-hounds, white-breasted and
spotted, in leashes, lying by his side. And certain was he that he
had never seen a youth of so royal a bearing as he. In the wood
opposite he heard hounds raising a herd of deer.

Peredur saluted the youth, and the youth greeted him in
return. There were three roads leading from the mound; two of
them were wide roads, and the third was more narrow. Peredur
inquired where the three roads went. "One of them goes to my
palace," said the youth, "and one of two things I would counsel
thee to do; either to proceed to my palace, which is before thee,
and where thou wilt find my wife, or else to remain here to see
the hounds chasing the roused deer from the wood to the plain.
And thou shalt see the best grey-hounds thou didst ever behold,
and the boldest in the chase, kill the deer by the water beside
us; and when it is time to go to meat, my page will come with
my horse to meet me, and thou shalt rest in my palace to-night."
"Heaven reward thee, but I cannot tarry, for onward must I go,"
said Peredur. "The other road leads to the town, which is near
here, and wherein food and liquor may be bought; and the road
which is narrower than the others goes towards the cave of the
Addanc." "With thy permission I will go that way."

And Peredur went towards the cave. He took the stone in his

left hand, and his lance in his right. As he went in he perceived the Addanc, and he pierced him through with his lance, and cut off his head. And as he came from the cave, behold there were three young men at the entrance, and they saluted Peredur, and told him that there was a prediction that he should slay that monster. Peredur gave the head to the young men, and they offered him in marriage whichever of their three sisters he might choose, and half their kingdom with her. "I came not hither to woo," said Peredur, "but if peradventure I took a wife, I should prefer one of your sisters to all others."

Then they said to him, "What seekst thou, Chieftain?" "I am seeking tidings of the Castle of Wonders." "Thy enterprise is greater, Chieftain, than thou wilt wish to pursue, nevertheless, thou shalt have tidings of the castle." Then they said to him, "Go over yonder mountain, and thou wilt find a lake, and in the middle of the lake there is a castle, and that is the castle that is called the Castle of Wonders, and we know not what wonders are therein, but thus it is called."

Peredur proceeded towards the castle, and the gate of the castle was open. And when he came to the hall, the door was open, and he entered. And he beheld a chess-board in the hall, and the chess-men were playing against each other, by themselves. The side that Peredur favoured lost the game, and thereupon the others set up a shout, as though they had been living men. Peredur was wroth, and took the chess-men in his lap, and cast the chess-board into the lake.

When he had done this, behold the black maiden came in, and she said to him, "The welcome of Heaven be not unto thee. Thou hadst rather do evil than good." "What complaint hast thou against me, maiden?" said Peredur. "That thou hast occasioned unto the Empress the loss of her chess-board, which she would not have lost for all her empire. And the way in which thou mayest recover the chess-board is to repair to the Castle of Ysbidinongyl, where is a Black Man, who lays waste the dominions of the Empress, and if thou canst slay him, thou wilt recover the chess-board. But if thou goest there, thou wilt not return alive." "Wilt thou direct me thither?" said Peredur. "I will show thee the way," she replied.

So Peredur went to the castle, and he fought with the Black Man who was there, and he overcame him. The Black Man besought mercy of Peredur. "Mercy will I grant thee," said he, "on condition that thou cause the chess-board to be restored to the place where it was when I entered the hall." Then Peredur went back to the Castle of Wonders.

Again the black maiden came to him, and said, "The malediction of Heaven attend thee for thy work, since thou hast left that monster alive, who lays waste all the possessions of the Empress." "I granted him his life," said Peredur, "that he might cause the chess-board to be restored." "The chess-board is not in the place where thou didst find it; go back, therefore, and slay him." So Peredur went back, and he fought with the Black Man, and he slew him.

And when he returned to the Castle of Wonders, he found the black maiden there. "Ah, maiden," said he, "where is the Empress?" "I declare to Heaven that thou wilt not see her now, unless thou dost slay the monster that is in yonder forest." "What monster is there?" "It is a stag that is as swift as the swiftest bird; he has one horn on his forehead, as long as the shaft of a spear, and as sharp as whatever is sharpest. He destroys the branches of the best trees in the forest, and he kills every animal that he meets with therein, and those that he doth not slay perish with hunger. And what is worse than that, he comes every night, and drinks up the fish-pond, and leaves the fishes exposed, so that for the most part they die before the water returns again." "Maiden," said Peredur, "wilt thou come and show me this animal?" "Not so," said the maiden, "for he has not permitted any mortal to enter the forest for above a twelvemonth. Behold, here is a little dog belonging to the Empress, which will rouse the stag, and will chase him towards thee."

Then the little dog went as a guide to Peredur, and roused the stag, and brought him towards the place where Peredur was. The stag attacked Peredur, and he let him pass by him, and as he did so, he smote off his head with his sword. And while he was looking on the head of the stag, he saw a lady on horseback coming toward him. She took the little dog in the lappet of her cape, and the head and the body of the stag lay before her. And around the stag's neck was a golden collar. "Ha! Chieftain," said she, "uncourteously hast thou acted in slaying the fairest jewel that was in my dominions." "I was entreated so to do, and is there any way by which I can obtain thy friendship?" "There is," she replied. "Go thou forward unto yonder mountain, and there thou wilt find a grove, and in the grove there is a cromlech; do thou there challenge a man three times to fight, and thou shalt have my friendship."

So Peredur proceeded onward, and came to the side of the grove, and challenged any man to fight. And a Black Man rose from beneath the cromlech, mounted upon a bony horse, and both he and the horse were clad in huge rusty armour. And they fought. As often as Peredur cast the Black Man to the earth, he would jump again into the saddle. And Peredur dismounted, and drew his sword, and thereupon the Black Man disappeared with Peredur's horse and his own, so that he could not gain sight of him a second time.

Then Peredur went along the mountain, and at the other side of the mountain he beheld a castle in the valley, wherein was a river. He went to the castle, and as he entered it, he saw a hall, and the door of the hall was open, and he went in. He saw a lame, hoary-headed man sitting on one side of the hall. And Peredur beheld his horse, which the Black Man had taken, in the stall. He went and seated himself on one side of the hoary-headed man.

Then, behold, a yellow-haired youth came, and bent upon the knee before Peredur, and besought his friendship. "Lord," said the youth, "it was I who came in the form of the black maiden to Arthur's Court, and when thou didst throw down the chess-board, and when thou didst slay the Black Man of Ysbidinongyl, and when thou didst slay the stag, and when thou didst go to fight the Black Man of the cromlech. And I came with the bloody head on the salver, and with the lance that streamed with blood from the point to the hand, all along the shaft; and the head was thy cousin's, and he was killed by the sorceresses of Gloucester, who also lamed thy uncle, this nobleman. And there is a prediction that thou art to avenge these things."

As they were being spoken about, the sorceresses came. And Peredur began to fight with them, and one of the sorceresses slew a man before Peredur's face, and Peredur bade her forbear. And the sorceress slew a man before Peredur's face a second time, and a second time he forbade her. And the third time the sorceress slew a man before the face of Peredur, and then Peredur drew his sword, and smote the sorceress on the helmet, and all her head-armour was split in two parts. And she set up a cry, and desired the other sorceresses to flee, and told them that this was Peredur, the man who had learnt chivalry with them, and by whom they were destined to be slain. Then Arthur and his household came, and they fell upon the sorceresses, and they slew the sorceresses of Gloucester every one. And thus is it related of Peredur in the Castle of Wonders.

THE STORY OF GERAINT
AND THE MAIDEN ENID

I

One Whitsuntide, as King Arthur was holding his Court at Caerleon upon Usk, there entered a tall, fair-haired youth clad in a coat and a surcoat of diapered satin, with a golden-hilted sword about his neck, and low shoes of leather upon his feet. He came and stood before Arthur. "Hail to thee, Lord," said he. "Heaven prosper thee," said the King, "and be thou welcome. Dost thou bring any new tidings?" "I do, Lord," said the youth. "Then tell me thine errand," said King Arthur.

"I am one of thy foresters in the Forest of Dean," said the youth. "In the forest I saw a stag, the like of which I never yet beheld. He is of pure white, and he does not herd with any other animal through stateliness and pride, so royal is his bearing. And I come to seek thy counsel, Lord, and to know thy will concerning him." "It seems best to me," said Arthur, "to go and hunt him to-morrow at break of day."

Then all in the palace received notice of the hunting that was to be at break of day. "Lord," said Queen Gwenhuivar to King Arthur, "wilt thou permit me to go to-morrow to see and hear the hunt of the stag of which the young man spoke?" "I will, gladly," said Arthur. "Then I will go," said she. And Gwalchmai said to Arthur, "Lord, if it seem well to thee, permit that into whose hunt soever the stag shall come, may that one cut off the stag's head, and give it to whom he pleases, whether to his own lady-love, or to the lady of his friend." "I grant it gladly," said Arthur. "And let the steward of the household be chastised if we are not all ready to-morrow for the chase."

When day came, they rose, and Arthur called the attendants who guarded his couch. They came to Arthur and saluted him, and arrayed him in his garments. Arthur wondered that Gwenhuivar did not awake, and did not move in her bed. The attendants wished to awaken her. "Disturb her not," said Arthur, "for she had rather sleep than see the hunting."

Then Arthur went forth, and he heard two horns sounding, one from near the lodging of the chief huntsman, and the other from near that of the chief page. The whole of the Court came to Arthur, and they took the road to the forest.

After Arthur had gone forth from the palace, Gwenhuivar awoke, and she called to her maidens, and apparelled herself. "Maidens," said she, "go one of you to the stable, and order hither a horse such as a woman may ride." And one of her maidens went, and she found but two horses in the stable, and Gwenhuivar and one of her maidens mounted them, and went through the Usk, and followed the track of the men and the horses.

As they rode thus, they heard a loud and rushing sound; and they looked behind them, and beheld a knight upon a hunter foal of mighty size; the rider was a fair-haired youth, bare-legged, and of princely mien, and a golden-hilted sword was at his side, and a robe and a surcoat of satin were upon him, and two low shoes of leather upon his feet; and around him was a scarf of purple, at each corner of which was a golden apple. And his horse stepped stately, and swift, and proud. The youth over-took Gwenhuivar, and saluted her.

"Heaven prosper thee, Geraint," said the Queen, "and the welcome of Heaven be unto thee. And why didst thou not go with thy lord to hunt?" "Because I knew not when he went," said Geraint. "I was asleep." "I was asleep, too," said the Queen. "But thou, O young man, art the most agreeable companion I could have in the whole kingdom; and it may be, that I shall be more amused with the hunting than they; for we shall hear the horns when they sound, and we shall hear the dogs when they are let loose, and begin to cry." So they went to the edge of the forest, and there they stood. "From this place," said the Queen, "we shall hear when the dogs are let loose."

While they were standing there they heard a loud noise, and they looked towards the spot whence it came, and they beheld a dwarf riding upon a horse, stately, and foaming, and prancing, and strong, and spirited. In the hand of the dwarf was a whip. And near the dwarf they saw a lady upon a beautiful white horse, of steady and stately pace; and she was clothed in a garment of gold brocade. Beside her was a knight upon a war horse of large size, with heavy and bright armour both upon himself and upon his horse. Those who were with the Queen thought that never before had they seen a knight, or a horse, or armour, of such remarkable size.

"Geraint," said Gwenhuivar, "knowest thou the name of that tall knight yonder?" "I know him not," said Geraint, "and the strange armour that he wears prevents my seeing either his face or his features." "Go, maiden," said Gwenhuivar, "and ask the dwarf who that knight is." Then the maiden went up to the dwarf; and the dwarf waited for the maiden, when he saw her coming towards him. The maiden inquired of the dwarf who the knight was. "I will not tell thee," he answered. "Since thou art so churlish as not to tell me," she said, "I will ask him himself." "Thou shalt not ask him, by my faith," said he. "Wherefore?" said she. "Because thou art not of sufficient honour to befit thee to speak to my lord." Then the maiden turned her horse's head towards the knight, upon which the dwarf struck her with the whip that was in his hand across the face and the eyes, until the blood flowed forth. And the maiden, through the hurt she received from the blow, returned to Gwenhuivar, complaining of the pain.

"Very rudely has the dwarf treated thee," said Geraint. "I will go myself to know who the knight is." "Go," said Gwenhuivar. Then Geraint went up to the dwarf. "Who is yonder knight?" said Geraint. "I will not tell thee," said the dwarf. "Then I will ask him myself," said Geraint. "Thou wilt not, by my faith," said the dwarf, "thou art not honourable enough to speak with my lord." Said Geraint, "I have spoken with men of equal rank with him." And saying that, he turned his horse's head towards the knight; but the dwarf overtook him, and struck him as he had done the maiden, so that the blood coloured the scarf that Geraint wore. Then Geraint put his hand on the hilt of his sword, but he took counsel with himself, and considered that it

The dwarf struck him as he had done the maiden.

would be no vengeance for him to slay the dwarf, and to be attacked unarmed by an armed knight, so he returned to where Gwenhuivar was.

"Thou hast acted wisely and discreetly," said she. "Lady," said he, "I will follow him yet, with thy permission; and at last he will come to some inhabited place, where I may have arms either as a loan or for a pledge, so that I may encounter the knight." "Go," said she, "and do not attack him until thou hast good arms, and I shall be very anxious concerning thee, until I hear tidings of thee." "If I am alive," said he, "thou shalt hear tidings of me by to-morrow afternoon." And saying that, he departed.

The road that the knight, the dwarf, and the lady took was below the palace of Caerleon, and across the ford of the Usk. Geraint followed, and they went along a fair and even and lofty ridge of ground, until they came to a town, and at the extremity of the town Geraint saw a fortress and a castle. As the knight passed through, all the people arose and saluted him, and bade him welcome. Geraint looked at every house to see if he knew any of those whom he saw there. But he knew none, and none knew him to do him the kindness to let him have arms either as a loan or for a pledge. And every house he saw was full of men, and arms, and horses. And the men were polishing shields, and burnishing swords, and washing armour, and shoeing horses. The knight and the lady and the dwarf rode up to the castle that was in the town, and every one was glad in the castle. From the battlements and the gates they risked their necks, through their eagerness to greet them, and to show their joy.

Geraint stood there to see whether the knight would remain in the castle; and when he was certain that he would do so, he looked around him; and at a little distance from the town he saw an old palace in ruins, wherein was a hall that was falling to decay. And as he knew not any one in the town, he went towards the old palace; and when he came near to the palace, he saw but one chamber, and a bridge of marble-stone leading to it. And upon the bridge he saw sitting a hoary-headed man, upon whom were tattered garments. Geraint gazed steadfastly upon him for a long time. Then the hoary-headed man spoke to him. "Young man," he said, "wherefore art thou thoughtful?" "I am thought-

ful," said Geraint, "because I know not where to go to-night."
"Wilt thou come forward this way?" said the hoary-headed man,
"and thou shalt have of the best that can be procured for thee."

Geraint went forward. In the hall he dismounted, and he left
there his horse. Then he went to the upper chamber with the
hoary-headed man. And in the chamber he beheld an aged
woman, sitting on a cushion, with old, tattered garments of satin
upon her; and it seemed to him that he had never seen a woman
fairer than she must have been, when in the fullness of youth.

And then he saw beside the aged woman a maiden, upon
whom were a vest and a veil, that were old, and beginning to be
worn out. And truly, he never saw a maiden more full of come-
liness, and grace, and beauty than she. The hoary-headed man
said to the maiden, "There is no attendant for the horse of this
youth but thyself." "I will render the best service I am able,"
said she, "both to him and to his horse." And the maiden disen-
cumbered the youth, and then she furnished the horse with
straw and with corn. The hoary-headed man said to her, "Go to
the town, and bring hither the best that thou canst find both of
food and drink." "I will, gladly, Lord," said she. And to the town
she went.

The hoary-headed man and Geraint conversed together while
the maiden was in the town. She came back, and a boy with her,
bearing on his back a costrel full of mead, and a quarter of a
young bullock; in her hands was a quantity of white bread, and
she had some manchet bread in her veil. "I could not obtain better than this," said she, "nor with better should I have been
trusted." "It is good enough," said Geraint. They caused the
meat to be cooked, and when their food was ready, they sat
down.

When they had finished eating Geraint talked with the hoary-
headed man, and he asked him, in the first place, to whom
belonged the palace that he was in. "Truly," said he, "it was I that
built it, and to me also belonged the town and the castle which
thou sawest." "Alas!" said Geraint, "how is it that thou hast lost
them now?" "I lost a great earldom as well as these," said he,
"and this is how I lost them. I had a nephew, the son of my
brother, and I took his possessions to myself; and when he came

to his strength, he demanded of me his property, but I withheld it from him. So he made war upon me, and wrested from me all I possessed."

Then Geraint said, "Good sir, wilt thou tell me wherefore came the knight and the lady and the dwarf just now into the town, and what is the preparation which I saw, and the putting of arms in order?" "I will tell thee." And then the old earl said:

"The preparations are for the game that is to be held to-morrow by the young earl, my nephew, which will be in this wise: In the midst of a meadow which is here, two forks will be set up, and upon the two forks a silver rod, and upon the silver rod a Sparrow Hawk, and for the Sparrow Hawk there will be a tournament. To the tournament will go all the array thou didst see in the city, of men, and of horses, and of arms. And with each man will go the lady he loves best; and no man can joust for the Sparrow Hawk, except the lady he loves best be with him. The knight whom thou sawest has gained the Sparrow Hawk these two years; and if he gains it the third year, they will, from that time, send it every year to him, and he himself will come here no more. And he will be called the Knight of the Sparrow Hawk from that time forth."

Said Geraint after he had heard all this, "Sir, what is thy counsel to me concerning this knight, on account of the insult which I received from the dwarf, and that which was received by the maiden of Gwenhuivar, the wife of Arthur?" And Geraint told the old earl what the insult was that he had received. "It is not easy to counsel thee, inasmuch as thou hast neither dame nor maiden belonging to thee, for whom thou canst joust. Yet I have arms here which thou couldst have; and there is my horse also, if he seems to thee better than thine own." "Ah, sir," said Geraint, "Heaven reward thee. My own horse, to which I am accustomed, together with thy arms, will suffice me. And if, when the appointed time shall come to-morrow, thou wilt permit me to challenge for yonder maiden who is thy daughter, I will engage, if I escape from the tournament, to love the maiden as long as I live." "Gladly will I permit thee," said the old earl, "and since thou dost thus resolve, it is necessary that thy horse and arms should be ready to-morrow at break of day. For then the Knight of the Sparrow Hawk will make proclamation, and ask the lady he loves best to take the Sparrow Hawk. 'For,' will he say to her, 'thou art the fairest of women, and thou didst possess it last year, and the year previous; and if any deny it thee to-day, by force will I defend it for thee.' And therefore," said the old earl, "it is needful for thee to be there at daybreak; and we three will be with thee." And thus was it settled.

Before the dawn they arose, and arrayed themselves; and by the time it was day, they were all four in the meadow. And there was the Knight of the Sparrow Hawk making the proclamation, and asking his lady-love to fetch the Sparrow Hawk. "Fetch it not," said Geraint, "for there is here a maiden, who is fairer, and more noble, and more comely, and who has a better claim to it than thou." "If thou maintainest the Sparrow Hawk to be due to her, come forward, and do battle with me." And Geraint went forward to the top of the meadow, having upon himself and upon his horse armour which was heavy, and rusty, and worthless, and of uncouth shape.

He and the knight encountered each other, and they broke a set of lances, and they broke a second set, and a third. And thus they did at every onset, and they broke as many lances as were brought to them. And when the young earl and his company saw the Knight of the Sparrow Hawk gaining the mastery, there was shouting, and joy, and mirth amongst them. And the old earl and his wife, and his daughter were sorrowful.

The old earl served Geraint lances as often as he broke them, and the dwarf served the Knight of the Sparrow Hawk. Then the old earl came to Geraint. "Oh! Chieftain," said he, "since no other will hold with thee, behold, here is the lance which was in my hand on the day when I received the honour of knighthood; and from that time to this I never broke it. And it has an excellent point." Then Geraint took the lance, thanking the old earl. The dwarf also brought a lance to his lord. "Bethink thee," said he, "that no knight ever withstood thee before so long as this one has done." "I declare to Heaven," said Geraint, "that unless death takes me quickly hence, he shall fare never the better for thy service."

Geraint pricked his horse towards him from afar, and warning him, he rushed upon him, and gave him a blow so severe, and furious, and fierce, upon the face of his shield, that he cleft it in two, and broke his armour, and burst his girths, so that both he and his saddle were borne to the ground over the horse's crupper. Geraint dismounted quickly. And he was wroth, and he drew his sword, and rushed fiercely upon him. Then the knight also arose, and drew his sword against Geraint. They fought on foot with their swords until their arms struck sparks of fire like stars from one another; and thus they continued fighting until the blood and sweat obscured the light from their eyes. When Geraint prevailed, the old earl and his wife, and daughter were glad; and when the knight prevailed, it rejoiced the young earl and his party.

Then the old earl saw Geraint receive a severe stroke, and he went up to him quickly, and he said to him, "Oh, Chieftain, remember the treatment which thou hadst from the dwarf; and wilt thou not seek vengeance for the insult to thyself, and for the insult to Gwenhuivar, the wife of Arthur?" Geraint was roused by what he said to him, and he called to him all his strength, and lifted up his sword, and struck the knight upon the crown of his head, so that he broke all his head-armour, and cut through even to the skull.

The knight fell upon his knees, and cast his sword from his hand, and besought mercy of Geraint. "Of a truth," said he, "I relinquish my overdaring and my pride in craving thy mercy; and unless I have time to commit myself to Heaven for my sins, and to talk with a priest, thy mercy will avail me little." "I will grant thee grace upon this condition," said Geraint, "that thou wilt go to Gwenhuivar, the wife of Arthur, to do her satisfaction for the insult which her maiden received from thy dwarf. As for myself, for the insult which I received from thee and thy dwarf, I am content with that which I have done unto thee. Dismount not from the time thou goest hence until thou comest into the presence of Gwenhuivar, to make her what atonement shall be adjudged at the Court of Arthur." "This will I do gladly. And who art thou?" said he. "I am Geraint. And declare thou also who thou art." "I am Edeyrn, the son of Nudd." Then he threw himself on his horse, and went forward to Arthur's Court, and the lady he loved best went before him and the dwarf, with much lamentation. And thus far this story up to that time.

Then came the young earl and his party to Geraint, and saluted him, and bade him to his castle. "I may not go," said Geraint, "but where I was last night, there will I be to-night also." "Since thou wilt have none of my inviting, thou shalt have abundance of all that I can command for thee, in the place thou wast last night. And I will order ointment for thee, to recover thee from thy fatigues, and from the weariness that is upon thee." "Heaven reward thee," said Geraint. And Geraint went with the old earl, and his wife and daughter.

When they reached the ruined palace, the household servants and attendants of the young earl had arrived, and they arranged all the chambers, dressing them with straw and with fire; and in a short time the ointment was ready, and Geraint came there, and they washed his head. Then came the young earl with forty knights. And when Geraint came from the anointing, the young earl asked him to go to the hall to eat. "Where is the old earl?" said Geraint, "and his wife and his daughter?" "They are in the chamber yonder," said the earl's chamberlain, "arraying them-selves in the garments which my master has caused to be brought for them." "Let not the maiden array herself," said Geraint, "except in her vest and her veil, until she come to the Court of Arthur, to be clad by Gwenhuivar in such garments as she may choose." So the maiden did not array herself.

They all entered the hall, and they washed, and went and sat down to meat. They were served abundantly, and they received a profusion of gifts. They conversed together, and the young earl invited Geraint to visit him next day. "I will not," said Geraint. "To the Court of Arthur will I go with the maiden to-morrow. The maiden's father is in poverty and trouble, and I go chiefly to gain a maintenance for him." "Ah, Chieftain," said the young earl, "it is not by my fault that he is without possessions. And with regard to the disagreement between me and him, I will gladly abide by thy counsel, and agree to what thou mayest judge right between us." "I but ask thee," said Geraint, "to restore to him what is his, and what he should have received from the time he lost his possessions, even until this day." "That I will gladly do, for thee," answered the young earl. "Then," said Geraint, "whosoever is here who owes homage to the old earl, let him come forward, and perform it on the spot." All the men gave their homage to him. And his castle, and his town, and all his possessions were restored to the old earl. And he received back all that he had lost, even to the smallest jewel.

Then spoke the old earl to Geraint. "Chieftain," said he, "behold the maiden Enid for whom thou didst challenge at the tournament, I bestow her upon thee." "She shall go with me," said Geraint, "to the Court of Arthur." And the next day they proceeded to Arthur's Court. So far concerning Geraint.

Now, this is how Arthur hunted the stag. The men and the dogs were were divided into hunting parties, and the dogs were let loose upon the stag. And the last dog that was let loose was the favourite dog of Arthur, Cavall. He left all the other dogs behind him, and turned the stag. At the second turn, the stag came towards the hunting party of Arthur. And Arthur set upon the stag. Before he could be slain by any other, Arthur cut off the stag's head. Then they sounded the death horn, and they all gathered around.

Then came Arthur's steward, and he said, "Lord, behold, yonder is the Queen, and none with her save only one maiden." "Command Gildas, the son of Caw, and all the scholars of the Court," said Arthur, "to attend Gwenhuivar to the palace." And they did so.

Then they all set forth, holding converse together concerning the head of the stag, to whom it should be given. One wished that it should be given to the lady best beloved by him, and another to the lady whom he loved best. And all they of the household, and the knights, disputed sharply concerning the head. They came to the palace. And when Arthur and Gwenhuivar heard them disputing about the head of the stag, Gwenhuivar said to Arthur, "My Lord, this is my counsel concerning the stag's head; let it not be given away until Geraint shall return from the errand he is upon." And Gwenhuivar told Arthur what that errand was.

And thus it was settled. The next day Gwenhuivar caused a watch to be set upon the ramparts for Geraint's coming. And after mid-day they beheld an unshapely little man upon a horse, and after him, as they supposed, a damsel, also on horseback, and after her a knight of large stature, bowed down, and hanging his head low and sorrowfully, and clad in broken and worthless armour.

Before they came near the gate, one of the watch went to Gwenhuivar, and told her what kind of people they saw, and what aspect they bore. "I know not who they are," said he. "But I know," said Gwenhuivar, "this is the knight whom Geraint pursued, and methinks that he comes not here by his own free will." Thereupon, behold, a porter came to the spot where Gwenhuivar was. "Lady," said he, "at the gate there is a knight, and I saw never a man of so pitiful an aspect to look upon as he. Miserable and broken is the armour that he wears, and the hue of blood is more conspicuous upon it than its own colour." "Knowest thou his name?" said she. "I do," said he, "he tells me that he is Edeyrn, the son of Nudd."

Gwenhuivar went to the gate to meet him, and he entered. And Gwenhuivar was sorry when she saw the condition he was in, even though he was accompanied by the churlish dwarf. Then Edeyrn saluted Gwenhuivar. "Heaven protect thee," said she. "Lady," said he, "Geraint, thy best and most valiant servant, greets thee." "Did he meet thee?" she asked. "Yes," said he, "and it was not to my advantage." "Sir," said she, "when thinkest thou that Geraint will be here?" "To-morrow, Lady, I think he will be here."

Then Arthur came to him, and he saluted Arthur; and Arthur gazed a long time upon him, and was amazed to see him thus. And thinking that he knew him, he inquired of him, "Art thou Edeyrn, the son of Nudd?" "I am, Lord," said he, "and I have met with much trouble, and received wounds unsupportable." Then he told Arthur and Gwenhuivar of all that had befallen him.

"Well," said Arthur, "from what I hear, it behooves Gwenhuivar to be merciful towards thee." "The mercy which thou desirest, Lord," said she, "will I grant to him." Then Arthur caused Morgan Tud to be called to him. He was the chief physician. "Take with thee Edeyrn, the son of Nudd, and cause a chamber to be prepared for him, and let him have the aid of medicine as thou wouldst do unto myself, if I were wounded, and let none into his chamber to molest him, but thyself and thy disciples, to administer to him remedies." "I will do so gladly, Lord," said Morgan Tud. Then said the steward of the household, "Whither is it right, Lord, to place the damsel who came with the knight?" "With Gwenhuivar and her maidens," said Arthur. And the steward of the household so placed her. Thus far concerning them.

The next day came Geraint towards the Court, and there was a watch set on the ramparts by Gwenhuivar, lest he should arrive unawares. And one of the watch came to the place where Gwenhuivar was. "Lady," said he, "methinks that I see Geraint, and a maiden with him. He is on horseback, but he has walking gear upon him, and the maiden appears to be in white, seeming to be clad in a garment of linen." "Assemble all the women," said Gwenhuivar, "and come to meet Geraint, to welcome him, and wish him joy." Gwenhuivar went to meet Geraint and the maiden, and when Geraint came to the place where Gwenhuivar was, he saluted her.

"Heaven prosper thee," said the Queen to him, "and welcome to thee. Thy career has been successful, and fortunate, and resistless, and glorious. And Heaven reward thee, that thou hast so proudly caused me to have retribution." "Lady," said Geraint, "I have earnestly desired to obtain thee satisfaction according to thy will; and, behold, here is the maiden through whom thou hadst thy revenge." "Verily," said Gwenhuivar, "the welcome of Heaven be unto her; and it is fitting that we should receive her joyfully." Then they went in. And Geraint came to where Arthur was and saluted him. "Heaven protect thee," said Arthur, "and the welcome of Heaven be unto thee. And since Edeyrn, the son of Nudd, has received his overthrow and wounds from thy hands, thou hast had a prosperous career." "Not upon me be the blame," said Geraint, "it was through the arrogance of Edeyrn himself that we were not friends." "Now," said Arthur, "where is the maiden for whom I heard thou didst give challenge?" "She is gone with the Queen to her chamber."

Then Arthur went to see the maiden. And he, and his companions, and his whole Court, were glad concerning the maiden Enid. And certain were they all, that had her array been suitable to her beauty, they had never seen a maiden fairer than she.

The choicest of all Gwenhuivar's apparel was given to Enid; and thus arrayed, she appeared most comely and graceful to all who beheld her. And that day and that night were spent in abundance of minstrelsy, and ample gifts, and a multitude of games. And from that time Enid became the bride of Geraint. She took up her abode in Arthur's palace; and she had many companions, both men and women, and there was no maiden more esteemed than she in the Island of Britain.

Then spake Gwenhuivar, the Queen. "Rightly did I judge," said she, "concerning the head of the stag, that it should not be given to any until Geraint's return; and, behold, here is a fit occasion for bestowing it. Let it be given to Enid, the most illustrious maiden. I do not believe that any will begrudge it her, for between her and everyone here there exists nothing but love and friendship." Much applauded was this by all of them, and Arthur also. And the head of the white stag was given to Enid. Thereupon her fame increased, and her friends thenceforward became more in number than before. And Geraint from that time forth loved hunting and the tournament, and hard encounters; and he came victorious from them all. A year, and a second, and a third, he proceeded thus, until his fame had flown over the face of the kingdom.

II

In another Whitsuntide Arthur was holding his Court at Caerleon upon Usk, and there came men before him, and they saluted him. "Heaven prosper you," said Arthur, "and the welcome of Heaven be unto you. And whence do you come?" "We come, Lord," said they, "from Cornwall, and we are ambassadors from Erbin, the Prince of Cornwall, thy uncle. And he greets thee as well, as an uncle should greet his nephew, and as a vassal should greet his lord. And he represents unto thee that he waxes feeble, and is advancing in years. And the neighbouring chiefs, knowing this, grow insolent towards him, and covet his land and possessions. And he earnestly beseeches thee, Lord, to permit Geraint, his son, to return to him, to protect his possessions, and to become acquainted with their boundaries. And unto him he represents that it were better for him to spend the flower of his youth and the prime of his age in preserving his own boundaries, than in tournaments, which are productive of no profit, although he obtains glory in them."

"Well," said Arthur, "go, and divest yourselves of your accoutrements, and refresh yourselves after your fatigue; and before you go forth hence you shall have an answer." Then the ambassadors went to eat. Arthur considered that it would go hard with him to let Geraint depart from him and from his Court; but neither did he think it fair that Geraint should be restrained from going to protect his dominions and his boundaries. No less was the grief and regret of Gwenhuivar, and all her women, and all her maidens, through fear that Enid would leave them.

Then Arthur spoke to Geraint about the coming of the ambassadors out of Cornwall. "Truly," said Geraint, "I will do according to thy will concerning this embassy." "Behold," said Arthur, "though it grieves me to part with thee, it is my counsel

that thou go to dwell in thine own dominions, and defend thy
boundaries, and to take with thee to accompany thee as many as
thou wilt of those thou lovest best among my faithful ones, and
among thy friends, and among thy companions in arms."
"Heaven reward thee; and this will I do," said Geraint. "What
discourse do I hear between you?" said Gwenhuivar. "Is it of
those who are to conduct Geraint to his own country?" "It is,"
said Arthur. "Then it will be needful for me to consider," said
she, "concerning companions and a provision for the Lady
Enid." "Thou wilt do well," said Arthur.

That night they went to sleep. And the next day the ambassadors were permitted to depart, and they were told that
Geraint would follow them. And on the third day Geraint set
forth, and many went with him. Never was there seen a fairer
host journeying towards the Severn. On the other side of the
Severn were the nobles of Erbin, the Prince of Cornwall, to welcome Geraint with gladness; and many of the women of the
court, with his mother, came to receive Enid. There was great
rejoicing and gladness throughout the court, and throughout all
the country, concerning Geraint, because of the greatness of
their love towards him, and of the greatness of the fame which
he had gained since he went from amongst them, and because
he was come to take possession of his dominions and to preserve
his boundaries.

In the court they had ample entertainment, and a multitude
of gifts, and a variety of minstrelsy and games. And to do honour to Geraint all the chief men of the country were invited that
night to visit him. At dawn next day Erbin arose, and summoned
to him Geraint, and the noble persons who had borne him company on the way. And he said to Geraint, "I am a feeble and aged
man, and whilst I was able to maintain the dominion for thee
and for myself, I did so. But thou art young, and in the flower of
thy vigour and thy youth; henceforth do thou preserve thy possessions. Into thy hands I give them, and this day also shalt thou
receive the homage of thy subjects."

Then Erbin desired Geraint to send messengers to the men,
to ask them whether it was displeasing to them that he should
come to receive their homage, and whether they had anything

to object to him. And they all said that it would be the fullness of joy and honour to them for Geraint to come and receive their homage. He received the homage of such as were there. After that, the followers of Arthur went; and Geraint went to bear them company, and Enid also, as far as Deganway; there they parted.

After that Geraint journeyed to the uttermost part of his dominions. And experienced guides, and the chief men of the country, went with him. And the furthermost point that they showed him he kept possession of.

As he had been used to do when he was at Arthur's Court, he frequented tournaments. He became acquainted with valiant and mighty men, until he had gained as much fame there as he had formerly done elsewhere. He ceased not until his fame had flown over the face of the whole kingdom.

When he knew that his fame was such, he began to love ease and pleasure, for there was no one who was worth his opposing. After that he came to like staying within his palace, with minstrelsy and diversions. For a long time he abode at home. And after that he began to shut himself up in the chamber of his wife, and he gave up the friendship of his nobles, together with his hunting and his amusements, and he lost the hearts of all the host in his court; and there was murmuring and scoffing concerning him among the inhabitants of the palace, on account of his relinquishing so completely their companionship for the love of his wife.

These tidings came to Erbin, Geraint's aged father. And when Erbin heard them, he spoke unto Enid, and inquired of her whether it was she who had caused Geraint to act thus, and to forsake his people and the men who fought for him. "Not I, by my confession unto Heaven," said Enid. And she knew not what she should do, for, although it were hard for her to own this to Geraint, yet it was not more easy for her to listen to what she heard, without warning Geraint concerning it. And Enid was very sorrowful.

One morning, in the summertime, Geraint lay upon the edge of Enid's couch. Enid was without sleep in the chamber which had windows of glass. And the sun shone through the windows upon the couch. The clothes had slipped from off Geraint's arms and his breast, and he was asleep. She gazed upon the marvellous beauty of his appearance, and she said, "Alas, and am I the cause that these arms and this breast have lost their glory and the warlike fame which they once so richly enjoyed!" And as she said this, the tears dropped from her eyes, and they fell upon his breast.

The tears she shed and the words she had spoken awoke him. Then he called his squire, and when he came to him, "Go quickly," he said, "and prepare my horse and my arms, and make them ready." And to Enid he said, "Do thou arise, and apparel thyself; and cause thy horse to be accoutred, and clothe thee in the worst riding dress that thou hast in thy possession. And evil betide me," he said, "if thou returnest here until thou knowest whether I have lost my strength so completely as thou didst say. And if it be so, it will then be easy for thee to seek the society thou didst wish for, of him of whom thou wast thinking." So Enid arose and clothed herself in her meanest garments. "I know nothing, Lord," said she, "of thy meaning." "Neither wilt thou know at this time," said he.

Then Geraint went to Erbin, his father. "Sir," said he, "I am going upon a quest, and I am not certain when I may come back. Take heed, therefore, unto thy possessions, until my return." "And who will proceed with thee?" his father asked. "But one person only will go with me," said Geraint. "Heaven counsel thee, my son," said Erbin.

Then went Geraint to the place where his horse was, and it was equipped with foreign armour, heavy and shining. He desired Enid to mount her horse, and to ride forward, and to keep a long way before him. "And whatever thou mayest see, and whatever thou mayest hear concerning me," said he, "do thou not turn back. And unless I speak unto thee, say not thou one word either." And then they set forward.

"Alas, and am I the cause that these arms have lost their glory!"

III

The road that Geraint chose was not the pleasantest and the most frequented road; it was the road that was wildest and most beset by thieves and robbers, and venomous animals. They followed the road till they saw a vast forest, and they went towards the forest.

Four armed horsemen came forth from the forest. When the horsemen beheld Geraint and Enid, one of them said to the others, "Behold, here is a good occasion for us to capture two horses and armour, and a lady likewise; for this we shall have no difficulty in doing against yonder single knight, who hangs his head so heavily." Enid heard this discourse. She knew not what she should do through fear of Geraint, who had told her to be silent. "The vengeance of Heaven be upon me," she said, "if I would not rather receive my death from his hand than from the hand of any other; and though he should slay me yet will I speak to him, lest I should have the misery to witness his death."

So Enid waited for Geraint until he came near to her. "Lord," said she, "didst thou hear the words of those men concerning thee?" Then he lifted up his eyes and looked at her angrily. "Thou hadst only," said he, "to hold thy peace as I bade thee. I wish but for thy silence, and not for warning." As he said that, the foremost of the men couched his lance, and rushed upon Geraint. Geraint received him, and that not feebly. But he let the thrust go by him, while he struck the horseman upon the centre of his shield in such a manner that the shield was split, and the man's armour broken, and the man himself sent to the earth, the length of a lance over his horse's crupper.

The second horseman then attacked him furiously, being wroth at the death of his companion. But with one thrust,

Geraint overthrew him also. Then the third set upon him, and he killed him in a like manner. And thus also he slew the fourth.

Then Geraint dismounted from his horse, and took the arms of the men he had slain, and placed them upon their saddles, and tied together the reins of the horses, and he mounted his horse again. "Behold what thou art to do," said he to Enid, "take the four horses, and drive them before thee, and proceed forward. And say not one word unto me, unless I speak first unto thee." "I will do, as far as I can, Lord," said she, "according to thy desire."

They went forward through the forest, and when they left the forest they came to a vast plain, in the centre of which was a thickly-tangled copse-wood. From out thereof they beheld three horsemen coming towards them, well equipped with armour, both they and their horses. Enid looked steadfastly upon them; and when they had come near, she heard them say to one another, "Behold, here is a good arrival for us; here are coming for us four horses and four suits of armour. We shall easily obtain them spite of yonder dolorous knight, and the maiden also will fall into our power." "This is but too true," said Enid to herself, "for my husband is tired with his former combat. The vengeance of Heaven will be upon me, unless I warn him of this." So she waited until Geraint came up to her. "Lord," said she, "dost thou not hear the discourse of yonder men concerning thee?" "What was it?" he asked. "They say to one another that they will easily obtain all this spoil." "I declare to Heaven," said he, "that their words are less grievous to me than that thou wilt not be silent, and abide by my counsel." "My Lord," said she, "I feared lest they should surprise thee unawares." And he said, "Do not I desire silence?"

Thereupon one of the horsemen couched his lance and attacked Geraint. Geraint received his thrust carelessly, and struck it aside, and then he rushed upon the horseman, and aimed at the centre of his person; the quantity of his armour did not avail the man, and the head of the lance and part of the shaft passed through him, so that he was carried to the ground an arm and a spear's length over the crupper of his horse.

Both the other horsemen came forward in their turn, but

their onset was not more successful than that of their companion. Enid stood by, looking at all this; and on one hand she was in trouble lest Geraint should be wounded in the encounter with the men, and on the other hand she was joyful to see him victorious. He dismounted and bound the three suits of armour upon the three saddles, and he fastened the reins of all the horses together, so that he had the seven horses with him.

Then he mounted his own horse, and he commanded Enid to drive forward the others. "It is no more use for me to speak to thee than to refrain, for thou wilt not attend to my advice." "I will do so, as far as I am able, Lord," said she, "but I cannot conceal from thee the fierce and threatening words which I may hear against thee, from such strange people as those that haunt this wilderness." "I desire nought but silence," said he; "therefore, hold thy peace." "I will, Lord, while I can."

Enid went on, with the horses before her, and she pursued her way straight onwards. And from the copse-wood already mentioned, they journeyed over a vast and dreary open plain. At a great distance from them they beheld a wood, and they could see neither end nor boundary to the wood, except on that side that was nearest to them, and they went towards it.

Then there came from out the wood five horsemen, eager and bold, mighty and strong, mounted upon chargers that were powerful, and large of bone, and high-mettled, and proudly snorting, and both the men and the horses were well equipped with armour. And when they drew near, Enid heard them say, "Behold, here is a fine booty coming towards us, which we shall obtain easily and without labour, for we shall have no trouble in taking all those horses and arms, and the maiden also, from yonder knight, so doleful and sad."

Sorely grieved was Enid upon hearing this discourse, so that she knew not in the world what she should do. At last, however, she determined to warn Geraint; so she turned her horse's head towards him. "Lord," said she, "if thou hadst heard as I did what yonder horsemen said concerning thee, thy dolefulness would be greater than it is." Angrily did Geraint look upon her, and he said, "Thee do I hear doing everything I forbade thee." And immediately, behold, the men met them, and victoriously and gallantly did Geraint overcome them all.

He placed the five suits of armour upon the five saddles, and tied together the reins of the twelve horses, and gave them in charge to Enid. "I know not," said he, "what good it is for me to order thee; but this time I charge thee in an especial manner." So Enid went forward towards the wood, keeping in advance of Geraint, as he had desired her, and she had much trouble with the care of the horses.

They reached the wood, and it was both deep and vast; and in the wood night overtook them. "Ah, maiden," said he, "it is vain to attempt proceeding forward." "Well, Lord," said she, "what-soever thou wishest, we will do." "It will be best for us," he said, "to turn out of the wood, and to rest, and wait for the day, in order to pursue our journey." "That will we, gladly," said she. And they did so. Having dismounted himself, he took her down from her horse. "I cannot, by any means, refrain from sleep, through weariness," said he. "Do thou, therefore, watch the horses, and sleep not." "I will, Lord," said she.

Then he went to sleep in his armour, and thus passed the night, which was not long at that season. And when she saw the dawn of day appear, she looked around her, to see if he were waking. Thereupon he awoke. "My Lord," said she, "I have desired to awake thee for some time." He arose, and said to her, "Take the horses, and ride on; and keep straight on before thee as thou didst yesterday." And early in the day they left the wood.

They left the wood, and they came to an open country, with meadows on one hand, and mowers mowing the meadows. There was a river before them, and the horses bent down, and drank the water. And they went up out of the river by a lofty steep; and there they met a slender stripling, with a satchel about his neck, and they saw that there was something in the satchel, but they knew not what it was. He had a small blue pitcher in his hand, and a bowl on the mouth of the pitcher.

The youth saluted Geraint. "Heaven prosper thee," said Geraint, "and whence dost thou come?" "I come," said he, "from the town that lies before thee." And then the youth said,

"Will it be displeasing to thee if I ask whence thou comest also?"
"By no means," said Geraint. "Through yonder wood did I
come." "Thou camest not through the wood to-day?" "No,"
replied Geraint, "we were in the wood last night." "I warrant,"
said the youth, "that thy condition there last night was not the
most pleasant, and that thou hadst neither meat nor drink." "No,
by my faith," said Geraint. "Wilt thou follow my counsel," said
the youth, "and take thy meal from me?" "What sort of a meal?"
inquired Geraint. "The breakfast which is sent to yonder mowers, nothing less than bread and meat and wine." "I will take it,"
said Geraint, "and Heaven reward thee for it."

Geraint alighted, and the youth took Enid from off her horse.
Then they washed, and took their repast. The youth cut the
bread in slices, and gave them drink, and served them withal.
And when they had finished, the youth arose, and said to
Geraint, "My Lord, with thy permission, I will now go and fetch
some food for the mowers." "Go," said Geraint, "and take a
lodging for me in the best place that thou knowest, and the most
commodious one for the horses, and take thou whichever horse
and arms thou choosest in payment for thy service and thy gift."
"Heaven reward thee, Lord," said the youth, "and this would be
ample to repay services much greater than those I have ren-
dered unto thee."

To the town the youth went, and he took the best and most
pleasant lodgings that he knew; and after that he went to the
palace, having the horse and armour with him, and proceeded
to the place where the earl was, and told him all his adventure.
"I go now, Lord," said he, "to meet the young man, and to conduct him to his lodging." "Go, gladly," said the earl, "and right
joyfully shall he be received here, if he so come."

The youth went to meet Geraint; he told him he would be
received gladly by the earl in his own palace; but Geraint would
go only to his own lodgings. He had a goodly chamber, in which
was plenty of straw, and drapery, and a spacious and commodious place he had for the horses; and the youth prepared for
them plenty of provender. "I must needs sleep," said Geraint.
"Well," said the youth, "and whilst thou sleepest, I will go to see
the earl." "Go gladly," said Geraint, "and come here again when

I require thee." Then Geraint went to sleep; and so did Enid also.

In the evening the earl came to visit Geraint, and his twelve honourable knights with him. Geraint rose up and welcomed him. "Heaven preserve thee," said the earl. Then they all sat down according to their precedence and honour. The earl conversed with Geraint, and inquired of him the object of his journey. "I have none," he replied, "but to seek adventures, and to follow my own inclination." Then the earl cast his eyes upon Enid, and looked at her steadfastly. And he thought he had never seen a maiden fairer or more comely than she.

And soon it came about that the earl had set all his thoughts and affections upon Enid. Then he asked of Geraint, "Have I thy permission to go and converse with yonder maiden, for I see that she is apart from thee?" "Thou hast it," said Geraint. So the earl went to the place where Enid was, and spake with her. "Ah, maiden," said he, "it cannot be pleasant for thee to journey with yonder man!" "It is not unpleasant for me," said she, "to journey the same road that he journeys." "Thou hast neither youths nor maidens to serve thee," said he. "Truly," she replied, "it is more pleasant for me to follow yonder man, than to be served by youths and maidens." "I will give thee good counsel," said he, "all my earldom will I place in thy possession, if thou wilt dwell with me." "That will I not, by Heaven," she said. "Yonder man was the first to whom my faith was ever pledged; and shall I prove inconstant to him!" "Thou art in the wrong," said the earl, "if I slay the man yonder, I can keep thee with me as long as I choose; and when thou no longer pleasest me I can turn thee away. But if thou goest with me by thine own good will, I protest that our union shall continue eternal and undivided as long as I remain alive."

Enid pondered these words of his, and she considered that it was advisable to encourage him in his request. "Behold, then, Chieftain, this is most expedient for thee to do to save me any needless imputation; come here to-morrow, and take me away as though I knew nothing thereof." "I will do so," said he. So the earl arose, and took his leave, and went forth with his attendants. And Enid told not then to Geraint any of the conversation which she had had with the earl, lest it should rouse his anger, and cause him uneasiness and care.

At the usual hour they went to sleep. And at the beginning of the night Enid slept a little; at midnight she arose, and placed all Geraint's armour together, so that it might be ready to put on. And although fearful of her errand, she came to the side of Geraint's bed, and she spoke to him softly and gently, saying, "My Lord, arise, and clothe thyself, for these were the words of the earl to me, and his intention concerning me." So she told Geraint all that had passed.

Although he was wroth with her, he took warning, and clothed himself. And she lighted a candle that he might have light to do so. "Leave there the candle," said he, "and desire the man of the house to come here." She went, and the man of the house came to him. "Dost thou know how much I owe thee?" asked Geraint. "I think thou owest but little," he said. "Take the eleven horses and the eleven suits of armour," said Geraint. "Heaven reward thee, Lord," said he, "but I spent not the value of one suit of armour upon thee." "For that reason," said Geraint, "thou wilt be the richer. And now, wilt thou come to guide me out of the town?" "I will, gladly," said he, "and in which direction dost thou intend to go?" "I wish to leave the town by a different way from that by which I entered it." So the man of the lodgings accompanied him as far as he desired.

Then Geraint bade Enid to go on before him; and she did so, and went straight forward, and his host returned home. And the man had only just reached his house, when, behold, the greatest tumult approached that was ever heard. And when he looked out, he saw fourscore knights in complete armour, around the house, with the earl at their head. "Where is the knight that was here?" said the earl. "By thy hand," said the man of the house, "he went hence some time ago." "Wherefore, villain," said the earl, "didst thou let him go without informing me?" "My Lord, thou didst not command me to do so, else would I not have allowed him to depart." "What way dost thou think that he took?" "I know not, except that he went along the high road."

Then the earl and his followers turned their horses' heads that way, and seeing the tracks of the horses upon the high road, they followed. And when Enid beheld the dawning of the day, she looked behind her, and saw vast clouds of dust coming nearer and nearer to her. And thereupon she became uneasy, and she thought that it was the earl and his host coming after them. And then she beheld a knight appearing through the mist. "By my faith," said she, "though he should slay me, it were better for me to receive my death at his hands, than to see him killed without warning him." And then she said to Geraint, "My Lord, seest thou yonder man hastening after thee, and many others with him?" "I do see him," said Geraint, "and in despite of all my orders, I see that thou wilt never keep silence."

Thereupon Geraint turned upon the knight, and with the first thrust he threw him down under his horse's feet. And as long as there remained one of the fourscore knights, he overthrew every one of them at the first onset. And from the weakest to the strongest, they all attacked him one after the other, except the earl; and last of all the earl came against him also. Geraint turned upon him, and struck him with his lance upon the centre of his shield, so that by that single thrust the shield was split, and all his armour broken, and he himself was brought over his horse's crupper to the ground, and was in peril of his life.

Geraint drew near to where he lay, and at the noise of the trampling of his horse the earl revived. "Mercy, Lord," said he to Geraint. And Geraint granted him mercy. But through the hardness of the ground where they had fallen, and the violence of the stroke which they had received, there was not a single knight amongst them who escaped without receiving a fall, severe, and grievously painful, and desperately wounding, from the hand of Geraint.

And now they were upon the high road. Enid went on first, and Geraint was behind her; and as they went on they beheld near them a valley which was the fairest ever seen, and which had a large river running through it, and the high road led to the bridge. Above the bridge upon the opposite side of the river, they beheld a fortified town, the fairest ever seen. And as they approached the bridge, Geraint saw coming towards them from a thick copse a man mounted upon a large and lofty steed, even of pace and spirited though tractable. "Ah, Knight," said

Geraint, "whence comest thou?" "I come," said he, "from the valley below us." "Canst thou tell me," said Geraint, "who is the owner of this fair valley and yonder walled town?" "I will tell thee, willingly," said he. "The owner is called the Little King." "Can I go by yonder bridge?" said Geraint, "and by the lower highway that is beneath the town?" Said the knight, "Thou canst not go by his tower on the other side of the bridge, unless thou dost intend to combat him; because it is his custom to encounter every knight who comes upon his lands." "I declare to Heaven," said Geraint, "that I will, nevertheless, pursue my journey that way." "If thou dost so," said the knight, "thou wilt probably meet with shame and disgrace in reward for thy daring."

Geraint proceeded along the road that led to the town, and the road brought him to a ground that was hard, and rugged, and high and ridgy. As he journeyed thus, he beheld a knight following him upon a war horse, strong, and large, and proudly-stepping, and wide-hoofed, and broad-chested. And he never saw a man of smaller stature than he who was upon the horse. Both the knight and his horse had complete armour. And when he had overtaken Geraint, he said to him, "Tell me, Chieftain, whether it is through ignorance or through presumption that thou seekest to insult my dignity, and to infringe my rules?" "Nay," answered Geraint, "I knew not this road was forbid to any." "Thou didst know it," said the other. "Come with me to my court, to give me satisfaction." "That will I not, by my faith," said Geraint, "I would not go even to thy lord's court, excepting Arthur were thy lord." "By the hand of Arthur himself," said the knight, "I will have satisfaction of thee, or receive my overthrow at thy hands." And immediately they charged one another.

They gave each other such hard and severe strokes that their shields lost all their colour. But it was very difficult for Geraint to fight with the knight on account of his small size, for he was hardly able to get a full aim at him with all the efforts he could make. They fought thus until their horses were brought down upon their knees; and at length Geraint threw the knight head-long to the ground; and then they fought on foot, and they gave one another blows so boldly fierce, so frequent, and so severely powerful, that their helmets were pierced, and their skullcaps were broken, and their arms were shattered, and the light of their eyes was darkened by sweat and blood.

At the last Geraint became enraged, and he called to him all his strength; and boldly angry, and swiftly resolute, and furiously determined, he lifted up his sword, and struck him on the crown of his head a blow so violent, so fierce, and so penetrating that it cut through all his head-armour, and the sword flew out of the hand of the Little King to the furthest end of the plain, and he besought Geraint that he would have mercy and compassion upon him. "Though thou hast been neither courteous nor just," said Geraint, "thou shalt have mercy, upon condition that thou wilt become my ally, and engage never to fight against me again, but to come to my assistance whenever thou hearest of my being in trouble." "This will I do gladly, Lord," said he. So he pledged Geraint his faith thereof. "And now, Lord, come with me," said he, "to my court yonder, to recover from thy weariness and fatigue." "That will I not, by Heaven," said Geraint.

Then the Little King beheld Enid where she stood, and it grieved him to see one of her noble mien appear so deeply afflicted. And he said to Geraint, "My Lord, thou doest wrong not to take repose, and refresh thyself a while; for if thou meetest with any difficulty in thy present condition, it will not be easy for thee to surmount it." But Geraint would do no other than proceed on his journey, and he mounted his horse in pain, and all covered with blood. And Enid went on first, and they proceeded towards the wood which they saw before them.

Now when they came into the wood, he stood under a tree, for the heat of the sun was very great, and through the blood and sweat, Geraint's armour cleaved to his flesh. And Enid stood under another tree. And lo! they heard the sound of horns, and a tumultuous noise.

The occasion of it was, that King Arthur and his company had come into that wood. While Geraint was considering which way he should go to avoid them, behold, he was espied by a footpage, who was an attendant on the Steward of the Household; and he went to the Steward, and told him what kind of man he had seen in the wood. Then the Steward caused his horse to be saddled, and he took his lance and his shield, and went to the place where Geraint was. "Ah, Knight," said he, "what dost thou here?" "I am standing under a shady tree, to avoid the heat and the rays of the sun." "Wherefore is thy journey, and who art thou?" "I seek adventures, and go where I list." "Indeed, then come with me to see Arthur, who is here hard by." "That will I not, by Heaven," said Geraint. "Thou must needs come."

Now Geraint knew that this was Kai, but Kai did not know Geraint. Kai attacked Geraint as best he could. And Geraint became wroth, and he struck him with the shaft of his lance, so that he rolled headlong to the ground. But chastisement worse than this Geraint would not inflict on Kai.

Scared and wildly Kai rose, and mounted his horse, and went back. And thence he proceeded to Gwalchmai's tent. "Oh, sir," said he to Gwalchmai, "I was told by one of the attendants, that he saw in the wood above a wounded knight, having on battered armour; and if thou dost right, thou wilt go and see if this be true." "I care not if I do so," said Gwalchmai. "Take, then, thy horse, and some of thy armour," said Kai, "for I hear that he is not over courteous to those who approach him." So Gwalchmai took his spear and his shield, and mounted his horse, and came to the spot where Geraint was.

"Sir Knight," said he, "wherefore is thy journey?" "I journey for my own pleasure, and to seek the adventures of the world." "Wilt thou tell me who thou art; or wilt thou come and visit Arthur, who is near at hand?" "I will make no alliance with thee, nor will I go and visit Arthur," said he. And Geraint knew that this was Gwalchmai, but Gwalchmai knew him not. "I purpose not to leave thee," said Gwalchmai, "till I know who thou art."

Then Gwalchmai gazed fixedly upon him, and he knew him. "Ah, Geraint," said he, "is it thou who art here?" "I am not Geraint," he said. "Geraint thou art, by Heaven," Gwalchmai replied, "and a wretched and insane expedition is this." Then he looked around, and beheld Enid, and he welcomed her gladly. "Geraint," said Gwalchmai again, "come thou and see Arthur; he is thy Lord and thy cousin." "I will not," said he, "for I am not in a fit state to go and see anyone."

Gwalchmai sent a page to appraise Arthur that Geraint was

there wounded, and that he would not go to visit him, and that it was pitiable to see the plight that he was in. This he did without Geraint's knowledge, inasmuch as he spoke in a whisper to the page. "Entreat Arthur," said he, "to have his tent brought near to the road, for Geraint will not meet him willingly, and it is not easy to compel him in the mood he is in."

King Arthur caused his tent to be removed unto the side of the road. And Gwalchmai led Geraint onwards along the road, till they came to the place where Arthur was encamped, and the pages were pitching his tent by the roadside. "Lord," said Geraint, "all hail unto thee." "Heaven prosper thee; and who art thou?" said Arthur. "It is Geraint," said Gwalchmai, "and of his own free will would he not come to meet thee." "Verily," said Arthur, "he is bereft of his reason." Then came Enid, and saluted Arthur. "Heaven protect thee," said he. And thereupon he caused one of his pages to take her from her horse. "Alas! Enid," said Arthur, "what expedition is this?" "I know not, Lord," said she, "save that it behooves me to journey by the same road that he journeys." "My Lord," said Geraint, "with thy permission we will depart." "Whither wilt thou go?" asked Arthur.

Arthur held him, but soon Geraint went forth, and he pursued his journey. And he desired Enid to go on, and to keep before him, as she had formerly done. And she went forward along the high road.

Now as they journeyed thus, they heard an exceedingly loud wailing near them. "Stay thou here," said he to Enid, "and I will go and see what is the cause of this wailing." "I will stay," said she. Then he went forward unto an open glade that was near the road. And in the glade he saw two horses, one having a man's saddle, and the other a woman's saddle upon it. And, behold, there was a knight lying dead in his armour, and a young damsel in a riding dress standing over him, lamenting.

"Ah, Lady," said Geraint, "what hath befallen thee?" "Behold," she answered, "I journeyed here with my beloved husband, when lo! three giants came upon us, and without any cause in the world, they slew him." "Which way went they hence?" said Geraint. "Yonder by the high road," she replied. So he returned to Enid. "Go," said he, "to the lady who is below yonder, and await me there till I come."

She was sorrowful when he ordered her to do thus, but nevertheless she went to the damsel, whom it was pitiful to hear, and she felt certain that Geraint would never return. Meanwhile Geraint followed the giants, and overtook them. And each of them was greater in stature than three other men, and a huge club was on the shoulder of each. Geraint rushed upon one of them, and thrust his lance through his body. And having drawn it forth again, he pierced another of them through likewise. But the third turned upon him, and struck him with his club, so that he split Geraint's shield, and crushed his shoulder, and opened his wounds anew, and all his blood began to flow from him.

But Geraint drew his sword, and attacked the giant, and gave him a blow on the crown of his head so severe, and fierce, and violent, that the giant fell dead.

Geraint left him thus, and returned to where Enid was. And when he saw her, he fell down from his horse. Piercing, and loud, and thrilling was the cry that Enid uttered. And she came and stood over him where he had fallen. And at the sound of her cries, the Earl of Limours and his company who were journeying that way, came to where she was.

The earl said to Enid, "Alas, Lady, what hath befallen thee?" "Ah! good Sir," said she, "the only man I have loved, or ever shall love, is slain." Then he said to the other, "And what is the cause of thy grief?" "They have slain my beloved husband also," said she. "And who was it that slew them?" "Giants," she answered, "slew my best-beloved, and the other knight went in pursuit of them, and came back in the state thou seest, his blood flowing excessively; but it appears to me that he did not leave the giants without killing some of them, if not all."

The earl caused the knight who was dead to be buried there, but he thought there still remained some life in Geraint; and to see if he yet would live, he had him carried with him in the hollow of his shield, and upon a bier. And Enid and the damsel went to the court; and when they arrived there, Geraint was placed upon a litter-couch in front of the table that was in the hall. Then they all took off their travelling gear, and the earl besought Enid to do the same, and to clothe herself in other garments.

But Enid, watching over Geraint, would not do this. "Ah! Lady," said the earl, "be not so sorrowful." "It were hard to persuade me to be otherwise," said she. "I will act towards thee in such wise," said he, "that thou needst not be sorrowful whether yonder knight live or die. Behold a good earldom, together with myself, will I bestow on thee; be, therefore, happy and joyful." "I declare to Heaven," said she, "that henceforth I will never be joyful while I live." "Come, then," said he, "and eat." "No, by Heaven, I will not," she answered. "But, by Heaven, thou shalt," said he.

So he took her with him to the table against her will, and many times desired her to eat. "I call Heaven to witness," said she, "that I will not eat until the man who is on yonder bier shall eat likewise." "Thou canst not fulfil that," said the earl, "yonder man is dead already." "I will prove that I can," said she. Then he offered her a goblet of wine. "Drink this goblet," he said, "and it will cause thee to change thy mind." "Evil betide me," she answered, "if I drink aught until he drink also." "Truly," said the earl, "it is of no more avail to me to be gentle with thee than ungentle." And he gave her a box on the ear.

Thereupon she raised a loud and piercing shriek, and her lamentations were much greater than they had been before, for she considered in her mind that had Geraint been alive, the earl durst not have struck her thus. And, behold, at the sound of her cry, Geraint revived from his swoon, and he sat up on the bier, and finding his sword in the hollow of his shield, he rushed to the place where the earl was, and struck him a fiercely-wounding, severely-venomous, and sternly-smiting blow upon the crown of his head. All who were there left the board, and fled away. And this was not so much through fear of the living as through the dread they felt at seeing the dead man rise up and slay their chieftain.

And now Geraint looked upon Enid. And as he looked on her he was grieved for two causes; one was, to see that Enid had lost her colour and her wonted aspect, and the other, to know that she had been in the right. "Lady," said he, "knowest thou where

He rushed to the place where the earl was.

our horses are?" "I know, Lord, where thy horse is," she replied, "but I know not where is the other. Thy horse is in the house yonder." So he went to the house, and brought forth his horse, and mounted him, and took up Enid from the ground, and placed her upon the horse with him. And he rode forward.

Now their road lay between two hedges, and as they went on the night was gaining on the day. And lo! they saw behind them the shafts of spears betwixt them and the sky, and they heard the trampling of horses, and the noise of a host approaching. "I hear something following us," said he, "and I will put thee on the other side of the hedge." And thus he did. Thereupon, behold, a knight pricked towards him, and couched his lance. When Enid saw this, she cried out from the other side of the hedge, saying, "Oh! Chieftain, whoever thou art, what renown wilt thou gain by slaying a dead man?" "Oh! Heaven," said he, "is it Geraint?" "Yes, in truth," said she. "And who art thou?" "I am the Little King," he answered, "coming to thy assistance, for I heard that thou wast in trouble."

Then said Geraint, "Nothing can happen without the will of Heaven, though much good results from counsel." "Yes," said the Little King, "and I know good counsel for thee now. Come with me to the court of a son-in-law of my sister, which is near here, and thou shalt have the best medical assistance in the kingdom." "We will first journey for one day more," said Geraint, "and return again."

Again they set forth. And more gladly and more joyfully did Enid journey with them that day than she had ever done. They came to the main road. And when they reached a place where the road divided in two, they beheld a man on foot coming towards them along one of these roads, and the Little King asked the man whence he came. "I come," said he, "from an errand in the country." "Tell me," said Geraint, "which is the best for me to follow of these two roads." "That is the best for thee to follow," answered he, "for if thou goest by this one, thou wilt never return. Below us," said he, "there is a hedge of mist, and within it are enchanted games, and no one who has gone there has ever returned. And the court of the Earl Owen is there."

They went into the town, and they ate, and they were amply served. And when they had finished eating they arose. And Geraint called for his horse, and he accoutred both himself and his horse. And they went forth until they came to the side of the hedge, and the hedge was so lofty that it reached as high as they could see in the air, and upon every stake in the hedge, except two, there was the head of a man, and the number of stakes throughout the hedge was very great. Then said the Little King, "May no one go on with the chieftain?" "No one may," said Owen. "Which way may I enter?" inquired Geraint. "I know not," said Owen, "but enter by the way thou wilt, and that seemeth easiest to thee."

Then fearlessly and unhesitatingly Geraint dashed forward into the mist. And on leaving the mist, he came to a large orchard; and in the orchard he saw an open space, wherein was a tent of red satin; and the door of the tent was open, and an apple tree stood in front of the door of the tent; and on a branch of the apple tree hung a large hunting-horn. Geraint dismounted, and went into the tent; and there was no one in the tent save one maiden sitting in a golden chair, and another chair was opposite to her, empty.

Geraint went to the empty chair, and sat down therein. "Ah! Chieftain," said the maiden, "I would not counsel thee to sit in that chair." "Wherefore?" said Geraint. "The man to whom that chair belongs has never suffered another to sit in it." "I care not," said Geraint, "though it displease him that I sit in the chair."

Thereupon there was a mighty tumult around the tent. Geraint looked to see what was the cause of the tumult. He beheld without a knight mounted upon a large war horse, proudly snorting, high-mettled, and large of bone; and a robe of honour in two parts was upon him and upon his horse, and beneath it was plenty of armour. "Tell me, Chieftain," said the knight to Geraint, "who it was that bade thee sit there?" "Myself," answered he. "It was wrong of thee to do me this shame and disgrace. Arise, and do me satisfaction for this insolence."

Then Geraint arose; and they encountered immediately; and they broke a set of lances, and a second set, and a third; and they gave each other fierce and frequent strokes; and at last Geraint became enraged, and he urged on his horse, and he rushed upon the knight, and he gave him a thrust on the centre of the shield, so that it was split, and so that the head of his lance went through his armour, and his girths were broken, and he himself was borne headlong to the ground the length of Geraint's lance and armour, over his horse's crupper. "Oh, my Lord," he cried, "thy mercy, and thou shalt have what thou wilt." "I only desire," said Geraint, "that this shall no longer exist here, nor the hedge of mist, nor magic, nor enchantment."

"Thou shalt have this gladly, Lord," the strange knight replied. "Cause, then, the mist to disappear from this place," said Geraint. "Sound yonder horn," said he, "and when thou soundest it, the mist will vanish; but it will not go unless the horn be blown by the knight by whom I am vanquished." Then Geraint went and sounded the horn.

Sad and sorrowful was Enid where she remained, through anxiety concerning Geraint. She heard the horn sound. And at the first blast, the mist vanished.

And the mist went from between Geraint and Enid, and from between Geraint and the host on the other side. They came together, and they all became reconciled to each other. Owen invited Geraint and the Little King to stay with him that night. The next morning they separated. Geraint went towards his own dominions with Enid; and thenceforth he reigned prosperously, and his warlike fame and splendour lasted with renown and honour both to him and to Enid from that time forth.

THE DREAM OF RONABBWAY

There was once a party of men who went upon a quest that need not be told of here. One of the men was called Ronabbway. And Ronabbway and some others came together to a house that they knew of. But when they came near, they saw an old hall, very black and having an upright gable, whence issued a great smoke; and on entering, they found the floor full of puddles and mounds; and it was difficult to stand thereon, so slippery was it with the mire of cattle. There were boughs of holly spread over the floor, whereof the cattle had browsed the sprigs. When the men came into the house, they beheld an old hag making a fire. And whenever she felt cold she cast a lapful of chaff upon the fire, and raised such a smoke that it was scarcely to be borne, as it rose up to the nostrils. On the other side of the house there was a yellow calfskin on the floor.

And when the men came within there arose a storm of wind and rain, so that it was hardly possible to go forth with safety. And being weary with their journey, they laid themselves down and sought to sleep. When they looked at the couch, it seemed to be made but of a little coarse straw full of dust and vermin, with the stems of boughs sticking up therethrough, for the cattle had eaten all the straw that was placed at the head and the foot. And upon it was stretched an old russet-coloured rug, threadbare and ragged; and a coarse sheet, full of slits, was upon the rug, and an ill-stuffed pillow, and a worn-out cover upon the sheet. And after much suffering from the vermin, and from the discomfort of their couch, a heavy sleep fell upon Ronabbway's companions. But Ronabbway, not being able either to sleep or to rest, thought he should suffer less if he went to lie upon the yellow calf-skin that was stretched out on the floor. And there he slept.

As soon as sleep came upon his eyes, it seemed to him that he was journeying with his companions across a plain, and he thought that he went towards the Severn. As he journeyed, he heard a mighty noise, the like whereof heard he never before; and looking behind him, he beheld a youth mounted on a chestnut horse, whereof the legs were grey from the top of the forelegs, and from the bend of the hindlegs downwards. The rider wore a coat of yellow satin sewn with green silk, and on his thigh was a gold-hilted sword, with a scabbard of new leather of Cordova, belted with the skin of a deer, and clasped with gold. And over this was a scarf of yellow satin wrought with green silk, the borders whereof were likewise green. The green of the caparison of the horse, and of his rider, was as green as the leaves of the fir-tree, and the yellow was as yellow as the blossom of the broom.

Now as this knight came toward them, his aspect was so fierce that fear seized upon Ronabbway and his companions, and they began to flee. The knight pursued them. And when his horse breathed forth, the men became distant from him, and when the horse drew in his breath, they were drawn near to him, even to the horse's chest. When the knight had overtaken Ronabbway and his companions, they besought his mercy. "You shall have it gladly," said he, "fear nought." "Ha, Chieftain, since thou hast mercy upon me, tell me also who thou art," said Ronabbway. "I am Iddog, yet not by my name, but by my nickname, am I best known." "And wilt thou tell me what thy nickname is?" "I will tell thee, but I will tell thee after this."

All this was in Ronabbway's dream. And he and his companions with the knight journeyed over the plain as far as a ford on the Severn. And for a mile around the ford on both sides of the road, they saw tents and encampments, and there was the clamour of a mighty host. And they came to the edge of the ford, and there they beheld King Arthur; he was on a flat island below the ford. And a tall, auburn-haired youth stood before him, with his sheathed sword in his hand, and clad in a coat and cap of jet-black satin. The youth's face was as white as ivory, and his eyebrows black as jet, and such part of his wrist as could be seen between his glove and his sleeve was whiter than the lily, and thicker than a warrior's ankle.

And in Ronabbway's dream, he and the knight and his companions stood before King Arthur and saluted him. "Heaven grant thee good," said Arthur to the knight, "and where didst thou find these little men?" said he, looking at Ronabbway and his companions. "I found them, Lord, up yonder on the road," said the knight. Then King Arthur smiled. "Lord," said the knight, "wherefore dost thou laugh?" "I laugh not," said Arthur; "but it pitieth me that men so small as these should have this Island in their keeping, after the men who guarded it in my time." Then said the knight to Ronabbway, "Dost thou see the ring with the stone set in it, that is upon the King's hand?" "I see it," he answered. "It is one of the properties of that stone to enable thee to remember what thou seest here to-night, and hadst thou not seen the stone, thou wouldst never have been able to remember aught thereof."

Then they heard a call made for Arthur's servant, and a red, rough, ill-favoured man, upon a tall red horse with the mane parted on each side, came forward, and he brought with him a large and beautiful sumpter pack. He dismounted before Arthur, and he drew a golden chair out of the pack, and a carpet of diapered satin. And he spread the carpet before Arthur, and he placed the chair upon the carpet. And so large was the chair that three armed warriors might have sat therein.

Then Ronabbway saw Arthur sitting on the chair within the carpet, and he saw Owen standing before him. "Owen," said Arthur, "wilt thou play chess?" "I will, Lord," said Owen. And Arthur's servant brought the chess for Arthur and Owen; golden pieces and a board of silver. And they began to play.

And while they were playing, behold they saw a white tent with a red canopy, and the figure of a jet-black serpent on the top of the tent, and red, glaring, venomous eyes in the head of the serpent, and a red flaming tongue. Then there came a young page who bore a heavy, three-edged sword with a golden hilt, in a scabbard of black leather tipped with fine gold. And he came to the place where King Arthur and Owen were playing at chess.

The youth saluted Owen. And Owen marvelled that the youth

should salute him, and should not have saluted the King. Arthur knew what was in Owen's thoughts, and he said, "Marvel not that the youth salutes thee now, for he saluted me erewhile; and it is unto thee that his errand is." Then said the youth to Owen, "Lord, is it with thy leave that the young pages and attendants of the King harass and torment and worry thy Ravens? And if it be not with thy leave, cause the King to forbid them." "Lord," said Owen to the King, "thou hearest what the youth says; if it seem good to thee, forbid them from my Ravens." "Play the game," said Arthur. They played, and the youth returned to the tent.

That game did they finish, and another they began, and when they were in the middle of the game, behold, a ruddy young man with auburn curling hair and large eyes, well-grown, and having his beard new-shorn, came forth from a bright yellow tent, upon the top of which was the figure of a bright red lion. In his hand there was a huge, heavy, three-edged sword with a scabbard of red deer-hide, tipped with gold. He came to the place where Arthur and Owen were playing at chess. He saluted Owen. And Owen was troubled at his salutation, but Arthur minded it no more than before. The youth said unto Owen, "Is it not against thy will that the attendants of the King harass thy Ravens, killing some and worrying others? If against thy will it be, beseech him to forbid them." "Lord," said Owen, "forbid thy men, if it seem good to thee." "Play thy game," said the King. And the youth returned to the tent.

And that game was ended and another begun. As they were beginning the first move of the game, they beheld at a small distance from them a tent speckled yellow, the largest ever seen, and the figure of an eagle of gold upon it, and a precious stone on the eagle's head. And coming out of the tent, they saw a youth with thick yellow hair upon his head, fair and comely, and a scarf of blue satin upon him, and a brooch of gold in the scarf upon his right shoulder as large as a warrior's middle finger. In the hand of the youth was a mighty lance, speckled yellow, with a newly sharpened head; and upon the lance a banner displayed.

Fiercely angry, and with rapid pace, came the youth to the place where Arthur was playing at chess with Owen. They perceived that he was wroth. And thereupon he saluted Owen, and told him that his Ravens had been killed, the chief part of them, and that such of them as were not slain were so wounded and bruised that not one of them could raise its wings a single fathom above the earth. "Lord," said Owen, "forbid thy men." "Play," said Arthur, "if it please thee." Then said Owen, speaking to the youth, "Go back, and wherever thou findest the strife at the thickest, there lift up the banner, and let come what pleases Heaven."

So the youth returned back to the place where the strife bore hardest upon the Ravens, and he lifted up the banner; and as he did so they all rose up in the air, wrathful and fierce and high of spirit, clapping their wings in the wind, and shaking off the weariness that was upon them. And recovering their energy and courage, furiously and with exultation did they, with one sweep, descend upon the heads of the men, who had erewhile caused them anger and pain and damage, and they seized some by the heads, and some by the ears, and others by the arms, and carried them up into the air; and in the air there was a mighty tumult with the flapping of the wings of the triumphant Ravens, and with their croaking; and there was another mighty tumult with the groaning of the men, who were being torn and wounded, and some of whom were slain.

And Arthur and Owen marvelled at the tumult as they played at chess; and, looking, they perceived a knight upon a dun-coloured horse coming towards them. Bright red was the horse's right shoulder, and from the top of his legs to the centre of his hoof was bright yellow. Both the knight and his horse were fully equipped with heavy foreign armour. A large gold-hilted one-edged sword had the knight upon his thigh. The belt of the sword was of dark green leather with golden slides and a clasp of ivory upon it, and a buckle of jet-black upon the clasp. A helmet of gold was upon the head of the knight, set with precious stones of great virtue, and at the top of the helmet was the image of a flame-coloured leopard with two ruby-red stones in its head, so that it was astounding for a warrior, however stout his heart, to look at the face of the leopard, much more at the face of the knight. He had in his hand a blue-shafted lance, but from the haft to the point it was stained crimson-red with the blood of the Ravens.

The knight came to the place where Arthur and Owen were seated at chess. And they perceived that he was harassed and vexed and weary as he came towards them. The youth saluted Arthur and told him that the Ravens of Owen were slaying his young men and attendants. And Arthur looked at Owen and said, "Forbid thy Ravens." "Lord," said Owen, "play thy game." They played. And the knight returned back towards the strife, and the Ravens were not forbidden any more than before.

When they had played a while, they heard a mighty tumult, and a wailing of men, and a croaking of Ravens, as they carried the men in their strength into the air, and, tearing them betwixt them, let them fall piecemeal to the earth. And during the tumult they saw a knight coming towards them, on a light grey horse, and the left foreleg of the horse was jet-black to the centre of his hoof. The knight and the horse were fully accoutred with huge, heavy blue armour. A robe of honour of yellow diapered satin was upon the knight, and the borders of the robe were blue. On the thigh of the knight was a sword, long, and three-edged, and heavy. The scabbard was of red cut leather, and the belt of new red deer-skin, having upon it many golden slides and a buckle of the bone of the sea-horse, the tongue of which was jet-black. A golden helmet was upon the head of the knight, wherein were set sapphire-stones of great virtue. At the top of the helmet was the figure of a flame-coloured lion, with a fiery-red tongue, issuing about a foot from his mouth, and with venomous eyes, crimson-red, in his head. And the knight came, bearing in his hand a thick ashen lance, the head whereof, which had been newly steeped in blood, was overlaid with silver.

The knight saluted King Arthur. "Lord," said he, "carest thou not for the slaying of thy pages, and thy young men, and the sons of the nobles of the Island of Britain, whereby it will be difficult to defend this island from henceforward for ever?" "Owen," said Arthur, "forbid thy Ravens." "Play this game, Lord," said Owen.

They finished the game and began another; and as they were finishing that game, lo, they heard a great tumult and a clamour of armed men, and a croaking of Ravens, and a flapping of

wings in the air, as they flung down the armour entire to the
ground, and the men and the horses piecemeal. Then they saw
coming a knight on a lofty-headed piebald horse. The left
shoulder of the horse was of bright red, and its right leg from
the chest to the hollow of the hoof was pure white. The knight
and horse were equipped with arms of speckled yellow. And
there was a robe of honour upon him, and upon his horse,
divided in two parts, white and black, and the borders of the
robe of honour were of purple. He wore a sword three-edged
and bright, with a golden hilt. And the belt of the sword was of
yellow goldwork, having a clasp upon it of the eyelid of a black
sea-horse, and a tongue of yellow gold to the clasp. Upon the
head of the knight was a bright helmet of yellow laton, with
sparkling stones of crystal in it, and at the crest of the helmet
was the figure of a griffin, with a stone of many virtues in its
head. He had an ashen spear in his hand, with a round shaft,
coloured with azure blue. And the head of the spear was newly
stained with blood.

Wrathfully came the knight to the place where Arthur was,
and he told him that the Ravens had slain his household and the
sons of the chief men of the Island of Britain, and he besought
him to cause Owen to forbid his Ravens. And Arthur besought
Owen to forbid them. Then Arthur took the golden chess-men
that were upon the board, and crushed them until they became
as dust. But he spoke no more to Owen. Then Owen ordered
the one he had sent to lower the banner. So it was lowered, and
all was peace.

Then spake a tall and stately man, of noble and flowing
speech, saying that it was a marvel that so vast a host should be
assembled in so narrow a space, and that it was a still greater
marvel that those should be there at that time when they had
promised to be by mid-day in the battle. Thereupon they heard
a call made for Arthur's sword-bearer, and behold he arose with
the sword of Arthur in his hand. The similitude of two serpents
was upon the sword in gold. And when the sword was drawn
from its scabbard, it seemed as if two flames of fire burst forth
from the jaws of the serpent, and then, so wonderful was the
sword, that it was hard for anyone to look upon it. And the host

became still, and the tumult ceased, and the sword-bearer returned to the tent.

"Iddog," said Ronabbway, "who is the man who bore the sword of Arthur?" "Kaddar, the Earl of Cornwall, whose duty it is to arm the King on the days of battle and warfare."

Then Iddog took Ronabbway behind him on his horse, and that mighty host moved forward, each troop in its order. And when they came to the middle of the ford of the Severn, Iddog turned his horse's head, and Ronabbway looked along the valley of the Severn. And he beheld two fair armies coming towards the ford. After they had dismounted he heard a great tumult and confusion amongst the host, and such as were then at the flanks turned to the centre, and such as had been in the centre moved to the flanks. And then, behold, he saw a knight coming, clad, both he and his horse, in mail, of which the rings were whiter than the whitest lily, and the rivets redder than the ruddiest blood. And this knight rode amongst the host.

"Iddog," said Ronabbway, "will yonder host flee?" "King Arthur never fled, and if this discourse of thine were heard, thou wert a lost man. But as to the knight whom thou seest yonder, it is Kai. The fairest horseman is Kai in all Arthur's Court; and the men who are at the front of the army hasten to the rear to see Kai ride, and the men who are in the centre flee to the side, from the shock of his horse. And this is the cause of the confusion of the host."

Then Kai said: "Whoever will follow Arthur, let him be with him to-night in Cornwall, and whosoever will not, let him be opposed to Arthur. For now the battle comes on."

Then Ronabbway turned to Iddog and said: "Wilt thou tell me what thy nickname is?" "I will tell thee," his companion said, "it is Iddog, the Stirrer-up of Britain." "Ha, Chieftain," said Ronabbway, "why art thou called thus?" "I will tell thee," said his companion. "I was at the battle the opening of which has been shown to thee. I was one of the messengers between Arthur and Medraud, his nephew, at the battle of Camlan; and I was then a reckless youth, and through my desire for battle, I kindled strife between them, and stirred up wrath, when I was sent by Arthur to reason with Medraud, and to show him that

Arthur was his foster-father and his uncle, and to seek for peace, lest the sons of the nobles of the Island of Britain should be slain. And whereas Arthur charged me with the fairest sayings he could think of, I uttered unto Medraud the harshest I could devise. And from this did the battle of Camlan ensue. And the nobles of the Island of Britain and the great companions of Arthur were slain in that battle, and an end was made to the Court of Arthur. And a magic sleep fell upon Arthur, and he stays within a hill. But he will come forth again when the Island of Britain is in danger and he will deliver his people."

Then again Ronabbway heard the voice of Kai saying, "Whosoever will follow Arthur, let him be with him to-night in Cornwall, and whosoever will not, let him be opposed to Arthur." And through the greatness of the tumult that ensued, Ronabbway awoke. And when he awoke he was upon the yellow calf-skin, having slept three days and three nights.

NOTES

How the Youth Kilhuch Came to King Arthur's Court

The story that begins with Kilhuch has in the Mabinogion the title "Kilhwch and Owen or the Twrch Trwyth." The maker of this story was evidently a man of brilliant invention and supreme literary equipment. Alfred Nutt places the date of its composition as about 1175, and he considers that it was shaped under Irish literary influences. He notes that a great patron of Welsh literature, Gruffydd ab Cynan, had passed his youth in Ireland and had drawn his forces for the conquest of North Wales from that country. "We must then, I think," he says of the makers of this and another story, "regard these Welsh story-tellers to whom we owe 'Kilhwch and Olwen,' and 'The Dream of Rhonabwy' as men fascinated by the spirit and style of Irish romance and introducing the same into Welsh literature." And he goes on to say with reference to this particular story, "Around this theme of immemorial antiquity the story-teller grouped numerous fairy-tale traits and incidents drawn undoubtedly from the rich store of popular tradition."

The elements that make up this story will be familiar to every student of folk-lore. There is, first of all, the widely spread folk-tale about the youth who comes to the enchanter-king as a suitor for his daughter, and who is given a number of difficult tasks. This story is told all the way from Ireland to the Malay Peninsula, and it has been given its greatest literary form in Greece in the story of Jason and Medea. The author of the story of Kilhuch and Olwen has tied this folk-tale up with another folk-tale—the tale of the hunting of a destructive boar. As in other Celtic variants of the suitor for the enchanter's daughter, it is the youth's jealous step-mother who starts him upon the dangerous quest.

In all other stories of this type the maiden helps her wooer to carry out the tasks. Olwen gives no help. But the story as we have it now is very fragmentary, and we do not know but that in some of the tasks Olwen helped. In the days when it was current there were probably many subsidiary episodes that were filled out by story-tellers—everything that was quite usual in the story would be left to the story-teller to develop. And amongst such usual incidents would be the fulfilling of certain tasks. Yspaddaden sets Kilhuch forty tasks. There is record of only eight tasks being accomplished. In retelling the story I have made Yspaddaden set only such tasks as were actually carried out.

When the maker of this story tied up the wooing with the hunting of the boar, he shifted the interest from Yspaddaden's castle and he left Kilhuch, as far as we can know, with hardly anything to do. Usually, in the folk-tales of this type, the suitor travels alone. But the shaper of this story gives Kilhuch the Skilful Companions that are out of another type of story: there is Kai who, when it pleased him, "could render himself as tall as the highest tree in the forest"; there is Bedour, who, although he was one-handed, "three warriors could not shed blood faster than he on the field of battle. Another quality he had: his lance could produce a wound equal to those of nine opposing lances"; there is Gwrhyr Gwalstawt Ieithoedd who knew all tongues, and there is Menw, who, if they were in a savage country, "could cast a charm and an illusion over them, so that none might see them whilst they could see everyone," and there is Gwalchmai who never returned home without achieving the adventure of which he went in quest. A surprising transformation makes three of these Skilful Companions—Kai, Bedour, and Gwalchmai—the Sir Kaye, the Sir Bedevere, and the Sir Gawaine of Malory's "Morte d'Arthur."

The Arthur of this story is the Celtic king to whom noble youths are sent for fosterage. His wife is Gwenhwyvar in the Mabinogion and Guenevere in the "Morte d'Arthur." Her name means "Fair Phantom," and it equates the name of another Celtic heroine, the Findabair of the Irish stories.

The Story of Puil, Prince of Dyved

The first part of "Puil, Prince of Dyved" (in the Mabinogion he is Pwyll) is on a theme that is peculiarly Celtic—the theme of the mortal hero going into the Realm of Faerie to aid one of the Chiefs of Faerie against another. The part that deals with the wooing of Rhiannon is not so obviously mythological; no doubt the theme of the second story—for it is a distinct story—is the winning of the Faery Bride, but Rhiannon herself, her father Heveid and her suitor Gwaul, have lost all their mythological traits. The story of the taking of Rhiannon's infant and the child's recovery is a folk-tale that is very widely spread. Often the tragic loss is due to an intrigue of jealous sisters or sisters-in-law.

Puil, Prince of Dyved, and The Story of Branwen and two other stories that are not given in this volume are the four stories that are definitely "mabinogion"; the other stories are not given this title in the Welsh manuscript. These four stories are all based on the mythology of the British Celts, but, as Alfred Nutt observes, "the crudity of the myth has disappeared in a dissolving mist of romance." Bran, with all his vastness, is obviously a divinity. Matholluch, the King of Ireland (in the Mabinogion he is Matholwch) may also be a figure out of some mythology; Mr. Roger Loomis of Columbia University has made the suggestion that, just as for the Irish story-tellers Spain was the other world, the world of the dead, so, for the British story-tellers, Ireland was the other world. In this case Matholluch might be a god of the dead; it may be that he is the same as that stern ruler of Ireland who comes into the Tristan story, Morhaut. Branwen (her name means "white bosom") comes into another cycle of romance as Brangwaine, the confidante of Iseult. "The Story of Branwen," Alfred Nutt considers, has been influenced by "The Woe of Gudrun," a story that the Welsh might have heard from their Norse allies. "The Story of Lud and Levellis" (in the Mabinogion "The Contention of Lludd and Llevelys") like "The Dream of Maxen the Emperor (in the Mabinogion "The Dream of Maxen Wledig") is based on British tradition history; both stories, scholars think, were given their present shape in the middle of the twelfth century.

THE KNIGHT OWEN AND THE LADY OF THE FOUNTAIN

In the Mabinogion his name appears as Owain, and he is the Yvain of the French romance. It is evident that the story of his stay in the castle of the Lady of the Fountain is the reminiscence of a story of a Celtic hero's going into the Land of Youth. When, in the Irish story, Oisin returns to his native land, old age comes upon him; he loses his heroic form and becomes decrepit. Something of the same kind happens to Owen after he returns to Arthur's court; he wanders to distant parts of the earth and to uncultivated mountains; his apparel becomes worn out; his body becomes wasted; his hair grows long, and he becomes familiar with wild beasts. Owen, it would seem, finds his way back to the Realm of Faerie.

The Arthur who appears in the three stories that make the second part of this book is a different Arthur from the King with whom Kilhuch claimed relationship. The Arthur of "Kilhuch and Olwen" was developed out of native Welsh tradition; the Arthur of the other stories has been shown to the Welsh by the Breton story-tellers who came into Britain with the Norman conquerors of England. At the end of the twelfth and the beginning of the thirteenth century, when the Welsh were making up new stories about Arthur, they were reading the lays and romances of the Anglo-Norman writers and they were influenced by them.

PEREDUR AND THE CASTLE OF WONDERS

Peredur is the Sir Perceval of Malory, and the Parsifal of the Wagnerian opera. In the Mabinogion the story of his adventures is repetitious and rather incoherent, and in retelling it I have condensed it a good deal. The mediæval story-tellers had many adventures to relate of Peredur's or of other heroes of the same type—the type is that of the Heroic Fool; the nights were long and neither they nor their audiences were very critical about like adventures succeeding like adventures. Peredur's great distinction came from the fact that he looked upon the dripping lance and the salver that had in it the man's head surrounded by a profusion of blood. The Anglo-Norman writers had it that the salver was the Cup of the Last Supper and that the lance was the Spear of the Passion. It is evident that the maker of the story in the Mabinogion had in his mind a reminiscence of some ritual that he did not understand. The elucidation that he gives at the end of the story is prosaic; the lance and the salver were undoubtedly symbols, but the teller of Peredur's adventures makes them literally a dripping lance and a salver with a head in it.

THE STORY OF GERAINT AND THE MAIDEN ENID

With this story the literature of knightly prowess and objective action seems about to pass into the literature of psychology and inner action. "Geraint and Enid" is undoubtedly the masterpiece of mediæval storytelling.

THE DREAM OF RONABBWAY

In the Mabinogion this story is "The Dream of Ronabbway." According to Alfred Nutt, "The Dream of Ronabbway" with "Kilhwch and Olwen" have been shaped under the influence of Irish romance. "With the instinctive rightness of genius," the men who had been so influenced "chose very archaic elements from out the great treasure house of Arthurian material which was undoubtedly open to them."

The marvellous achievement of the writer of "The Dream of Ronabbway" is that he has been able to combine the utmost precision of detail with a wholly visionary quality. Certain lines have been added by the present reteller of the tale. They are the lines about the magic sleep falling upon Arthur, about his staying within a hill, and about his coming forth to deliver the Island of Britain from danger. These lines are not in the story in the Mabinogion. But they belong to the legend of Arthur. A writer of about 1200 declared that in his time resentment would have been aroused in Brittany by the denial of Arthur's expected return. And Henry the Second, according to Mr. Roger Loomis (Introduction to The Romance of Tristram and Ysolt) instigated the exhuming of the bodies of Arthur and Guinevere . . . "with the deliberate purpose of destroying the hope of the Welsh and the Cornish that Arthur would come again to deliver them from the invader."

The battle that looms through "The Dream of Ronabbway" is the battle of Camlan. According to the legend, Arthur gained the victory, but he received a mortal wound at the hand of Medraud, his nephew. He was conveyed to Avalon, and the crown of Britain descended to the son of Kadwr, his kinsman. A mystery hung over the final fate of Arthur.

A CATALOG OF SELECTED
DOVER BOOKS
IN ALL FIELDS OF INTEREST

A CATALOG OF SELECTED DOVER
BOOKS IN ALL FIELDS OF INTEREST

CONCERNING THE SPIRITUAL IN ART, Wassily Kandinsky. Pioneering work by father of abstract art. Thoughts on color theory, nature of art. Analysis of earlier masters. 12 illustrations. 80pp. of text. 5⅜ x 8½. 23411-8

ANIMALS: 1,419 Copyright-Free Illustrations of Mammals, Birds, Fish, Insects, etc., Jim Harter (ed.). Clear wood engravings present, in extremely lifelike poses, over 1,000 species of animals. One of the most extensive pictorial sourcebooks of its kind. Captions. Index. 284pp. 9 x 12. 23766-4

CELTIC ART: The Methods of Construction, George Bain. Simple geometric techniques for making Celtic interlacements, spirals, Kells-type initials, animals, humans, etc. Over 500 illustrations. 160pp. 9 x 12. (Available in U.S. only.) 22923-8

AN ATLAS OF ANATOMY FOR ARTISTS, Fritz Schider. Most thorough reference work on art anatomy in the world. Hundreds of illustrations, including selections from works by Vesalius, Leonardo, Goya, Ingres, Michelangelo, others. 593 illustrations. 192pp. 7⅛ x 10¼. 20241-0

CELTIC HAND STROKE-BY-STROKE (Irish Half-Uncial from "The Book of Kells"): An Arthur Baker Calligraphy Manual, Arthur Baker. Complete guide to creating each letter of the alphabet in distinctive Celtic manner. Covers hand position, strokes, pens, inks, paper, more. Illustrated. 48pp. 8¼ x 11. 24336-2

EASY ORIGAMI, John Montroll. Charming collection of 32 projects (hat, cup, pelican, piano, swan, many more) specially designed for the novice origami hobbyist. Clearly illustrated easy-to-follow instructions insure that even beginning papercrafters will achieve successful results. 48pp. 8¼ x 11. 27298-2

THE COMPLETE BOOK OF BIRDHOUSE CONSTRUCTION FOR WOODWORKERS, Scott D. Campbell. Detailed instructions, illustrations, tables. Also data on bird habitat and instinct patterns. Bibliography. 3 tables. 63 illustrations in 15 figures. 48pp. 5¼ x 8½. 24407-5

BLOOMINGDALE'S ILLUSTRATED 1886 CATALOG: Fashions, Dry Goods and Housewares, Bloomingdale Brothers. Famed merchants' extremely rare catalog depicting about 1,700 products: clothing, housewares, firearms, dry goods, jewelry, more. Invaluable for dating, identifying vintage items. Also, copyright-free graphics for artists, designers. Co-published with Henry Ford Museum & Greenfield Village. 160pp. 8¼ x 11. 25780-0

HISTORIC COSTUME IN PICTURES, Braun & Schneider. Over 1,450 costumed figures in clearly detailed engravings–from dawn of civilization to end of 19th century. Captions. Many folk costumes. 256pp. 8⅜ x 11¾. 23150-X

STICKLEY CRAFTSMAN FURNITURE CATALOGS, Gustav Stickley and L. & J. G. Stickley. Beautiful, functional furniture in two authentic catalogs from 1910. 594 illustrations, including 277 photos, show settles, rockers, armchairs, reclining chairs, bookcases, desks, tables. 183pp. 6½ x 9¼. 23838-5

AMERICAN LOCOMOTIVES IN HISTORIC PHOTOGRAPHS: 1858 to 1949, Ron Ziel (ed.). A rare collection of 126 meticulously detailed official photographs, called "builder portraits," of American locomotives that majestically chronicle the rise of steam locomotive power in America. Introduction. Detailed captions. xi+ 129pp. 9 x 12. 27393-8

AMERICA'S LIGHTHOUSES: An Illustrated History, Francis Ross Holland, Jr. Delightfully written, profusely illustrated fact-filled survey of over 200 American lighthouses since 1716. History, anecdotes, technological advances, more. 240pp. 8 x 10¾. 25576-X

TOWARDS A NEW ARCHITECTURE, Le Corbusier. Pioneering manifesto by founder of "International School." Technical and aesthetic theories, views of industry, economics, relation of form to function, "mass-production split" and much more. Profusely illustrated. 320pp. 6⅛ x 9¼. (Available in U.S. only.) 25023-7

HOW THE OTHER HALF LIVES, Jacob Riis. Famous journalistic record, exposing poverty and degradation of New York slums around 1900, by major social reformer. 100 striking and influential photographs. 233pp. 10 x 7⅞. 22012-5

FRUIT KEY AND TWIG KEY TO TREES AND SHRUBS, William M. Harlow. One of the handiest and most widely used identification aids. Fruit key covers 120 deciduous and evergreen species; twig key 160 deciduous species. Easily used. Over 300 photographs. 126pp. 5⅜ x 8½. 20511-8

COMMON BIRD SONGS, Dr. Donald J. Borror. Songs of 60 most common U.S. birds: robins, sparrows, cardinals, bluejays, finches, more–arranged in order of increasing complexity. Up to 9 variations of songs of each species.
Cassette and manual 99911-4

ORCHIDS AS HOUSE PLANTS, Rebecca Tyson Northen. Grow cattleyas and many other kinds of orchids–in a window, in a case, or under artificial light. 63 illustrations. 148pp. 5⅜ x 8½. 23261-1

MONSTER MAZES, Dave Phillips. Masterful mazes at four levels of difficulty. Avoid deadly perils and evil creatures to find magical treasures. Solutions for all 32 exciting illustrated puzzles. 48pp. 8¼ x 11. 26005-4

MOZART'S DON GIOVANNI (DOVER OPERA LIBRETTO SERIES), Wolfgang Amadeus Mozart. Introduced and translated by Ellen H. Bleiler. Standard Italian libretto, with complete English translation. Convenient and thoroughly portable–an ideal companion for reading along with a recording or the performance itself. Introduction. List of characters. Plot summary. 121pp. 5¼ x 8½. 24944-1

TECHNICAL MANUAL AND DICTIONARY OF CLASSICAL BALLET, Gail Grant. Defines, explains, comments on steps, movements, poses and concepts. 15-page pictorial section. Basic book for student, viewer. 127pp. 5⅜ x 8½. 21843-0

THE CLARINET AND CLARINET PLAYING, David Pino. Lively, comprehensive work features suggestions about technique, musicianship, and musical interpretation, as well as guidelines for teaching, making your own reeds, and preparing for public performance. Includes an intriguing look at clarinet history. "A godsend," *The Clarinet,* Journal of the International Clarinet Society. Appendixes. 7 illus. 320pp. 5⅜ x 8½. 40270-3

HOLLYWOOD GLAMOR PORTRAITS, John Kobal (ed.). 145 photos from 1926-49. Harlow, Gable, Bogart, Bacall; 94 stars in all. Full background on photographers, technical aspects. 160pp. 8⅜ x 11¼. 23352-9

THE ANNOTATED CASEY AT THE BAT: A Collection of Ballads about the Mighty Casey/Third, Revised Edition, Martin Gardner (ed.). Amusing sequels and parodies of one of America's best-loved poems: Casey's Revenge, Why Casey Whiffed, Casey's Sister at the Bat, others. 256pp. 5⅜ x 8½. 28598-7

THE RAVEN AND OTHER FAVORITE POEMS, Edgar Allan Poe. Over 40 of the author's most memorable poems: "The Bells," "Ulalume," "Israfel," "To Helen," "The Conqueror Worm," "Eldorado," "Annabel Lee," many more. Alphabetic lists of titles and first lines. 64pp. 5³⁄₁₆ x 8¼. 26685-0

PERSONAL MEMOIRS OF U. S. GRANT, Ulysses Simpson Grant. Intelligent, deeply moving firsthand account of Civil War campaigns, considered by many the finest military memoirs ever written. Includes letters, historic photographs, maps and more. 528pp. 6⅛ x 9¼. 28587-1

ANCIENT EGYPTIAN MATERIALS AND INDUSTRIES, A. Lucas and J. Harris. Fascinating, comprehensive, thoroughly documented text describes this ancient civilization's vast resources and the processes that incorporated them in daily life, including the use of animal products, building materials, cosmetics, perfumes and incense, fibers, glazed ware, glass and its manufacture, materials used in the mummification process, and much more. 544pp. 6¹⁄₈ x 9¹⁄₄. (Available in U.S. only.) 40446-3

RUSSIAN STORIES/RUSSKIE RASSKAZY: A Dual-Language Book, edited by Gleb Struve. Twelve tales by such masters as Chekhov, Tolstoy, Dostoevsky, Pushkin, others. Excellent word-for-word English translations on facing pages, plus teaching and study aids, Russian/English vocabulary, biographical/critical introductions, more. 416pp. 5⅜ x 8½. 26244-8

PHILADELPHIA THEN AND NOW: 60 Sites Photographed in the Past and Present, Kenneth Finkel and Susan Oyama. Rare photographs of City Hall, Logan Square, Independence Hall, Betsy Ross House, other landmarks juxtaposed with contemporary views. Captures changing face of historic city. Introduction. Captions. 128pp. 8¼ x 11. 25790-8

AIA ARCHITECTURAL GUIDE TO NASSAU AND SUFFOLK COUNTIES, LONG ISLAND, The American Institute of Architects, Long Island Chapter, and the Society for the Preservation of Long Island Antiquities. Comprehensive, well-researched and generously illustrated volume brings to life over three centuries of Long Island's great architectural heritage. More than 240 photographs with authoritative, extensively detailed captions. 176pp. 8¼ x 11. 26946-9

NORTH AMERICAN INDIAN LIFE: Customs and Traditions of 23 Tribes, Elsie Clews Parsons (ed.). 27 fictionalized essays by noted anthropologists examine religion, customs, government, additional facets of life among the Winnebago, Crow, Zuni, Eskimo, other tribes. 480pp. 6⅛ x 9¼. 27377-6

FRANK LLOYD WRIGHT'S DANA HOUSE, Donald Hoffmann. Pictorial essay of residential masterpiece with over 160 interior and exterior photos, plans, elevations, sketches and studies. 128pp. 9¼ x 10¾. 29120-0

THE MALE AND FEMALE FIGURE IN MOTION: 60 Classic Photographic Sequences, Eadweard Muybridge. 60 true-action photographs of men and women walking, running, climbing, bending, turning, etc., reproduced from rare 19th-century masterpiece. vi + 121pp. 9 x 12. 24745-7

1001 QUESTIONS ANSWERED ABOUT THE SEASHORE, N. J. Berrill and Jacquelyn Berrill. Queries answered about dolphins, sea snails, sponges, starfish, fishes, shore birds, many others. Covers appearance, breeding, growth, feeding, much more. 305pp. 5¼ x 8¼. 23366-9

ATTRACTING BIRDS TO YOUR YARD, William J. Weber. Easy-to-follow guide offers advice on how to attract the greatest diversity of birds: birdhouses, feeders, water and waterers, much more. 96pp. 5³⁄₁₆ x 8¼. 28927-3

MEDICINAL AND OTHER USES OF NORTH AMERICAN PLANTS: A Historical Survey with Special Reference to the Eastern Indian Tribes, Charlotte Erichsen-Brown. Chronological historical citations document 500 years of usage of plants, trees, shrubs native to eastern Canada, northeastern U.S. Also complete identifying information. 343 illustrations. 544pp. 6½ x 9¼. 25951-X

STORYBOOK MAZES, Dave Phillips. 23 stories and mazes on two-page spreads: Wizard of Oz, Treasure Island, Robin Hood, etc. Solutions. 64pp. 8¼ x 11. 23628-5

AMERICAN NEGRO SONGS: 230 Folk Songs and Spirituals, Religious and Secular, John W. Work. This authoritative study traces the African influences of songs sung and played by black Americans at work, in church, and as entertainment. The author discusses the lyric significance of such songs as "Swing Low, Sweet Chariot," "John Henry," and others and offers the words and music for 230 songs. Bibliography. Index of Song Titles. 272pp. 6½ x 9¼. 40271-1

MOVIE-STAR PORTRAITS OF THE FORTIES, John Kobal (ed.). 163 glamor, studio photos of 106 stars of the 1940s: Rita Hayworth, Ava Gardner, Marlon Brando, Clark Gable, many more. 176pp. 8⅜ x 11¼. 23546-7

BENCHLEY LOST AND FOUND, Robert Benchley. Finest humor from early 30s, about pet peeves, child psychologists, post office and others. Mostly unavailable elsewhere. 73 illustrations by Peter Arno and others. 183pp. 5⅜ x 8½. 22410-4

YEKL and THE IMPORTED BRIDEGROOM AND OTHER STORIES OF YIDDISH NEW YORK, Abraham Cahan. Film Hester Street based on *Yekl* (1896). Novel, other stories among first about Jewish immigrants on N.Y.'s East Side. 240pp. 5⅜ x 8½. 22427-9

SELECTED POEMS, Walt Whitman. Generous sampling from *Leaves of Grass*. Twenty-four poems include "I Hear America Singing," "Song of the Open Road," "I Sing the Body Electric," "When Lilacs Last in the Dooryard Bloom'd," "O Captain! My Captain!"–all reprinted from an authoritative edition. Lists of titles and first lines. 128pp. 5³⁄₁₆ x 8¼. 26878-0

THE BEST TALES OF HOFFMANN, E. T. A. Hoffmann. 10 of Hoffmann's most important stories: "Nutcracker and the King of Mice," "The Golden Flowerpot," etc. 458pp. 5⅜ x 8½.   21793-0

FROM FETISH TO GOD IN ANCIENT EGYPT, E. A. Wallis Budge. Rich detailed survey of Egyptian conception of "God" and gods, magic, cult of animals, Osiris, more. Also, superb English translations of hymns and legends. 240 illustrations. 545pp. 5⅜ x 8½.   25803-3

FRENCH STORIES/CONTES FRANÇAIS: A Dual-Language Book, Wallace Fowlie. Ten stories by French masters, Voltaire to Camus: "Micromegas" by Voltaire; "The Atheist's Mass" by Balzac; "Minuet" by de Maupassant; "The Guest" by Camus, six more. Excellent English translations on facing pages. Also French-English vocabulary list, exercises, more. 352pp. 5⅜ x 8½.   26443-2

CHICAGO AT THE TURN OF THE CENTURY IN PHOTOGRAPHS: 122 Historic Views from the Collections of the Chicago Historical Society, Larry A. Viskochil. Rare large-format prints offer detailed views of City Hall, State Street, the Loop, Hull House, Union Station, many other landmarks, circa 1904-1913. Introduction. Captions. Maps. 144pp. 9⅜ x 12¼.   24656-6

OLD BROOKLYN IN EARLY PHOTOGRAPHS, 1865-1929, William Lee Younger. Luna Park, Gravesend race track, construction of Grand Army Plaza, moving of Hotel Brighton, etc. 157 previously unpublished photographs. 165pp. 8⅞ x 11¾.
                                                                                23587-4

THE MYTHS OF THE NORTH AMERICAN INDIANS, Lewis Spence. Rich anthology of the myths and legends of the Algonquins, Iroquois, Pawnees and Sioux, prefaced by an extensive historical and ethnological commentary. 36 illustrations. 480pp. 5⅜ x 8½.   25967-6

AN ENCYCLOPEDIA OF BATTLES: Accounts of Over 1,560 Battles from 1479 B.C. to the Present, David Eggenberger. Essential details of every major battle in recorded history from the first battle of Megiddo in 1479 B.C. to Grenada in 1984. List of Battle Maps. New Appendix covering the years 1967-1984. Index. 99 illustrations. 544pp. 6½ x 9¼.   24913-1

SAILING ALONE AROUND THE WORLD, Captain Joshua Slocum. First man to sail around the world, alone, in small boat. One of great feats of seamanship told in delightful manner. 67 illustrations. 294pp. 5⅜ x 8½.   20326-3

ANARCHISM AND OTHER ESSAYS, Emma Goldman. Powerful, penetrating, prophetic essays on direct action, role of minorities, prison reform, puritan hypocrisy, violence, etc. 271pp. 5⅜ x 8½.   22484-8

MYTHS OF THE HINDUS AND BUDDHISTS, Ananda K. Coomaraswamy and Sister Nivedita. Great stories of the epics; deeds of Krishna, Shiva, taken from puranas, Vedas, folk tales; etc. 32 illustrations. 400pp. 5⅜ x 8½.   21759-0

THE TRAUMA OF BIRTH, Otto Rank. Rank's controversial thesis that anxiety neurosis is caused by profound psychological trauma which occurs at birth. 256pp. 5⅜ x 8½.   27974-X

A THEOLOGICO-POLITICAL TREATISE, Benedict Spinoza. Also contains unfinished Political Treatise. Great classic on religious liberty, theory of government on common consent. R. Elwes translation. Total of 421pp. 5⅜ x 8½.   20249-6

MY BONDAGE AND MY FREEDOM, Frederick Douglass. Born a slave, Douglass became outspoken force in antislavery movement. The best of Douglass' autobiographies. Graphic description of slave life. 464pp. 5⅜ x 8½.   22457-0

FOLLOWING THE EQUATOR: A Journey Around the World, Mark Twain. Fascinating humorous account of 1897 voyage to Hawaii, Australia, India, New Zealand, etc. Ironic, bemused reports on peoples, customs, climate, flora and fauna, politics, much more. 197 illustrations. 720pp. 5⅜ x 8½.   26113-1

THE PEOPLE CALLED SHAKERS, Edward D. Andrews. Definitive study of Shakers: origins, beliefs, practices, dances, social organization, furniture and crafts, etc. 33 illustrations. 351pp. 5⅜ x 8½.   21081-2

THE MYTHS OF GREECE AND ROME, H. A. Guerber. A classic of mythology, generously illustrated, long prized for its simple, graphic, accurate retelling of the principal myths of Greece and Rome, and for its commentary on their origins and significance. With 64 illustrations by Michelangelo, Raphael, Titian, Rubens, Canova, Bernini and others. 480pp. 5⅜ x 8½.   27584-1

PSYCHOLOGY OF MUSIC, Carl E. Seashore. Classic work discusses music as a medium from psychological viewpoint. Clear treatment of physical acoustics, auditory apparatus, sound perception, development of musical skills, nature of musical feeling, host of other topics. 88 figures. 408pp. 5⅜ x 8½.   21851-1

THE PHILOSOPHY OF HISTORY, Georg W. Hegel. Great classic of Western thought develops concept that history is not chance but rational process, the evolution of freedom. 457pp. 5⅜ x 8½.   20112-0

THE BOOK OF TEA, Kakuzo Okakura. Minor classic of the Orient: entertaining, charming explanation, interpretation of traditional Japanese culture in terms of tea ceremony. 94pp. 5⅜ x 8½.   20070-1

LIFE IN ANCIENT EGYPT, Adolf Erman. Fullest, most thorough, detailed older account with much not in more recent books, domestic life, religion, magic, medicine, commerce, much more. Many illustrations reproduce tomb paintings, carvings, hieroglyphs, etc. 597pp. 5⅜ x 8½.   22632-8

SUNDIALS, Their Theory and Construction, Albert Waugh. Far and away the best, most thorough coverage of ideas, mathematics concerned, types, construction, adjusting anywhere. Simple, nontechnical treatment allows even children to build several of these dials. Over 100 illustrations. 230pp. 5⅜ x 8½.   22947-5

THEORETICAL HYDRODYNAMICS, L. M. Milne-Thomson. Classic exposition of the mathematical theory of fluid motion, applicable to both hydrodynamics and aerodynamics. Over 600 exercises. 768pp. 6⅛ x 9¼.   68970-0

SONGS OF EXPERIENCE: Facsimile Reproduction with 26 Plates in Full Color, William Blake. 26 full-color plates from a rare 1826 edition. Includes "The Tyger," "London," "Holy Thursday," and other poems. Printed text of poems. 48pp. 5¼ x 7.   24636-1

OLD-TIME VIGNETTES IN FULL COLOR, Carol Belanger Grafton (ed.). Over 390 charming, often sentimental illustrations, selected from archives of Victorian graphics—pretty women posing, children playing, food, flowers, kittens and puppies, smiling cherubs, birds and butterflies, much more. All copyright-free. 48pp. 9¼ x 12¼.   27269-9

PERSPECTIVE FOR ARTISTS, Rex Vicat Cole. Depth, perspective of sky and sea, shadows, much more, not usually covered. 391 diagrams, 81 reproductions of drawings and paintings. 279pp. 5⅜ x 8½. 22487-2

DRAWING THE LIVING FIGURE, Joseph Sheppard. Innovative approach to artistic anatomy focuses on specifics of surface anatomy, rather than muscles and bones. Over 170 drawings of live models in front, back and side views, and in widely varying poses. Accompanying diagrams. 177 illustrations. Introduction. Index. 144pp. 8⅜ x11¼. 26723-7

GOTHIC AND OLD ENGLISH ALPHABETS: 100 Complete Fonts, Dan X. Solo. Add power, elegance to posters, signs, other graphics with 100 stunning copyright-free alphabets: Blackstone, Dolbey, Germania, 97 more–including many lower-case, numerals, punctuation marks. 104pp. 8⅛ x 11. 24695-7

HOW TO DO BEADWORK, Mary White. Fundamental book on craft from simple projects to five-bead chains and woven works. 106 illustrations. 142pp. 5⅜ x 8. 20697-1

THE BOOK OF WOOD CARVING, Charles Marshall Sayers. Finest book for beginners discusses fundamentals and offers 34 designs. "Absolutely first rate . . . well thought out and well executed."–E. J. Tangerman. 118pp. 7¾ x 10⅝. 23654-4

ILLUSTRATED CATALOG OF CIVIL WAR MILITARY GOODS: Union Army Weapons, Insignia, Uniform Accessories, and Other Equipment, Schuyler, Hartley, and Graham. Rare, profusely illustrated 1846 catalog includes Union Army uniform and dress regulations, arms and ammunition, coats, insignia, flags, swords, rifles, etc. 226 illustrations. 160pp. 9 x 12. 24939-5

WOMEN'S FASHIONS OF THE EARLY 1900s: An Unabridged Republication of "New York Fashions, 1909," National Cloak & Suit Co. Rare catalog of mail-order fashions documents women's and children's clothing styles shortly after the turn of the century. Captions offer full descriptions, prices. Invaluable resource for fashion, costume historians. Approximately 725 illustrations. 128pp. 8⅜ x 11¼. 27276-1

THE 1912 AND 1915 GUSTAV STICKLEY FURNITURE CATALOGS, Gustav Stickley. With over 200 detailed illustrations and descriptions, these two catalogs are essential reading and reference materials and identification guides for Stickley furniture. Captions cite materials, dimensions and prices. 112pp. 6½ x 9¼. 26676-1

EARLY AMERICAN LOCOMOTIVES, John H. White, Jr. Finest locomotive engravings from early 19th century: historical (1804–74), main-line (after 1870), special, foreign, etc. 147 plates. 142pp. 11⅜ x 8¼. 22772-3

THE TALL SHIPS OF TODAY IN PHOTOGRAPHS, Frank O. Braynard. Lavishly illustrated tribute to nearly 100 majestic contemporary sailing vessels: Amerigo Vespucci, Clearwater, Constitution, Eagle, Mayflower, Sea Cloud, Victory, many more. Authoritative captions provide statistics, background on each ship. 190 black-and-white photographs and illustrations. Introduction. 128pp. 8⅞ x 11¾. 27163-3

LITTLE BOOK OF EARLY AMERICAN CRAFTS AND TRADES, Peter Stockham (ed.). 1807 children's book explains crafts and trades: baker, hatter, cooper, potter, and many others. 23 copperplate illustrations. 140pp. 4⅝ x 6. 23336-7

VICTORIAN FASHIONS AND COSTUMES FROM HARPER'S BAZAR, 1867–1898, Stella Blum (ed.). Day costumes, evening wear, sports clothes, shoes, hats, other accessories in over 1,000 detailed engravings. 320pp. 9⅜ x 12¼. 22990-4

GUSTAV STICKLEY, THE CRAFTSMAN, Mary Ann Smith. Superb study surveys broad scope of Stickley's achievement, especially in architecture. Design philosophy, rise and fall of the Craftsman empire, descriptions and floor plans for many Craftsman houses, more. 86 black-and-white halftones. 31 line illustrations. Introduction 208pp. 6½ x 9¼. 27210-9

THE LONG ISLAND RAIL ROAD IN EARLY PHOTOGRAPHS, Ron Ziel. Over 220 rare photos, informative text document origin (1844) and development of rail service on Long Island. Vintage views of early trains, locomotives, stations, passengers, crews, much more. Captions. 8⅞ x 11¾. 26301-0

VOYAGE OF THE LIBERDADE, Joshua Slocum. Great 19th-century mariner's thrilling, first-hand account of the wreck of his ship off South America, the 35-foot boat he built from the wreckage, and its remarkable voyage home. 128pp. 5⅜ x 8½. 40022-0

TEN BOOKS ON ARCHITECTURE, Vitruvius. The most important book ever written on architecture. Early Roman aesthetics, technology, classical orders, site selection, all other aspects. Morgan translation. 331pp. 5⅜ x 8½. 20645-9

THE HUMAN FIGURE IN MOTION, Eadweard Muybridge. More than 4,500 stopped-action photos, in action series, showing undraped men, women, children jumping, lying down, throwing, sitting, wrestling, carrying, etc. 390pp. 7⅞ x 10⅝. 20204-6 Clothbd.

TREES OF THE EASTERN AND CENTRAL UNITED STATES AND CANADA, William M. Harlow. Best one-volume guide to 140 trees. Full descriptions, woodlore, range, etc. Over 600 illustrations. Handy size. 288pp. 4½ x 6⅜. 20395-6

SONGS OF WESTERN BIRDS, Dr. Donald J. Borror. Complete song and call repertoire of 60 western species, including flycatchers, juncoes, cactus wrens, many more–includes fully illustrated booklet. Cassette and manual 99913-0

GROWING AND USING HERBS AND SPICES, Milo Miloradovich. Versatile handbook provides all the information needed for cultivation and use of all the herbs and spices available in North America. 4 illustrations. Index. Glossary. 236pp. 5⅜ x 8½. 25058-X

BIG BOOK OF MAZES AND LABYRINTHS, Walter Shepherd. 50 mazes and labyrinths in all–classical, solid, ripple, and more–in one great volume. Perfect inexpensive puzzler for clever youngsters. Full solutions. 112pp. 8⅛ x 11. 22951-3

PIANO TUNING, J. Cree Fischer. Clearest, best book for beginner, amateur. Simple repairs, raising dropped notes, tuning by easy method of flattened fifths. No previous skills needed. 4 illustrations. 201pp. 5⅜ x 8½. 23267-0

HINTS TO SINGERS, Lillian Nordica. Selecting the right teacher, developing confidence, overcoming stage fright, and many other important skills receive thoughtful discussion in this indispensible guide, written by a world-famous diva of four decades' experience. 96pp. 5⅜ x 8½. 40094-8

THE COMPLETE NONSENSE OF EDWARD LEAR, Edward Lear. All nonsense limericks, zany alphabets, Owl and Pussycat, songs, nonsense botany, etc., illustrated by Lear. Total of 320pp. 5⅜ x 8½. (Available in U.S. only.) 20167-8

VICTORIAN PARLOUR POETRY: An Annotated Anthology, Michael R. Turner. 117 gems by Longfellow, Tennyson, Browning, many lesser-known poets. "The Village Blacksmith," "Curfew Must Not Ring Tonight," "Only a Baby Small," dozens more, often difficult to find elsewhere. Index of poets, titles, first lines. xxiii + 325pp. 5⅝ x 8¼. 27044-0

DUBLINERS, James Joyce. Fifteen stories offer vivid, tightly focused observations of the lives of Dublin's poorer classes. At least one, "The Dead," is considered a masterpiece. Reprinted complete and unabridged from standard edition. 160pp. 5$\frac{3}{16}$ x 8¼. 26870-5

GREAT WEIRD TALES: 14 Stories by Lovecraft, Blackwood, Machen and Others, S. T. Joshi (ed.). 14 spellbinding tales, including "The Sin Eater," by Fiona McLeod, "The Eye Above the Mantel," by Frank Belknap Long, as well as renowned works by R. H. Barlow, Lord Dunsany, Arthur Machen, W. C. Morrow and eight other masters of the genre. 256pp. 5⅜ x 8½. (Available in U.S. only.) 40436-6

THE BOOK OF THE SACRED MAGIC OF ABRAMELIN THE MAGE, translated by S. MacGregor Mathers. Medieval manuscript of ceremonial magic. Basic document in Aleister Crowley, Golden Dawn groups. 268pp. 5⅜ x 8½. 23211-5

NEW RUSSIAN-ENGLISH AND ENGLISH-RUSSIAN DICTIONARY, M. A. O'Brien. This is a remarkably handy Russian dictionary, containing a surprising amount of information, including over 70,000 entries. 366pp. 4½ x 6⅛. 20208-9

HISTORIC HOMES OF THE AMERICAN PRESIDENTS, Second, Revised Edition, Irvin Haas. A traveler's guide to American Presidential homes, most open to the public, depicting and describing homes occupied by every American President from George Washington to George Bush. With visiting hours, admission charges, travel routes. 175 photographs. Index. 160pp. 8¼ x 11. 26751-2

NEW YORK IN THE FORTIES, Andreas Feininger. 162 brilliant photographs by the well-known photographer, formerly with *Life* magazine. Commuters, shoppers, Times Square at night, much else from city at its peak. Captions by John von Hartz. 181pp. 9¼ x 10¾. 23585-8

INDIAN SIGN LANGUAGE, William Tomkins. Over 525 signs developed by Sioux and other tribes. Written instructions and diagrams. Also 290 pictographs. 111pp. 6⅛ x 9¼. 22029-X

ANATOMY: A Complete Guide for Artists, Joseph Sheppard. A master of figure drawing shows artists how to render human anatomy convincingly. Over 460 illustrations. 224pp. 8⅜ x 11¼. 27279-6

MEDIEVAL CALLIGRAPHY: Its History and Technique, Marc Drogin. Spirited history, comprehensive instruction manual covers 13 styles (ca. 4th century through 15th). Excellent photographs; directions for duplicating medieval techniques with modern tools. 224pp. 8⅜ x 11¼. 26142-5

DRIED FLOWERS: How to Prepare Them, Sarah Whitlock and Martha Rankin. Complete instructions on how to use silica gel, meal and borax, perlite aggregate, sand and borax, glycerine and water to create attractive permanent flower arrangements. 12 illustrations. 32pp. 5⅜ x 8½. 21802-3

EASY-TO-MAKE BIRD FEEDERS FOR WOODWORKERS, Scott D. Campbell. Detailed, simple-to-use guide for designing, constructing, caring for and using feeders. Text, illustrations for 12 classic and contemporary designs. 96pp. 5⅜ x 8½. 25847-5

SCOTTISH WONDER TALES FROM MYTH AND LEGEND, Donald A. Mackenzie. 16 lively tales tell of giants rumbling down mountainsides, of a magic wand that turns stone pillars into warriors, of gods and goddesses, evil hags, powerful forces and more. 240pp. 5⅜ x 8½. 29677-6

THE HISTORY OF UNDERCLOTHES, C. Willett Cunnington and Phyllis Cunnington. Fascinating, well-documented survey covering six centuries of English undergarments, enhanced with over 100 illustrations: 12th-century laced-up bodice, footed long drawers (1795), 19th-century bustles, 19th-century corsets for men, Victorian "bust improvers," much more. 272pp. 5⅜ x 8¼. 27124-2

ARTS AND CRAFTS FURNITURE: The Complete Brooks Catalog of 1912, Brooks Manufacturing Co. Photos and detailed descriptions of more than 150 now very collectible furniture designs from the Arts and Crafts movement depict davenports, settees, buffets, desks, tables, chairs, bedsteads, dressers and more, all built of solid, quarter-sawed oak. Invaluable for students and enthusiasts of antiques, Americana and the decorative arts. 80pp. 6½ x 9¼. 27471-3

WILBUR AND ORVILLE: A Biography of the Wright Brothers, Fred Howard. Definitive, crisply written study tells the full story of the brothers' lives and work. A vividly written biography, unparalleled in scope and color, that also captures the spirit of an extraordinary era. 560pp. 6⅛ x 9¼. 40297-5

THE ARTS OF THE SAILOR: Knotting, Splicing and Ropework, Hervey Garrett Smith. Indispensable shipboard reference covers tools, basic knots and useful hitches; handsewing and canvas work, more. Over 100 illustrations. Delightful reading for sea lovers. 256pp. 5⅜ x 8½. 26440-8

FRANK LLOYD WRIGHT'S FALLINGWATER: The House and Its History, Second, Revised Edition, Donald Hoffmann. A total revision–both in text and illustrations–of the standard document on Fallingwater, the boldest, most personal architectural statement of Wright's mature years, updated with valuable new material from the recently opened Frank Lloyd Wright Archives. "Fascinating"–*The New York Times*. 116 illustrations. 128pp. 9¼ x 10¾. 27430-6

PHOTOGRAPHIC SKETCHBOOK OF THE CIVIL WAR, Alexander Gardner. 100 photos taken on field during the Civil War. Famous shots of Manassas Harper's Ferry, Lincoln, Richmond, slave pens, etc. 244pp. 10⅝ x 8¼.   22731-6

FIVE ACRES AND INDEPENDENCE, Maurice G. Kains. Great back-to-the-land classic explains basics of self-sufficient farming. The one book to get. 95 illustrations. 397pp. 5⅜ x 8½.   20974-1

SONGS OF EASTERN BIRDS, Dr. Donald J. Borror. Songs and calls of 60 species most common to eastern U.S.: warblers, woodpeckers, flycatchers, thrushes, larks, many more in high-quality recording.   Cassette and manual 99912-2

A MODERN HERBAL, Margaret Grieve. Much the fullest, most exact, most useful compilation of herbal material. Gigantic alphabetical encyclopedia, from aconite to zedoary, gives botanical information, medical properties, folklore, economic uses, much else. Indispensable to serious reader. 161 illustrations. 888pp. 6½ x 9¼. 2-vol. set. (Available in U.S. only.)   Vol. I: 22798-7
                                                                              Vol. II: 22799-5

HIDDEN TREASURE MAZE BOOK, Dave Phillips. Solve 34 challenging mazes accompanied by heroic tales of adventure. Evil dragons, people-eating plants, blood-thirsty giants, many more dangerous adversaries lurk at every twist and turn. 34 mazes, stories, solutions. 48pp. 8¼ x 11.   24566-7

LETTERS OF W. A. MOZART, Wolfgang A. Mozart. Remarkable letters show bawdy wit, humor, imagination, musical insights, contemporary musical world; includes some letters from Leopold Mozart. 276pp. 5⅜ x 8½.   22859-2

BASIC PRINCIPLES OF CLASSICAL BALLET, Agrippina Vaganova. Great Russian theoretician, teacher explains methods for teaching classical ballet. 118 illustrations. 175pp. 5⅜ x 8½.   22036-2

THE JUMPING FROG, Mark Twain. Revenge edition. The original story of The Celebrated Jumping Frog of Calaveras County, a hapless French translation, and Twain's hilarious "retranslation" from the French. 12 illustrations. 66pp. 5⅜ x 8½.
                                                                              22686-7

BEST REMEMBERED POEMS, Martin Gardner (ed.). The 126 poems in this superb collection of 19th- and 20th-century British and American verse range from Shelley's "To a Skylark" to the impassioned "Renascence" of Edna St. Vincent Millay and to Edward Lear's whimsical "The Owl and the Pussycat." 224pp. 5⅜ x 8½.
                                                                              27165-X

COMPLETE SONNETS, William Shakespeare. Over 150 exquisite poems deal with love, friendship, the tyranny of time, beauty's evanescence, death and other themes in language of remarkable power, precision and beauty. Glossary of archaic terms. 80pp. 5³⁄₁₆ x 8¼.   26686-9

THE BATTLES THAT CHANGED HISTORY, Fletcher Pratt. Eminent historian profiles 16 crucial conflicts, ancient to modern, that changed the course of civilization. 352pp. 5⅜ x 8½.   41129-X

THE WIT AND HUMOR OF OSCAR WILDE, Alvin Redman (ed.). More than 1,000 ripostes, paradoxes, wisecracks: Work is the curse of the drinking classes; I can resist everything except temptation; etc. 258pp. 5⅜ x 8½. 20602-5

SHAKESPEARE LEXICON AND QUOTATION DICTIONARY, Alexander Schmidt. Full definitions, locations, shades of meaning in every word in plays and poems. More than 50,000 exact quotations. 1,485pp. 6½ x 9¼. 2-vol. set.

Vol. 1: 22726-X
Vol. 2: 22727-8

SELECTED POEMS, Emily Dickinson. Over 100 best-known, best-loved poems by one of America's foremost poets, reprinted from authoritative early editions. No comparable edition at this price. Index of first lines. 64pp. 5³⁄₁₆ x 8¼. 26466-1

THE INSIDIOUS DR. FU-MANCHU, Sax Rohmer. The first of the popular mystery series introduces a pair of English detectives to their archnemesis, the diabolical Dr. Fu-Manchu. Flavorful atmosphere, fast-paced action, and colorful characters enliven this classic of the genre. 208pp. 5³⁄₁₆ x 8¼. 29898-1

THE MALLEUS MALEFICARUM OF KRAMER AND SPRENGER, translated by Montague Summers. Full text of most important witchhunter's "bible," used by both Catholics and Protestants. 278pp. 6⅝ x 10. 22802-9

SPANISH STORIES/CUENTOS ESPAÑOLES: A Dual-Language Book, Angel Flores (ed.). Unique format offers 13 great stories in Spanish by Cervantes, Borges, others. Faithful English translations on facing pages. 352pp. 5⅜ x 8½. 25399-6

GARDEN CITY, LONG ISLAND, IN EARLY PHOTOGRAPHS, 1869–1919, Mildred H. Smith. Handsome treasury of 118 vintage pictures, accompanied by carefully researched captions, document the Garden City Hotel fire (1899), the Vanderbilt Cup Race (1908), the first airmail flight departing from the Nassau Boulevard Aerodrome (1911), and much more. 96pp. 8⅞ x 11¾. 40669-5

OLD QUEENS, N.Y., IN EARLY PHOTOGRAPHS, Vincent F. Seyfried and William Asadorian. Over 160 rare photographs of Maspeth, Jamaica, Jackson Heights, and other areas. Vintage views of DeWitt Clinton mansion, 1939 World's Fair and more. Captions. 192pp. 8⅞ x 11. 26358-4

CAPTURED BY THE INDIANS: 15 Firsthand Accounts, 1750-1870, Frederick Drimmer. Astounding true historical accounts of grisly torture, bloody conflicts, relentless pursuits, miraculous escapes and more, by people who lived to tell the tale. 384pp. 5⅜ x 8½. 24901-8

THE WORLD'S GREAT SPEECHES (Fourth Enlarged Edition), Lewis Copeland, Lawrence W. Lamm, and Stephen J. McKenna. Nearly 300 speeches provide public speakers with a wealth of updated quotes and inspiration—from Pericles' funeral oration and William Jennings Bryan's "Cross of Gold Speech" to Malcolm X's powerful words on the Black Revolution and Earl of Spenser's tribute to his sister, Diana, Princess of Wales. 944pp. 5⅜ x 8⅜. 40903-1

THE BOOK OF THE SWORD, Sir Richard F. Burton. Great Victorian scholar/adventurer's eloquent, erudite history of the "queen of weapons"—from prehistory to early Roman Empire. Evolution and development of early swords, variations (sabre, broadsword, cutlass, scimitar, etc.), much more. 336pp. 6⅛ x 9¼. 25434-8

AUTOBIOGRAPHY: The Story of My Experiments with Truth, Mohandas K. Gandhi. Boyhood, legal studies, purification, the growth of the Satyagraha (nonviolent protest) movement. Critical, inspiring work of the man responsible for the freedom of India. 480pp. 5⅜ x 8½. (Available in U.S. only.) 24593-4

CELTIC MYTHS AND LEGENDS, T. W. Rolleston. Masterful retelling of Irish and Welsh stories and tales. Cuchulain, King Arthur, Deirdre, the Grail, many more. First paperback edition. 58 full-page illustrations. 512pp. 5⅜ x 8½. 26507-2

THE PRINCIPLES OF PSYCHOLOGY, William James. Famous long course complete, unabridged. Stream of thought, time perception, memory, experimental methods; great work decades ahead of its time. 94 figures. 1,391pp. 5⅜ x 8½. 2-vol. set.
Vol. I: 20381-6 Vol. II: 20382-4

THE WORLD AS WILL AND REPRESENTATION, Arthur Schopenhauer. Definitive English translation of Schopenhauer's life work, correcting more than 1,000 errors, omissions in earlier translations. Translated by E. F. J. Payne. Total of 1,269pp. 5⅜ x 8½. 2-vol. set. Vol. 1: 21761-2 Vol. 2: 21762-0

MAGIC AND MYSTERY IN TIBET, Madame Alexandra David-Neel. Experiences among lamas, magicians, sages, sorcerers, Bonpa wizards. A true psychic discovery. 32 illustrations. 321pp. 5⅜ x 8½. (Available in U.S. only.) 22682-4

THE EGYPTIAN BOOK OF THE DEAD, E. A. Wallis Budge. Complete reproduction of Ani's papyrus, finest ever found. Full hieroglyphic text, interlinear transliteration, word-for-word translation, smooth translation. 533pp. 6½ x 9¼. 21866-X

MATHEMATICS FOR THE NONMATHEMATICIAN, Morris Kline. Detailed, college-level treatment of mathematics in cultural and historical context, with numerous exercises. Recommended Reading Lists. Tables. Numerous figures. 641pp. 5⅜ x 8½.
24823-2

PROBABILISTIC METHODS IN THE THEORY OF STRUCTURES, Isaac Elishakoff. Well-written introduction covers the elements of the theory of probability from two or more random variables, the reliability of such multivariable structures, the theory of random function, Monte Carlo methods of treating problems incapable of exact solution, and more. Examples. 502pp. 5⅜ x 8½. 40691-1

THE RIME OF THE ANCIENT MARINER, Gustave Doré, S. T. Coleridge. Doré's finest work; 34 plates capture moods, subtleties of poem. Flawless full-size reproductions printed on facing pages with authoritative text of poem. "Beautiful. Simply beautiful."–*Publisher's Weekly.* 77pp. 9¼ x 12. 22305-1

NORTH AMERICAN INDIAN DESIGNS FOR ARTISTS AND CRAFTSPEOPLE, Eva Wilson. Over 360 authentic copyright-free designs adapted from Navajo blankets, Hopi pottery, Sioux buffalo hides, more. Geometrics, symbolic figures, plant and animal motifs, etc. 128pp. 8⅜ x 11. (Not for sale in the United Kingdom.) 25341-4

SCULPTURE: Principles and Practice, Louis Slobodkin. Step-by-step approach to clay, plaster, metals, stone; classical and modern. 253 drawings, photos. 255pp. 8⅛ x 11.
22960-2

THE INFLUENCE OF SEA POWER UPON HISTORY, 1660–1783, A. T. Mahan. Influential classic of naval history and tactics still used as text in war colleges. First paperback edition. 4 maps. 24 battle plans. 640pp. 5⅜ x 8½. 25509-3

THE STORY OF THE TITANIC AS TOLD BY ITS SURVIVORS, Jack Winocour (ed.). What it was really like. Panic, despair, shocking inefficiency, and a little heroism. More thrilling than any fictional account. 26 illustrations. 320pp. 5⅜ x 8½.
20610-6

FAIRY AND FOLK TALES OF THE IRISH PEASANTRY, William Butler Yeats (ed.). Treasury of 64 tales from the twilight world of Celtic myth and legend: "The Soul Cages," "The Kildare Pooka," "King O'Toole and his Goose," many more. Introduction and Notes by W. B. Yeats. 352pp. 5⅜ x 8½.
26941-8

BUDDHIST MAHAYANA TEXTS, E. B. Cowell and others (eds.). Superb, accurate translations of basic documents in Mahayana Buddhism, highly important in history of religions. The Buddha-karita of Asvaghosha, Larger Sukhavativyuha, more. 448pp. 5⅜ x 8½.
25552-2

ONE TWO THREE . . . INFINITY: Facts and Speculations of Science, George Gamow. Great physicist's fascinating, readable overview of contemporary science: number theory, relativity, fourth dimension, entropy, genes, atomic structure, much more. 128 illustrations. Index. 352pp. 5⅜ x 8½.
25664-2

EXPERIMENTATION AND MEASUREMENT, W. J. Youden. Introductory manual explains laws of measurement in simple terms and offers tips for achieving accuracy and minimizing errors. Mathematics of measurement, use of instruments, experimenting with machines. 1994 edition. Foreword. Preface. Introduction. Epilogue. Selected Readings. Glossary. Index. Tables and figures. 128pp. 5⅜ x 8½.   40451-X

DALÍ ON MODERN ART: The Cuckolds of Antiquated Modern Art, Salvador Dalí. Influential painter skewers modern art and its practitioners. Outrageous evaluations of Picasso, Cézanne, Turner, more. 15 renderings of paintings discussed. 44 calligraphic decorations by Dalí. 96pp. 5⅜ x 8½. (Available in U.S. only.)   29220-7

ANTIQUE PLAYING CARDS: A Pictorial History, Henry René D'Allemagne. Over 900 elaborate, decorative images from rare playing cards (14th–20th centuries): Bacchus, death, dancing dogs, hunting scenes, royal coats of arms, players cheating, much more. 96pp. 9¼ x 12¼.   29265-7

MAKING FURNITURE MASTERPIECES: 30 Projects with Measured Drawings, Franklin H. Gottshall. Step-by-step instructions, illustrations for constructing handsome, useful pieces, among them a Sheraton desk, Chippendale chair, Spanish desk, Queen Anne table and a William and Mary dressing mirror. 224pp. 8⅛ x 11¼.
29338-6

THE FOSSIL BOOK: A Record of Prehistoric Life, Patricia V. Rich et al. Profusely illustrated definitive guide covers everything from single-celled organisms and dinosaurs to birds and mammals and the interplay between climate and man. Over 1,500 illustrations. 760pp. 7½ x 10⅛.   29371-8